CHUCK & DEANNE

GREAT COUPLE. GREAT FRIENDS!

ARSEN

JIM TINDLE

ISBN: 978-1-4834-8845-5 (sc)
ISBN: 978-1-4834-8847-9 (hc)
ISBN: 978-1-4834-8846-2 (e)

Library of Congress Control Number: 2018908483

Lulu Publishing Services rev. date: 07/24/2018

ARSEN

Who looks outside, dreams; who looks inside, awakes.
—Carl Jung

How on earth are you ever going to explain in terms of chemistry and physics so important a biological phenomenon as first love?
—Albert Einstein

1

Panama City, Panama
Saturday, June 10th

One of her nipple-tassels rotated clock-wise and the other in the opposite direction . . . in perfect rhythm. Near the young lady, on each side of the main stage, were two pole-dancers in cages, completely nude and smiling as the wadded-up currency was being thrown at their feet. Some of the larger amounts were wrapped in note paper with names and phone numbers included. The cages provided some comfort from the laser like stares and the provocative language also being thrown at the performers. It was 10:30 p.m. and the heavy beat, electronica sound emanating from the multiple-speaker system, along with the nudity, was stirring the clientele in The Crazy Bull Show Club to a shouting, drink spilling, frenzy. Everyone except Arsen.

Arsen was seated at a small, round table with four soft-cushion, red chairs. The middle-aged stranger seated across from him was in the process of getting a ten-dollar lap dance. The chair next to Arsen was vacant, although several girls had made efforts to make themselves available. One glance from Arsen was all it took for them to look elsewhere for free drinks. It wasn't his slight frown or his apparent lack of enthusiasm that caused them to leave, and they had no idea the mustache and goatee were fake. It was the message sent when they looked into his penetrating, steel blue eyes peering from the black-rimmed glasses. *Wrong table, ladies.*

Prostitution was legal in Panama, and for a mere one hundred dollars paid to the club, and another two hundred paid to the woman, Arsen could have had company all night. But Arsen was focused on the three men sitting next to the stage, especially the one in the middle. The men on each side appeared to dwarf him in size. They were both dressed in black, both had shaved heads, and both were constantly scanning their surroundings, snatching glances at the club entrance, and occasionally nodding at each other. Their shoulders seemed muscular and oversized. Arsen knew what was causing the lumps in their sports jackets. The man in the middle was wearing silver-rimmed glasses and a blue-striped suit. His elbows were resting on the stage, his hands full of dollar bills.

Arsen had been following the three gentlemen for the past five days. He was so familiar with the trio, he could recognize any one of them in the dark. Even though Panama City boasted a population of close to a million, the men had been easy to follow, and easy to predict in their movements, especially in the evenings. This was their third visit to the Crazy Bull. Women and entertainment were abundant in this city of international banking, commerce . . . and money laundering.

Arsen had strategically located his seat. He was two tables away from the three men at the stage, with the main entrance to the club about twenty yards directly behind him. A bar with ten stools was on his right, and red couches lined the wall to his left. Every seat in the club, except for the one next to Arsen, was occupied. The remainder of the room was filled with circular tables, cushioned chairs, red carpet, and noise. A noise that had morphed into near pandemonium.

The Latin stripper with the tassels, probably Columbian, was removing her G-string at the same time Arsen was reaching inside his plaid jacket. A jacket that matched his Scottish touring cap. A lower, inside pocket of the jacket contained an EG18X Smoke Grenade with a wire-pull ignition system. The clamor of the crowd masked the pop of the canister as Arsen rolled it under the chair to the left of the three targets. A huge cloud of white smoke immediately filled the area around the stage and began spreading into the remainder of the club's interior. Even though it was only smoke, someone yelled "FIRE!" The scream penetrated the din of the crowd and additional shouts moved through the room like shock waves. Drinks were spilled as most of the confused patrons stood and began pushing their way to the nearest exit.

Both bodyguards jumped to their feet, survival instinct causing them to bolt toward the main entrance of the club. The one on the left hesitated after a few steps and looked back at his employer. The man with the silver-rimmed glasses was now standing and stuffing dollar bills into his suit pockets.

The music was blaring and the whiteness was billowing as Arsen slipped on a pair of thin, leather gloves and pulled the eight-inch, double-edged stiletto from inside his jacket.

Let's bring it on home.

Three steps toward the man with the glasses and one upward thrust left the knife protruding from under his jaw, the blade reaching into his brain. The limp body hit the floor like a sparrow with a broken wing, except in this case, the sparrow was dead. The man's days of sex trafficking, drugs, and small-arms sales were over in a pool of blood.

Arsen vaulted onto the stage and ran through the beaded curtain separating the platform from the narrow hallway leading past the dressing room. Women in various stages of dress were scurrying down the hall toward the exit.

The warm, humid night air wrapped its arms around Arsen as he stepped through the door to the alley. The strippers and several other male customers pushed their way through the door and turned left toward Avenida Balboa, the main thoroughfare in front of the club. Arsen turned right and hurried deeper into the alleyway. He hesitated at two dumpsters he had spotted during his reconnaissance earlier in the day and deposited his cap and jacket in one of the bins and his mustache, goatee, and glasses in the other. This was the fifth time he had discarded his disguise during an assignment. He walked casually to the street and began the fifteen-minute journey to his hotel, the InterContinental Italia.

Arsen ran his hands through his short-cut, dark brown hair and untucked the golf shirt he'd been wearing under the plaid jacket. As he walked, he removed a phone from his pants pocket and sent a simple text: "Business finished." After dropping the phone on the pavement and grinding it with his heel, he kicked the remains down a storm drain. A wire transfer for $250,000 would be deposited within the next hour in a Cayman Island bank account, no questions asked.

The lounge at the InterContinental Italia was busy. A hint of a satisfied, confident smile was on Arsen's lips as he approached the long, curving bar. He was aware of the glances from several of the women as he sat down. This was nothing new.

After ordering a Tito's martini, straight up with two olives, Arsen turned in his seat and observed the crowd in the lounge. His thoughts turned to his trip scheduled for the following morning. It would take a full twelve hours to travel from the Tocumen International Airport in Panama City to Texas. He would fly to Miami, then to Dallas, and finally to Midland. A fifteen-minute drive would have him in Odessa, his home base.

Jim Tindle

The vodka was smooth, the music was calming, and it appeared there were ample free-range women in the lounge. The "business trip" had been successful and it was time to relax. Arsen noticed a dark-haired beauty looking at him from the end of the bar. As their eyes met, Arsen raised his martini glass and nodded.

Arsen worked hard . . . and he played hard. Time to play.

THREE WEEKS LATER

2

El Paso, Texas
Sunday, July 2nd

It was late in the evening as Jack Pope and his gang sat patiently in their white Dodge Grand Caravan. He called it a gang, even though, including himself, it consisted of only three people. The van could seat a total of seven adults, and that was Jack's goal, a gang with seven, hand-picked members. Seven was Jack's lucky number.

They had been observing the small grocery store on Mundy Avenue for the past fifteen minutes. Jack knew everything he needed to know about the couple who owned Big City Grocery: their children, their grandchildren and where they all lived. He was thorough. Very thorough.

Even though the humidity was low and the sun was only minutes from disappearing behind the smog being generated across the river in Juarez, it was hot in El Paso at this time of the year. The air conditioner was running on full blast and yet it was still warm in the back seat of the van.

"How're you doing back there, Burk?" Jack didn't really care how Burk was doing, but he asked anyway. He was into the basic principles of good management.

"It's a wee bit warm. That's how I'm doing!" Burk had a high-pitched voice, which masked his true self. Jack had known Burk for two months and had never heard him utter a curse word. Mild manner, vicious nature. Perfect combination.

Turning to the young lady sitting in the driver's seat, Jack asked, "How about you, Robin?"

With a slight narrowing of her eyes and a sultry smile, Robin said, "I'm always ready."

Jack smiled and felt a slight twinge in his groin. Robin had long, sexy natural red hair that enhanced her good looks. She was five-eight and had long legs to go with her spitfire personality. Robin had one flaw in the twenty-first century culture: her soul was as dark as a mile-deep coal mine at midnight. Jack appreciated all of her traits.

A young couple exited the store, each carrying a paper bag full of groceries, and walked to their car parked at the curb. As they drove away, no other cars or customers were in view.

"Let's go," Jack ordered. "Time to realize our potential and move up the scale of life."

The two owners of the store were standing behind the counter when Jack and his friends entered. Robin strode to the counter while Jack stopped and surveyed the interior of the store, his iPad in his hand. Burk flipped the "open" sign on the door to "closed."

The fifty-something Hispanic man opened his mouth to protest just as Robin leaned forward and slapped him on the side of the head. She was wearing a padded, black glove containing a thin piece of metal in the palm. He staggered back a step, gray hair swirling.

Burk quickly moved behind the counter and grabbed the frightened and confused woman who could do little to protest. His right arm was around her waist and his left arm was loosely draped around her neck as he pulled her close to his body. She also appeared to be in her early fifties, maybe late forties. Burk immediately pressed his body against her.

Jack was first to speak. "Hello, folks. I'm Jack Pope. Now listen closely, 'cause I don't want to repeat myself."

Jack was tall with strawberry-blonde hair combed straight back on the top and on both sides. He wasn't overweight, but he appeared to be somewhat "soft." He was what most women would describe as nice looking, but it was his natural charisma that caused him to be noticed.

Robin moved behind the counter, looked around, and nodded at Jack. "All clear."

Jack continued. "If you're thinking at this point that we're going to rob you, then you're wrong. We're here to enhance your business. Grow your profits. Okay? Let me get to the point. We're going to supply you with a variety of drugs and you're going to sell them. In addition to the people that buy bread and milk, you'll be developing a new customer base. Any questions?"

"You can't make us do that!" The gray-haired owner looked at his wife who was being held only a few feet away.

"Oh, Mr. Rodriguez, we *can* make you do it. You will do it not only for your wife's sake, but also for your two daughters, Rosa and Kasie. And for

Rosa's two small children, Ben and Amy. You'll do it for your daughters and grandchildren. Right?"

The owner's mouth was open, but no words came out.

It was time for Jack to relay an important bit of information. "Rosa and her family live at 58 Desert Holly Drive, about fifteen minutes from here, and Kasie lives in the Royal Palms Apartments at 265 Park Street, also about fifteen minutes away. Now, let me show you and your wife a . . . ahh . . . let's just call it a training video."

Burk pushed the woman against the counter, his arms still around her waist and neck. Robin shoved Rodriguez against the counter, next to his wife, as Jack pushed a couple of keys on his iPad and placed it in front of the couple.

The first image displayed a close-up of the address on Desert Holly Drive. Next, Rosa and her two children exited the front door and got into a silver Honda parked in the driveway. There were intermittent scenes of the Honda on various streets, finally parking in a shopping-mall parking lot. A twelve-second video showed the other daughter, Kasie, wearing a two-piece bathing suit at the apartment swimming pool.

Jack smirked as he said, "Now, that's one fine looking specimen of a woman! I know twenty guys across the river that would love to have their way with that babe. All in one day."

Mr. Rodriguez took his wife's hand and shook his head, a deeply worried look etched in his face. His wife was sobbing silently.

The video ended with a five-second image of a body with a mangled face lying in a pool of blood. Vacant eyes stared at the camera.

Jack retrieved the iPod and switched it off. "I wish we could follow up with a cartoon of some kind, but that's it for today, folks. Surely, you're convinced at this point that I mean business, but we have one last reminder."

Jack walked behind the counter and quickly moved behind Rodriguez, wrapping his arm tightly around the man's neck. Burk continued pressing the woman against the counter, and his free hand found the front of her blouse and pulled in a downward motion. Several buttons popped off and skidded across the counter top. Robin walked to the other side of the counter, leaned over, and grabbed a handful of the woman's hair.

"Stay still, bitch, and we'll get this over with in a hurry," Burk said, as he removed a switch-blade knife and a small bottle from the pocket of his jeans.

Raising the blouse from the woman's back, Burk proceeded to make two precise cuts on her left shoulder. As the woman groaned and began to cry, he poured the ink from the bottle into the cuts.

"Damn, that's one of the best *sevens* I've ever made," Burk squeaked.

The more Mr. Rodriguez struggled, the tighter Jack's grip became on his throat. When the homemade tattoo procedure was finished, the gang moved to the other side of the counter and glared at the two store owners. The woman was still crying, her husband's body slumped in helpless desperation.

Jack continued the conversation as if he were sitting at a dinner table with friends. "We'll be back this Thursday for a training session, and then we'll deliver the first shipment of produce to you on Friday. Yeah, *produce*. Remember, you get to keep part of the profits . . . a small amount, but nevertheless, something."

Burk looked at Mr. Rodriguez and said, "Shape up, old man, or I'll cut a seven in your forehead."

Jack had one final warning. "And don't forget. Your names and the names of your children and grandchildren have been entered into the … let's call it the *system*. The *system* consists of my total organization and the rest of the organization across the river. Know what I mean? If you contact the police, or anyone else, your family will be eliminated. Maybe not tomorrow, or even next week, but eventually someone will be making a video of you. You know, like the one you just saw. Or maybe the video will star one of your grandchildren. No talk, no problems. *Comprende?*"

This was Jack's "insurance policy." No one in their right mind would ever repeat his name or the details of the visit after seeing the video. This was absolute fear insurance. After a few moments without receiving an answer, Jack screamed, *"Comprende?"*

Mr. Rodriguez nodded without speaking.

"Remember," Jack said, "we'll be back this Thursday for a training session on how to handle the produce, and then we'll deliver the first product to you on Friday. You'll receive all the information you need to begin your new business venture. So, stay tuned."

Jack took a Snickers bar from the candy display on the counter. Without smiling, he placed a five-dollar bill on the counter and said, "Keep the change."

3

Odessa, Texas
Monday, July 3rd

Arsen was sitting on his back porch gazing at the garden. He was focused on the raised, cedar-lined garden bed he had purchased at Home Depot for eighty-three dollars. It was brimming with plants: tomatoes, peppers, carrots, and green onions. He was particularly proud of the large red tomatoes. It was 1:00 p.m., the sun was peeking through the partly cloudy sky, the west Texas humidity was low. Life was good.

Speaking slowly, the old lady sitting in the lawn chair next to Arsen said, "I wish I had a dollar for every time I changed your diaper when you were just a baby. Your mother worked her hands to the bone and your daddy was always working in the oil patch. It's been twenty-eight years or so. Am I correct?"

Arsen nodded. This wasn't the first time he'd heard Evelyn reminiscing about his childhood.

"I can still see the look on your face when I gave you that red wagon for your fourth birthday. You were one happy young man. I was proud to have helped raise you, even if I was only a part-time baby sitter."

"Yep, that was one fine wagon."

"I'm glad your job is working out so well. I've never heard of anyone only working for a week or so at a stretch, and then taking off for a couple of months. Back in my day, the men worked twelve to fifteen hours a day, all year long. Mercy me, how do you do it?"

"Like I told you, Evelyn, these international consulting assignments pay nice bonuses."

"Well, I can see why a company would want to pay you a lot of money. I knew you'd make it at whatever you put your mind to. You've always been a complicated young man, but a moral one. And that's what counts."

Arsen didn't consider himself a Good Samaritan, but he wouldn't hesitate to help a deserving person in need. He had taken strays and injured animals to the vet more times than he could count. He always rooted for the underdog and had a particular dislike for bullies. Still . . . he was a contract assassin. Not a killer. The fine distinction in his justification was due to the fact that a government agency was selecting the targets. The designated victims weren't exactly the cream of the crop, the elite of social dignity. Arsen didn't know which government agency was pulling the strings because he had never met anyone. He only had a phone number and the name of one person: Nils. They contacted him, they provided detailed information, they paid on time, and the targets appeared to be deserving of death. That's how his mind worked. He knew there was a large amount of rationalization in this line of thinking, but so what. He liked his job.

"Your parents would've been proud. I can't believe they've been gone for eight years. They had to leave us way too early."

"Evelyn, you've been a big help, and you know how much I appreciate it."

She *harrumphed* as she placed her hands on the arms of the lawn chair and attempted to stand.

"Time to go. Help me out of this aluminum contraption, and off the porch, Arsen."

After Arsen walked Evelyn to the back gate and returned to the porch, his cell phone rang. He thought of it as his personal cell phone since only clients and special friends had this number. This wasn't a throwaway.

Clearing his throat, Arsen answered with a simple, "Yes."

"Arsen, this is Miguel. How are you doing?"

Miguel Burbano and Arsen had been in the army together for four years.

"Darn good, you little runt. What are you up to?"

"I'm *still* up to about five-eleven. Haven't grown an inch since I last saw you."

"You're *still* a funny guy."

Miguel got straight to the subject of the call. "Do you have any spare time during the next week or so, or are you in the middle of one of your business deals?"

Miguel didn't know the exact nature of Arsen's business, but he assumed that the CIA, or some other government agency, had recruited Arsen from the private security firm in Dallas where they had been employed. They had been in regular contact over the past three years.

"I'll answer both of your questions. Yes, to the first and no to the second."

Miguel was quiet for a second and said, "You're not retired, are you?"

"You know better than that. I just finished a successful business trip earlier this month and I'm now hanging out at my tomato farm."

Laughing, Miguel said, "Oh yeah, I saw your farm last summer. Seems to me you only had about three tomatoes on those spindly vines you planted."

"Yuck it up. You'll change your tune when I start shipping these lovely red things all over the country." Getting serious again, Arsen asked, "How can I help you?"

"I was involved in a . . . using your terms, a *business trip* to Cancun a few months ago and I met a young man from Dallas. His name is Jamie Rodriguez. I won't bore you with the details, but I want you to know that Jamie is an exceptional guy and I would like to help him. We just got off the phone, and he has a little problem. I'd try to assist him myself, but I'm leaving for Quito, Ecuador, in the morning and may be gone for a while. My mother had a stroke and I need to be with her."

"I'm so sorry." Arsen knew Miguel hadn't hesitated to buy a ticket home to be close to his parents. "Hope all goes well."

"Thanks. Now here's the situation. Jamie's parents own a small grocery store in El Paso, near downtown. Jamie's mother called him this morning and sounded worried about something, but she wouldn't elaborate. Jamie called his father, and after some prodding found out that several thugs showed up at their store and roughed them up."

"Why doesn't your friend, Jamie, call the police? Sounds like an open and shut case of assult and battery."

"This is where it gets strange. There were three gang members involved and they demanded that Jamie's parents start selling drugs for them out of their store. They knew the names and addresses of Jamie's two sisters, who also live in El Paso. One of the sisters has two kids. They even showed videos of the sisters and the kids. To top it off, they said their gang, or someone in Juarez, would kill all of them if they notified the authorities. I guess they implied that one of the Juarez cartels was involved. You know, the short-term, long-term thing. We'll get to you sooner or later and chop off your heads. Know what I mean?"

"Hmm." Arsen was getting more interested in the story.

"That's not all. After slapping around Jamie's father, they tore off his mother's blouse and cut a small seven in her shoulder. Poured ink in the wound."

Sounds more exciting than growing tomatoes. "How can I help?"

"Well, I'm not sure. Would it be okay if Jamie called and filled you in on the details? He'll be passing through Odessa on his way to El Paso.

Maybe you could offer some advice. I don't know, maybe you could even go to El Paso with him. I'm afraid that Jamie will beat the stuffing out of someone and get up to his ass in alligators.

He's got a short fuse."

"What's Jamie's background? Where does he live?"

"As I said, I got to know Jamie pretty well during our trip to Cancun. He's about our age, twenty-seven or so. He lives here in Dallas, getting ready to start medical school. He used to be a MMA fighter. I'll let him fill you in. Oh, by the way, I'll take care of your expenses if you decide to help him."

Laughing, Arsen said, "This is my bread and butter. I'll write it off as charity work on my next tax return."

"Thanks, Arsen. Okay if I give Jamie your private phone number?"

"Sure. If you can remember it," Arsen said with a chuckle.

Arsen's private cell phone number was 277-362-7736, but his clients and friends didn't remember it by the numbers . . . they remembered it by simply punching in ARSEN ARSEN.

Someone in the government also had a sense of humor.

"Thanks. I knew I could count on you. Jamie will be calling you shortly since he plans on driving to El Paso right away. *Preocupado como mierda.* He's worried as shit."

Arsen thought for a second. "Well, it's a five-hour drive from Dallas to Odessa and another four hours from here to El Paso. Tell him to call me and we can make plans."

"Thanks again, Arsen. You're not nearly as bad as all the women say."

"I'm glad you recognize that fact. Let me know how your mother is doing. Have a safe trip to Ecuador."

Arsen frowned as he sat back in the lawn chair with his hands clasped behind his head. It was possible this was just a few kids trying to shake down a small business or it could be a gang with cartel ties starting up a creative drug distribution model. There wouldn't be a $250,000 bonus involved, but it did sound interesting.

Exactly four minutes later, Arsen answered his cell phone. "Yes."

"Hello, is this Arsen?" There seemed to be a quiet hum in the background.

"It is indeed. This must be Jamie, Miguel's friend."

"Yes, it is. I'm not sure how much Miguel told you, but my parents in El Paso have a problem and I'm on my way to see them. He said that you might have some thoughts on the matter."

"Where are you right now?"

"On the outskirts of Dallas, just getting ready to exit onto I-20."

Arsen thought for a few seconds and then said, "I suppose Miguel told you I live in Odessa, right?"

"Yep. He said you used to work together in a security firm in Dallas."

"Okay. You should be here around six thirty or so. Are you familiar with Odessa?"

"Not really. I've driven through, but never had a reason to stop."

"Most people don't." Arsen tried to take some tension out of the conversation. "Let's meet at a bar called J.D.'s After Dark. When you get to Odessa, take a right on Exit 116. That'll put you on Highway 385. The bar is three miles on the left. Blue building with a big parking lot. Hard to miss. I'll be sitting at the bar wearing a black shirt and shorts. I'll probably be the only person in the bar that's not outfitted in Levis and a hat of some kind."

"Easy enough. See you in about five hours."

Arsen leaned back in his chair, the garden no longer in focus. His thoughts took him back two years to Agua Prieta, Mexico, in the state of Sonora. The Sinaloa Cartel had complete control of the city. Bodies piled up, including young boys and women. The cartel had hired an architect to construct a short underground passage running roughly four hundred feet from an attorney's house in Agua Prieta to a cartel-owned warehouse in Douglas, Arizona. Arsen's assignment was to eliminate both the attorney and the architect.

The task had taken one day to complete. With the help of the information supplied by his contact, Arsen had broken the attorney's neck and shot the architect in the back of the head, all in one evening. The project had gone smoothly, without a hitch. The only issue occurred the next morning when Arsen learned that both victims had families . . . wives and children. Guilt swept over him, but the drugs smuggled into the U.S. would undoubtedly ruin lives and probably lead to numerous deaths. He equated it with the "Hiroshima Syndrome" . . . many innocent lives lost, but many more innocent lives saved.

Arsen's logic process had been completed and filed away for future use.

Miguel's mention of a cartel possibly being involved had triggered Arsen's interest in this case.

The same Sinaloa Cartel was now based in Juarez and in charge of most illegal drug smuggling activities into the United States. They had recruited some extremely ruthless members.

For some deep, hidden reason, Arsen looked forward to ruthless versus ruthless.

4

El Paso, Texas
Monday, July 3rd

Jack sat in the swivel chair, feet on his desk. He was wearing a pair of dark blue slacks and a short sleeve, white shirt. His office was about two hundred square feet and was located at the back of the bar he owned . . . the Seventh Avenue Lounge. A one-way mirror allowed him to keep an eye on the bartender, the five early morning patrons, and the front door. The interior was standard "dive bar" and consisted of a juke box, a pool table, three booths, ten tables that could each seat four, and the bar with eight stools.

Jack was fully aware of the trite, unoriginal, clichéd appearance the ownership of a bar presented. Every crime family and mob movie made in the past thirty years depicted the bad guys as owning nightclubs and bars, complete with an office in the back. It just seemed like the thing to do under the circumstances. The previous owner was the first person Jack and his "gang" had strong-armed and forced to sell drugs. After two weeks in the drug business, the owner, sporting the black *seven* tattoo on his shoulder, approached Jack and offered to sell the bar and all its contents for a mere twenty-five thousand dollars. The negotiations took about fifteen minutes and the owner agreed to let go of the bar for eight thousand dollars, with no down payment, and paid-out over a two-year time frame. Jack had a legitimate business and all the paperwork to prove it.

Jack had slowly progressed into the world of crime. It started in high school because he couldn't throw a football with a tight spiral. He had some athletic ability, but he only wanted to be the quarterback on the team. The coach felt he should play another position since all his pass attempts in practice were end-over-end. Jack quit the team and moved into sports another way---sports wagering. He became a small-time bookie his junior year in high school and continued through college.

A new member initiation was taking place in Jack's office. Lester Anderson, the new inductee, raised his head from the desk, just inches away from Jack's feet, and said, "That didn't hurt at all."

"Maybe I should have made the two cuts a little deeper." The excited tone of Burk's high-pitched voice reflected the pleasure he derived from making the *shoulder-seven* tattoos.

Jack removed his feet from his desk and said, "Welcome to the organization." Now that he had four members, he'd decided to call the group an *organization* rather than a mere gang.

Robin chimed in. "Congratulations, Lester. I'm certain we'll have a good time working together. Glad to have you on board."

Lester squinted at Jack. "Okay, now that you've checked me out in every possible way and branded me, tell me about the details of our gan . . ., I mean organization." Lester was as plain as a man could possibly be. Plain looking, plain personality. His head was perfectly round, and his long, straight, lifeless hair accentuated it.

Jack rose slowly from his chair and stood behind his desk. He folded his arms across his chest and made eye contact with his three employees. He'd read that a leader should stand and look down on his audience for maximum effect. In his mind, the degree in psychology and the Basic Principles of Management course he had taken his sophomore year had totally prepared him to run a gang, a night club, or even a large company. He was sure that the big score was just around the corner.

"Yes, we *have* checked you out in every way. You're educated and you've never been arrested. That minimizes the chance of anyone profiling us. Our sources have told us that you're aggressive and that you know how to fight."

"All those fights were started by someone else," Lester said. "I just finished 'em."

Jack completely ignored the comments and continued. "Plus, you've worked at a Best Buy store repairing computers, and at a couple of gun ranges. We can use that knowledge in our drug distribution business."

"We're not going up against the cartels, are we?" Lester asked.

Jack smiled. "Quite the opposite. One of my best friends is a ranking member in the Sinaloa Cartel in Juarez. He'll supply the product and all we have to do is distribute it. He's okay with us starting out small and growing . . . as long as we don't have any problems with the DEA or any of the other Feds."

Lester tilted his head, a puzzled look on his face. "Look, I appreciate the two-thousand dollars a month salary, and I realize that the big money will be coming from my share of the drug profits. My question is this. Do you have a network of dealers to sell the stuff?"

"The good news is, no. The brilliant news is that we don't use street corner dealers or low-rent junkies selling out of their pads like everyone else in the world. We're recruiting legitimate businesses to sell the product."

"Oh, I get it. A person wants to get high, so he just goes to JC Penney's and buys what he needs. Right?" Lester smirked.

Jack pursed his lips. Using sheer willpower to keep his emotions under control, he said, "Not exactly. We engage with small businesses to conduct our sales. You know, like 'mom and pop' type businesses. Small grocery stores, independent pharmacies, ice cream shops, bars, etcetera. Our cartel friends put the word out to recreational and hard-core users over here and it travels like wildfire, you know, like a *rave*. I'm told that the businesses we enlist will have plenty of customers the first day they start selling."

"How do you find someone at these businesses that's willing to work for us?"

Jack felt it was time to get down to basics with Lester. "We threaten to kill them and their families if they don't cooperate, or if they go to the police." He tried to smile, but his face twisted into something sinister instead. "Same with the members of our organization should they want to leave. Once a seven is cut into your shoulder, you're a member for life. Okay?"

"Sounds good to me. I'm sick and tired of repairing computers. And all the noise at the gun range gives me headaches. Tell me what to do. I'm ready to get started."

"Our background check indicated you have a license to carry a handgun. Correct?"

"Yep. I paid the hundred forty bucks to the Great State of Texas for the honor of carrying a concealed weapon." Lester grinned. "Soooo . . . I'm getting the distinct feeling that this is not a Boy Scout troop. You guys really get into it, don't you?"

Jack knew about the concealed weapon permit, due to Robin's inquiries, but didn't know the exact type of weapon Lester had purchased. "What kind of handgun do you have?"

Lester smiled. "Smith and Wesson .38 Special, four-inch barrel. It's a . . ."

"Good. Keep it with you at all times, except when you come into this bar. We don't want to have any problems with the law. Understand? Now, put your shirt back on."

"Got it."

Jack could see the satisfaction on Lester's face as he talked about his Smith & Wesson. Lester would never be his best friend, but he had talents that would benefit their business.

It was nearing noon and the bar had been open for two hours. Jack had only one employee running the bar. He could see Shelly Jones standing behind the counter talking to one of the customers.

Jack was swinging into action. He was aware of the time and he was aware that his 20 milligram Ritalin pill was overdue. He had been taking Ritalin since he was twelve. His hyperactivity and impulse control were somewhat under control, but he relied on the three doses a day to maintain an even keel.

Still standing, he looked at the three employees. "Okay, I've made some major decisions. First of all, our name is going to be the Seventh Avenue Crew, not *organization*, but *crew*. It may appear that I'm going against my own philosophy of staying in the weeds, you know, under the radar. However, a name with *crew* in it will help put fear in the store owners we use to distribute our product. Okay?" He wasn't asking a question, he wanted approval of whatever came out of his mouth.

"We need at least two businesses on-line by the end of the week. Robin has a new one she'll discuss with you in a minute. Our first drug shipment will be here this Friday and there should be enough product to last two distribution sites for a week." Jack was proud of himself for using real business terms such as *product* and *distribution sites*. The small grocery store owned by the Rodriguez couple was the only "distribution site" currently ready to be put into operation. All they needed was the product and a short training session.

"We'll be adding a few more members to our crew in the coming days, but for now here's how we're going to be organized. Robin will continue conducting research on small businesses and private inquiries about their families. She'll also conduct the product training at these places. All of us will conduct the initial visits to the potential distribution sites to insure they're completely on-board with the program. You know, rough 'em up if necessary, carve the seven. Get their full attention. I'll coordinate with my friend in Juarez and keep the inventory under control. Any questions?"

Lester raised his hand. "How do we get the inventory? Do you go to Juarez each week and bring the . . . what do you call it . . . *produce* across the bridge?"

Jack tried not to rolled his eyes. "Of course, not." He was trying hard to remain calm. "The Mexico-US border is like a block of Swiss cheese.

The weekly inventory will arrive each Friday morning at six and I'll be here to meet it. Believe me." Jack hoped the crew would be impressed with their leader sacrificing his sleep to handle the most dangerous part of the operation.

Jack walked to the only closet in the office, opened the door, and said, "Look at this!" The dark gray safe took up most of the closet space. "This baby is five-feet tall with two-inch thick steel, weighs eight hundred thirty-seven pounds, and has a biometric locking mechanism. It only recognizes fingerprints from me or Robin."

Burk cleared his throat. "Say boss, exactly what kind of drugs are we going to be pushing?"

Jack spun around to face him. "Don't use the term *pushing*! We distribute *produce*. Got it?" Jack needed his Ritalin . . . the sooner, the better. "We have just four items to start with. We may expand the selection later on. For now, we're wading into the program. Reduces mistakes." Jack took a deep breath. "Ten-dollar bags of weed, you know, dime bags. Quarter grams of crystal meth for twenty bucks, ecstasy capsules for five-dollars each, and cocaine eight-balls for one-twenty each. Okay?"

Lester ventured one more question. "How about Molly? It's an offshoot of Ecstasy."

Jack finally lost control. "Goddam it! I just told you about the four items we're starting with. We can always add more later. At some point we may buy it in bulk and package it ourselves. Got it?" Jack reached into his top desk drawer and palmed the bottle of Ritalin. "I need to check on our bartender. Robin, give them instructions on the potential new business site we'll be visiting today."

Jack walked to the door and Robin took his place behind the desk. Burk knew that Robin was Jack's second-in-command, his right-hand woman . . . and more.

Robin stood and nodded. "The Rodriguez grocery store on Mundy Avenue, our first distribution site, will serve our clientele in the downtown area. The pharmacy we're visiting today is on the other side of the mountain near Ft. Bliss, on Montana Avenue. There should be more than adequate business there, so it's important we handle it correctly. The owner and his wife have operated the store for over ten years. I have a video clip of their daughter and her husband who live in the area, so there shouldn't be any problems. The pharmacy closes at six so we'll need to be there a few minutes earlier."

Lester started to say something.

Robin was way ahead of him. "And before you ask, yes, we're all riding together in Jack's van."

Jack returned to the office as Robin was finishing her spiel. "Okay, guys, let's meet back here at no later than five. It'll take twenty minutes to get there, so don't be late. I'll buy you a drink before we leave."

Jack peered through the one-way mirror and watched his two male employees walk through the bar to the front door. He turned, nodded at Robin, and locked the office door. Jack had read how top executives developed their own power moves. He knew that few words, combined with simple nods or facial expressions, could exhibit dominance and control.

Robin casually got up from her chair and smiled. After unbuttoning her blouse, she pulled her G-string down to her ankles and stepped out of it.

Jack's tongue involuntarily ran across his upper lip as he unzipped his pants. "My thirtieth birthday is only a month away. Let's practice blowing out my candles."

Another dessert-before-lunch day for Jack Pope.

5

Odessa, Texas
Monday, July 3rd

The sun was leaning toward the west as Arsen walked through the door of J. D.'s After Dark.

The sign on the wall highlighted the bar's philosophy: *"If It's Dark, We're Doin' It."* He was wearing a short-sleeved black T-shirt, tan shorts, and black tennis shoes. He estimated the bar to be about a third occupied. Still a little early for the hard-core crowd.

After getting the bartender's attention, he asked, "Where's your restroom?"

The bartender pointed to his left without speaking. Arsen didn't need to use the facilities, he only wanted to know where the back exit was located and what type of lock it had, if any. He'd only been here one other time, and that was several years ago. Satisfied, he returned to the bar and ordered his favorite vodka. He was amused at the country song playing on the juke box. One phrase in particular caught his attention: *"Don't cry over my shoulder 'cause you might rust my spurs."*

Even though Arsen had traveled all over the world during his time in the army and in his current job, he was comfortable in Odessa. He understood these people, he essentially was one of them. He especially liked impecunious bars such as this one. Genuinely unpretentious. Most of the people coming to this type bar worked in the oil fields or in a related business. The hours were long and the work was hard. Some relaxed, some let off steam.

The music switched from country-western to Chicago blues. The noise level in the bar was increasing as several couples moved toward the tiny dance floor.

A young man wearing jeans and a white T-shirt approached the stool next to Arsen and said,

"You must be Arsen."

"Therefore, you must be Jamie."

The two shook hands and Arsen made a quick appraisal of the new-comer. He was fairly tall, nice looking, probably in his mid to late twenties, and had a firm grip. He was solidly built with well-defined arms. His thick, black hair was cut short in front and it gave him a classy, masculine look.

Pointing to the bar stool beside him, Arsen said, "Have a seat and I'll buy you a drink. How was the drive?"

"Not bad, once I got out of the Dallas traffic. Pretty easy after that. Plus, your directions to this establishment were right-on." Jamie's voice cracked, his eyes narrowed.

The bartender leaned against the bar and said, "What'll it be?"

Without hesitating, Jamie replied, "Any kind of light beer."

Arsen was still evaluating his most recent drinking partner, aware that he was stressed.

Continuing with the small talk, he said, "How long have you known Miguel Burbano?"

"Only a few months. He assisted a friend of mine and me with a situation in Cancun. He's super-good at what he does. Like him a lot. And by-the-way, he speaks very highly of you.

Where did you guys meet?"

The bartender brought Jamie's drink and said to Arsen, "Ready for another one?"

"Not yet, but don't get too far away." Arsen was still trying to keep the mood light and casual.

Putting his elbows on the bar, he answered Jamie's question. "Miguel and I met in the army during Special Forces training. You know, airborne, survival, hand-to-hand and so forth. Sixteen months of torture. Miguel is one tough guy. Not only because he survived the training, but because of what he did for me in Jordan."

Jamie's eyes widened. "What did he do?"

"After our training was over, we, along with ten other brothers, were sent to Jordan. We were on loan to a CIA outfit near the Syrian border. It was supposed to be strictly training and reconnaissance, but one night we ventured into Syria and bumped into the bad guys. We were engaged in a fire-fight and I took one in the side. Broke a couple of ribs and starting bleeding like crazy. To make a long story short, Miguel, who's four inches shorter than I, and at the time was forty pounds lighter, stopped the bleeding and then carried, pushed, and drug me for over a mile back to our base. I know it may sound a bit dramatic, but he probably saved my life. I've never met anyone as tough or more trustworthy than Miguel. Owe him."

"How long were you guys in the army?"

"Four years."

"Miguel said the two of you worked together at a private investigation firm in Dallas."

"Yeah, for about a year after we got out of the service. Following that, I was recruited to a job with an international consulting firm specializing in security services and moved back here three years ago. I live in the same house in which I was raised. My parents passed away around eight years ago, and the house had been leased-out for most of that time."

"Interesting. What's it like living here?"

"It's a typical small West Texas town. The area came into prominence in the early 1930s when two major oil fields were discovered. You may remember how the city was glamorized in a book . . . *Friday Night Lights*. It chronicled the Permian High School Panthers as they made a run toward the state football championship in 1988. I was born that year." Smiling, Arsen asked,

"Any other facts you want to know?"

Nodding, Jamie said, "Very thorough. It must have been nice growing up in a small city."

"Were you in the military?" Arsen asked.

"I was in the army for two years. Nothing exciting like you and Miguel. I was stationed at Ft. Bliss in El Paso the entire time. I even got special treatment because I was on the army boxing team. In addition, I learned some martial arts skills. Simple, boring story."

"Miguel mentioned that you were an MMA cage fighter for a while. That couldn't have been very boring."

Jamie settled back on his bar stool. "After the army, I began training in Brazilian jiu-jitsu and wrestling, and competed in several local competitions in El Paso. I finally got discovered by the UFC and received a thirty-five thousand dollar signing bonus."

"Impressive."

"Not really. The good news is that I received the signing bonus, the bad news is that I gave it back two months later."

Arsen raised his eyebrows and said, "How'd that happen?"

"My UFC career, that's the Ultimate Fighting Championship, only lasted a total of fifty-two seconds."

"I've got to hear the ending to this story."

"That consisted of three fights. I knocked out my opponent in the first fight in twelve seconds, and knocked out the guy in the second fight in twenty-two seconds. I may have become a little over confident, because eighteen seconds into the third fight I got kicked squarely on the side of my head and was out for a couple of minutes. I met with my manager the next day and told him to give the money back. I started nursing school the very next week."

He has an honest, humble approach to life. "Miguel says you're about to start medical school. Getting out of the fight business was an excellent idea."

"I think so. So far, I've been very lucky. I imagine you had a lot of martial arts training in the special forces."

Thinking a second before answering, Arsen said, "Well, my experience was probably different than yours. When we got someone on the ground, they didn't tap out or holler *uncle*. They just never got up again."

Nodding, Jamie smiled. "That's awesome!"

Arsen appreciated Jamie's enthusiasm. *It's hard not to like this fellow. Not an ounce of bullshit in him.*

The bartender brought Arsen another drink and pointed his index finger at Jamie's glass.

Jamie shook his head and said, "Nothing more for me. I've still got a few miles to drive this evening." Turning his attention back to Arsen, he stated apologetically, "Oh yeah, I don't mean to be rude, but I don't even know your last name."

"Arsen."

A confused expression crossed Jamie's face. "What's your first name?"

"Arsen." Shrugging, Arsen explained the anomaly. "My dad worked in the oil fields around here most of his life. He was completely embarrassed, if not ashamed, of his name . . . Percy Arsen. Thought it had a sissy sound to it, always tried to go by his last name. You know, some people hear the name Arsen, and it evokes images of something sinister, of someone setting a fire. Anyway, when I was born he tagged me with both names. So, here I am . . . Arsen Arsen."

"So that's how your phone number came about."

"Yep." Arsen decided to get down to business. "Tell me exactly what your parents told you about the people that roughed them up."

Jamie recounted the story, not leaving out any details.

Arsen thought for a few seconds. "And this Jack Pope fellow implied that either they, or someone from across the river, would exact revenge if they went to the authorities?"

"Yes. That message and the videos of my sisters and the two kids have my parents pretty shook up."

Arsen leaned back on his bar stool, crossing his arms. "My immediate response is for both of us to head out for El Paso, find these three hoodlums, and beat the crap out of them … including the girl. My professional sense tells me that something very unusual is going on. This could be a conundrum in which nothing is as dire as it seems, or it could be an extremely dangerous situation with lots of fall-out potential."

"I suppose you're right. Have any recommendations?"

"I might, but first I need to make a couple of phone calls and try to get a line on this Jack Pope character. It may bring things into better focus. I'll call you tomorrow and we can proceed from there."

Jamie nodded and said, "What's your standard fee for this type of assistance?"

"Zero. Nothing. Don't worry about it. I told you I owe Miguel Burbano and he's the one who referred you. Miguel and I do favors for one another. No more talk about fees. Okay?"

"Sure. Anything you can find out will be appreciated."

Several details about the story bothered Arsen, but the thing that bothered him most was the video showing the two children. *Some lines can't be crossed!*

Arsen looked around the place. The dance floor was packed, it was after dark, and the crowd was "doin' it."

An attractive, and very inebriated, young lady pushed her way next to Jamie at the bar. Her long brown hair brushed his shoulder as she leaned against him. She placed her hand on the back of his neck and loudly purred over the noise, "Let's dance, honey."

With a surprised look, Jamie stuttered, "I'm, I'm kind of tied up at the moment, but thanks for the invitation."

The words had barely left Jamie's mouth when a barrel-chested hulk approached from behind the young lady. He was wearing a red and white cap that proudly proclaimed *City Pipe & Supplies*. He was flanked by two, equally large friends. His message was clear and simple, even if it wasn't literally accurate. "No cocksucker messes with my woman!" The beer bottle in his right hand was beginning an arc towards Jamie's head.

The edge of Jamie's hand quickly sliced into the hulk's wrist and the beer bottle flipped into the air, hitting the top of the bar, spewing foam. Almost simultaneously, Jamie rose from a seated position and leaned into a straight-right hand that hit the man's jaw, making a cracking sound.

Jamie watched as the drunk crumpled to the floor, his red and white cap lying next to him.

Arsen slowly stood and stared at the hulk's two large friends who seemed confused. One look into Arsen's eyes suggested they back-off and tend to their friend who was moaning on the wet floor. The bartender, who had witnessed the entire scene, was waving a baseball bat and barking orders to the two men. "Get him out of here. Now!"

Arsen looked at Jamie and shrugged. "Good work. He deserved it."

Jamie seemed unusually calm. "Apparently, that guy is not wired correctly."

Arsen shook his head and said, "Well, I don't know about his brain, but based on the sound I just heard, his jaw is going to be wired for quite a while."

"The drunk was easy to handle, but you only had to stare down his two friends! Man, you scared the shit out of them." Jamie grinned.

"Hey, my friend, I think you're the one who scared them. The drunk dude hit the floor like a bag of wet laundry."

"Sorry to cause you problems in your home-town. I guess I'd better hit the road."

"Are you sure you want to make that four-hour drive tonight?"

"Yeah, I've got to get on with it. Besides, my parents are expecting me."

Several gawkers stood in a semi-circle watching the hulk's friends drag him toward the restroom. The rest of the crowd was dancing, playing pool, and drinking the night away.

Arsen thought for a second, and said, "Look. I know this is personal for you, but depending on what I find out, what would you think about me meeting you in El Paso sometime tomorrow? I need to take care of some personal business there, anyway." The second part of the statement was not entirely accurate.

"That would be great. You've got my number. Look forward to hearing from you."

"Be careful."

As Jamie walked away, Arsen returned to the bar and looked at the young lady who had caused the scene. She was wearing a low-cut blouse that fully displayed abundant cleavage.

The recent altercation already forgotten, she asked with a slight slur, "Are you looking at my tits?"

"You know, it seems like they're looking at me. Want to go to my place and have another drink?"

"Thought you'd never ask. I've been wanting to get a closer look at your big shoulders and manly arms ever since you got here."

Since this had the potential to be a very strenuous work week, Arsen decided to play hard tonight.

It's only July third, but let the fireworks begin.

6

Juarez, Mexico
Monday, July 3rd

Carlos Delgado pointed to the framed newspaper article hanging on the garage wall. It was a *2011 Los Angeles Times* report crowning the Sinaloa Cartel as "Mexico's most powerful organized crime group."

"That was true then, and it's true now. Sinaloa is powerful. Sinaloa is strong. Sinaloa is the *'blood alliance.'* Do you understand?" Carlos was considerably taller than the young man standing in front of him.

"Yes, Mr. Delgado, I understand." Tears ran down the young man's face as he spoke, but he couldn't wipe them away; his hands were tied behind his back.

Delgado was in charge of Sinaloa's enforcement wing and had been living in Juarez for most of his life. He had risen quickly through the ranks, partly due to his involvement in the fight against the Juarez Cartel for the control of the Juarez corridor and partly due to Joaquin "El Chapo" Guzman being his biological father. There were currently three hundred members in his organization, one hundred of which were located in Juarez.

"You understand now, but you should have understood before you killed one of my men. Now you have to pay the price for not understanding soon enough."

The young man was sobbing uncontrollably. "I will do anything for you. Please don't kill me! Please."

Two of Delgado's men were in the process of rolling a fifty-five-gallon barrel through the garage's double doors on a hand-dolly. Two other men were each carrying forty-pound sacks of lime on their shoulders.

"We are going to stuff you in this barrel, fill it with lime, put the lid on, and then deposit it in your front yard tonight. You should thank me for getting you back to your family." Delgado's hollow, grating laugh was a direct reflection of his personality.

Three of the men, using a high voltage stun gun, managed to get the victim into the barrel, while the other one opened the sacks and poured the lime. After the lid was hammered into place, the muffled screams lasted only a few seconds.

"I've changed my mind. Don't put the barrel in his front yard, put it on the porch. That'll make it more convenient for his wife and kids."

It was only a short time ago that Juarez was reported to be the murder capital of the world. Carlos Delgado was doing his best to maintain the city's reputation.

7

El Paso, Texas
Monday, July 3rd

Robin was driving the van while Jack sat in the passenger seat pontificating about something he had learned in one of his psychology courses. Their destination was the Jiffy Pharmacy on Montana Avenue, near the Ft. Bliss Army base. To no one's surprise, the van's air conditioner was finding it difficult to keep up with the late afternoon heat.

Burk and Lester had endured fifteen minutes of psychological babble about realizing their full potential and how they could raise themselves to the top of Maslow's *Hierarchy of Needs*. Jack was of the opinion that they were at the "Love and Belonging" stage, with "Self-Actualization" in the cards if this new venture was successfully implemented by the crew over the coming months.

Lester glanced at Burk and rolled his eyes. When an opening in the conversation finally came, he said, "The location of this pharmacy is ideal for our business. Not only does Ft. Bliss have thousands of soldiers, civilians and retirees living there, the post has over 900,000 acres for training."

Robin said sarcastically, "You're a walking, talking Wikipedia, Lester. Any other pearls you can share with us?" Earlier, she had mentioned to Jack that she was not completely comfortable with Lester's vanilla personality, even if he did carry a Smith & Wesson under his shirt.

Completely missing the sarcasm, Lester continued, "Yeah, Ft. Bliss is home to the First Armored Division. I used to date a girl stationed there and she gave me all these facts."

Burk, with a high-pitched laugh, said, "I'll bet that wasn't all she gave you! Maybe you can get a free penicillin shot at this pharmacy we're visiting."

Lester was not amused. "Fuck you, you skinny bitch. I'll take your carving knife and shove it up your ass!"

"Uh huh. Dream on, dick-head." Burke sat back in the seat with an amused look on his face.

"Gentlemen!" Jack interrupted the argument. "Save this aggression for the pharmacy. This business is full of surprises, stay focused."

Jack was studying the report Robin had prepared regarding the pharmacy owners. The salient facts about the couple were simple enough: Bob and Alice Murphy were both forty-three, they lived at 296 Vista Sage Drive with their pet dog, Bogey, and they had one married daughter.

Jack was sure the psychological impact would be greater if he reeled off the facts to the owners by memory, rather than reading from a piece of paper. He had a video of the daughter, and a video of a bludgeoned corpse he could show at the end of his threatening speech.

The Jiffy Pharmacy was located at the end of a strip center just off Montana Avenue. There were no cars parked in front of the business, but Robin parked several spaces away in front of a jewelry store.

Jack opened his door and said. "Let's move. They'll be closing in a *jiffy*." He had read that an effective leader added humor during stressful situations.

A man in a white smock was standing behind the counter of the small drug store. He looked up from his computer screen as the foursome entered.

"Come in. I'll be right with you."

Jack approached the counter and said in a low key, friendly tone, "Bob, how much for a bottle of twenty-milligram Ritalin?"

Looking up from the computer screen and adjusting his glasses, the pharmacist replied, "Do you have a prescription, sir?"

Jack decided to impress his three cohorts and said in a loud, threatening manner, "I didn't say I wanted to fill a prescription, I asked about the cost of a twenty-milligram bottle of Ritalin. Is the question too difficult for you?"

The pharmacist stood and removed his glasses as Robin walked around the counter and entered a door that led to a storage room. Burk pulled the shade on the front door as Lester casually strolled behind the counter. Robin emerged from the back room pushing a middle-aged lady in a wheelchair. The lady's eyes were wide, her complexion pale.

"Well, hello," Jack said. You must be Alice. How long have you been riding the chair?"

Alice didn't respond, her face was as white as the smock she was wearing.

Jack was not through with his bullying. "Bob, does Alice ignore you the way she's ignoring me? Has the cat got her tongue?"

"She's ill. Leave her alone." It was a pleading tone, as opposed to anger.

Jack puffed out his chest. "Bob, this is your lucky day. My name is Jack Pope. Don't forget it."

With a sweep of his hand in a grand fashion, he continued, "Meet the Seventh Avenue Crew. We're soon going to supply you with several pharmaceutical products that will make you extra money. Cash money! Can you believe it?"

Burk took Robin's place behind the wheel chair and put his hands on Alice's shoulders. He leaned over and started moving both hands down her chest. She made a coughing sound and slowly slumped forward. Burk placed both hands on her breasts and pulled her back to a sitting position. The look on his face indicated that he was enjoying his work.

In a quick movement, the pharmacist got on his knees and was reaching under the counter. He retrieved a .45 caliber hand-gun and started fumbling with the safety. Lester casually pulled his revolver from his waist band, placed it on the back of the pharmacist's head . . . and was the most surprised person in the pharmacy when the gun discharged. The body lurched forward and fell face down in front of the wheelchair.

Lester was staring at his gun as if it was a poisonous snake. "Shit!" His vocabulary was down to one word. "Shit! Shit! It was an accident!"

"You idiot!" Jack said. "What's wrong with you! What happened?"

Robin lifted the limp head of the pharmacist's wife. She put her index finger on the woman's neck, trying to find a pulse, and said calmly, "Her face is blue . . . I think she's dead."

Burk was almost as nonchalant as Robin. "Well, I guess we can forget about this distributor ever coming on-line."

Jack stood frozen, visibly shaken. "Everybody shut up. Are you sure she's dead?" There was no question about the pharmacist being deceased. "Drag the bodies to the back room and let's get out of here. I've got to think this through."

Robin wheeled the lifeless body of the wife to the back room while Burk and Lester dragged the dead pharmacist down the aisle, blood smearing the floor. Lester stopped, bent over, and gagged. Burk continued with the task of getting the body through the door to the storage room.

Jack was beginning to regain his composure and started issuing orders. "Okay, let's get it together. Lester, find the shell casing. Robin, wipe down anyplace that might have any of our fingerprints. The wheelchair, door knobs, the counter. Anything! Move! We need to get out of here as soon as possible."

Burk, still calm and in control of his emotions, said to Lester, "You know, the police can analyze the contents of your throw-up and get DNA from it."

"You perverted bastard. I didn't throw-up, something was caught in my throat."

Jack's composure disappeared. He swallowed a Ritalin pill without water and screamed, "Now! Get rid of the fingerprints and get to the van!"

Robin brushed by Burk and said, "Come on, perv, let's go."

Everyone was silent during the first five minutes of the drive back to the bar. The evening sky was already being punctuated with the signature trail of sparks from several day-early bottle rockets.

Jack finally broke the silence. "This is not all bad. My friend, Carlos Delgado, will be impressed with our aggressiveness and commitment. I'll let him know how we handle a situation when someone doesn't cooperate. Yes, he'll like the way we do business." Jack was talking himself into the more positive aspects of extortion and murder. He looked back at Lester. "Good work, man. The pharmacist could have killed us all." He was back to his basic principles of good management.

Lester was still pale and could only utter a grunting sound.

Burk leaned over and whispered, "Good work, killer. The Seventh Avenue Crew rides again."

When Robin glanced in the rear-view mirror and saw the flashing red lights, she said, "Uh oh." She knew the difference between skyrockets and police car flashers. "Everyone, shut the fuck up. We're being stopped."

Jack put his head in both hands. The Ritalin had kicked-in, but the events of the evening had him on edge. His "crew" had just killed someone, and accident or not, he could go to prison for the rest of his life.

Lester was fidgeting in his seat, jabbing his finger-tips against his forehead. "I didn't mean for the gun to go off. It wasn't my fault. It wasn't my fault."

Burk slid open the blade of his knife and calmly said, "I will not be arrested for something this asshole did."

"I told you to shut up. I'll handle this." Robin lowered her window.

"Good evening, ma'am." The officer was polite and didn't show any signs of reaching for his weapon.

Managing a sultry smile, Robin replied, "And good evening to you, officer."

Leaning forward and looking into the van, he said, "Do you know why I stopped you?"

"No sir, I don't."

"Either both of your tail-lights are out, or else you didn't stop before making a right turn at the red light when you exited Montana Avenue." It was apparent that the officer was making an attempt at lighthearted sarcasm.

"I guess I just rolled through it, officer. I promise to pay better attention." Robin slowly lowered her head and raised her eyelids as she said *officer*.

The officer took one last look at the passengers in the van and said, "Okay. Pay attention to your driving and have a good evening."

As Robin pulled the van back onto the street, she shook her head. "Goddammit, I'm renaming this the *pussy van*, because we have a bunch of 'em in here."

8

Odessa/El Paso, Texas
Tuesday, July 4th

It was 8:30 a.m. and the temperature was close to ninety when Arsen walked to his car in the parking lot. It was supposed to be hot in early July . . . and it was. He had taken his impromptu date back to her car at the bar, and afterwards stopped at Denny's for breakfast. He leaned on the hood of his black Lexus LS 460 and entered a number on his cell phone. It was for, Nils, his only contact. He had never asked any personal questions regarding Nil's location, whom he represented, or his last name.

"Yes. How can I assist you, Arsen?" No matter when Arsen called, day or night, there was always an answer on the first or second ring.

"Good morning, Nils." Arsen knew it could be noon or midnight depending on where Nils was located. "I have a personal favor. I'm working on a situation for a friend. Could you get me any information on a fellow by the name of Jack Pope who lives in El Paso or thereabouts?"

"I'll call you back." Nils rarely wasted time on small talk.

It took Arsen exactly ten minutes to arrive in his driveway. The three-bedroom, white frame house blended nicely with the other residences in the middle-income neighborhood. Small front yards, spacious back yards. His phone rang before he could open the car door.

"Yes."

"Jack Pope graduated from New Mexico State in Las Cruces about five years ago with a degree in psychology. His college degree and his experience as a bookie while in school evidently didn't prepare him for the real world. He sold shoes, managed a small apartment building, and tried his luck at being a travel agent. Failure was his constant friend in each endeavor."

"Interesting. What's he doing now?"

"He recently bought a bar in El Paso and passed all the necessary qualifications in order to own that type of business. No criminal record. The name of the establishment is the Seventh Avenue Lounge and it's located at 1566 Seventh Avenue, near the Santa Fe Street Bridge. Mr. Pope takes a twenty-milligram Ritalin pill, which is a heavy dosage, three times a day."

"How do you know so much about someone who doesn't have a criminal record?"

"Never thought you'd ask. During his college days, Pope testified for a friend during a rape investigation. Jack provided credible testimony that he and his girlfriend were absolutely, positively with the friend at the time of the alleged rape and there was no way he could have been involved. Got him off. The friend was Carlos Delgado, the illegitimate son of Joaquin Guzman, also known as El Chapo. Delgado is now a lieutenant in the Sinaloa Cartel in Juarez. They're still friends and still in contact. Not sure why, but we have our suspicions."

"Thanks, Nils."

"Oh, one more item. The authorities believe that Carlos reciprocated a month later when he and two cohorts beat one of Jack's deadbeat bookie clients nearly to death. Couldn't be proven."

"Carlos must be a really bad dude."

"Indeed, he is. Arsen, keep me informed. As you can tell, there's interest in some things going on in Juarez."

"Will do. Nils, do you have the number for a *transfer site* in El Paso?"

Without hesitating, Nils reeled off the number. He ended the conversation on an upbeat note.

"Have a happy Fourth of July and be careful."

Arsen had memorized the address of the Seventh Avenue Lounge and the phone number for the *transfer site*. A transfer site referred to a funeral home with a crematorium. Arsen didn't have any doubts as to what had happened to Jimmy Hoffa.

Arsen entered another number as he entered the front door and walked to the living room couch.

"Hello." The voice had a neutral tone.

Arsen was adept at detecting anger, fear, or elation from the sound of someone's voice. He listened to the pitch, the rhythm, and the frequency of sounds for clues. Nothing stood out so far.

Leaning back on the couch with his feet planted on a coffee table, Arsen responded, "Jamie, this is Arsen. How're your parents doing?"

"Not so good. They're still pretty shook up from the visit they had at the store. You mentioned last night that you might be able to get information about these guys. Any luck?"

"A few items. I'll be in El Paso by two-thirty this afternoon. I think we should talk before you take any action. Okay?"

"Sounds good to me. Let's meet at my parent's grocery store. The name of the store is Big City Grocery and it's located at 803 Mundy Drive, near downtown. Since it's a holiday, they'll be closing early at four. I'll wait for you in the parking lot in case you're late."

"I won't be late. See you at two-thirty." Another address committed to memory.

Arsen took a shower and packed a small hand-carry bag with enough clothes for a week. He also removed a golf bag from a closet. The bag consisted of only two golf clubs: a five-iron and a three-wood, with head cover. The pockets also contained a Glock 17 with a seventeen-round clip and a threaded barrel for a silencer, a Glock 42 with an ankle holster, ten additional clips, and a switch-blade knife with an ankle holster. The last item in the bag was a small, hand-held, battery operated dental drill.

This should prepare me for any hazards I find on the golf course.

Arsen called Evelyn and arranged for her to tend his backyard garden while he was gone. She spent more time in the garden than he did due to his travels. The next phone call was to the transfer site.

"Yes." The voice was even and calm.

"This is Arsen. Nils referred me to you."

"Yes, I know."

"How late will you be open this week?"

"How late do you want me to be open?"

"Could be early, could be very late."

"Just call and give me five-minutes notice."

"And what is your address and what is the name of the closest hotel to your facility?"

"3412 Wyoming. Gardner Hotel on Franklin. My name is Spencer." Spencer was very specific, almost rude.

"Thanks."

Arsen made on-line reservations at the Gardner, and ten minutes later the Lexus was headed west on Interstate 20. El Paso was only four hours away. The tomatoes would be fine.

———•◦•———

It was exactly 2:30 p.m. when Arsen pulled into the small parking lot on the side of Big City Grocery. The red brick, one-story building was located at the corner of Mundy and Yandell Drive. As he entered the door, he made a quick appraisal of the interior, which was larger than he expected. A man behind the counter on the left, was sacking several items for a customer. There were five aisles of food products, and the white tile floors appeared to be spotless. A bank of frozen food cases lined the wall at the back of the store.

Jamie Rodriquez appeared from one of the aisles, followed by a middle-aged woman wearing a white smock. Arsen assumed she was Jamie's mother.

Jamie smiled as he spoke. "For some reason, I figured you would be here right on time."

Arsen returned the smile. "I'm lucky to be on time. Seems like the Fourth of July traffic was all headed toward El Paso. The highway was awfully crowded."

As the only customer in the store walked out the door, Jamie said, "Arsen, I'd like you to meet my parents. This is my mother, Luanna, and this is my father, Reynaldo."

Arsen nodded at Mrs. Rodriguez and shook hands with Reynaldo. As they were exchanging pleasantries, a customer walked into the store.

Jamie said, "We're having a Fourth of July cookout at my parents' home this evening. How about coming over? We can talk in private. Besides, I owe you a drink."

"Sounds good. Tell me where and what time."

"I should have the grill going by six. The address is 296 West Cliff Drive. Need to write it down?"

"Nope. Got it. See you at six."

"By the way, where are you staying?"

"Gardner Hotel on Franklin."

"Oh, good. That's probably the oldest hotel in El Paso. As I recall, the building was built in 1920. I hear it's pretty nice, though."

The drive to the hotel took fifteen minutes. The three-story structure was identified by a blue and white sign on the top corner of the building and another over the front door. It wasn't the most fashionable hotel in the area, but the location, at the intersection of Franklin and Stanton Street, was perfect. The Stanton Street Bridge and the Santa Fe Street Bridge, both of which crossed over the Rio Grande to Juarez, were only five minutes away. The downtown area was close, and the *transfer site* was nearby.

Parking in the hotel lot, Arsen could see a fire escape ascending to the second and third floors.

A six-story office building was adjacent to the parking area.

Arsen walked through the double doors into a small lobby. The registration desk was at the back of the lobby, a marble staircase on the left. A door next to the staircase led into a restaurant.

"Good afternoon, sir." The attractive lady behind the desk smiled as she welcomed the new guest.

"Arsen. I believe you have reservations for me."

Looking at her computer screen, the clerk appeared confused. "Yes, we do, Mr. Arsen. It is *Mr. Arsen* . . . correct?

Arsen had been confronted with this situation many times in his life. Without explanation, he said, "Yes. Any chance I could get a room on the second floor near the fire escape?"

Looking again at her computer screen, the clerk said, "Absolutely. As a matter of fact, would you like to stay in the same room as John Dillinger?"

"Is he still in the room?" Arsen grinned.

"Well, you know what I mean. Dilinger stayed in Room 221 in January, 1934. He registered under the name of John D. Ball and was captured later that month."

"Fine with me, but only if you can guarantee I won't be arrested."

The clerk smiled at Arsen's teasing. "I can't guarantee it, but I'll give you a heads-up if the Feds storm the lobby."

Nearing the end of the second-floor hallway, Arsen could see a window leading to the fire escape. He unlocked the door and placed his travel bag on the double bed. The golf bag with his accessories was safely locked in the trunk of the Lexus. The mechanic at the body shop who customized the trunk had assured Arsen it would take a thief with a blow torch at least two hours to get it open.

The room was small, but neat. The furnishings consisted of a double bed, an antique chest-of- drawers, an end table with a telephone, and a chair near the window. The hardwood floor appeared to be well maintained.

Arsen walked into the hallway and inspected the window exit to the fire escape. The window had a double latch and a small sign indicating the window should remained locked at all times.

How can you get out if the window is always locked? Arsen smiled at his simple attempt at levity. *In this line of work, you can't be too cautious. The bad guys could sneak in at any time.*

Returning to his room, Arsen removed his shoes and reclined on the bed. No sooner had his head hit the pillow, his cell phone rang.

"Yes?"

For some reason, Arsen knew it was Nils the second the phone rang.

"How's the Gardner?" Nils was well informed.

"I would definitely give it five stars, maybe six. How's Washington D.C.?"

"Never been there." This was one of the few times Nils had shown any sign of a personality.

"This is a total coincidence, but since you're in El Paso, I have a job for you."

"Does it pay well?"

"Two-fifty. Same as Panama, but different."

"Tell me about it."

"Have you ever been to Socorro? I'm talking about a suburb of El Paso, not the city in Mexico."

"Yes. I know exactly where it is. It's about thirty minutes south on Loop 375."

"This assignment needs to take place at midnight tomorrow tonight. Not earlier, not later. I'm aware that you've called the number I gave you for the transfer site. Spencer is expecting you this afternoon. He'll give you additional equipment and instructions. Okay?"

Looking at his watch, Arsen said, "I'll be leaving in a few minutes."

The conversations today with Nils had caused some concerns. Several thoughts whirled through Arsen's mind: *If the gang that threatened Jamie's parents actually has ties with the Sinaloa Cartel, things could get messy. Really messy. Good thing I'm in a messy kind of mood.*

The drive to the transfer site at 3412 Wyoming took five minutes. A sign on the front lawn indicated the Dunleavy Funeral Home & Crematorium had been assisting families for over twenty years. A wooden bench was situated under a large tree in front of the building, adding a feeling of serenity to circumstances usually associated with distress and discomfort.

Arsen entered the large, oak double doors and was met by an imposing man in his mid-thirties.

He was tall, tanned, and appeared to have a well-developed body under his tight, European style trousers, and white dress shirt.

"You must be Spencer." Arsen suspected this wasn't the man's real name, but played along anyway.

Without speaking, Spencer motioned toward an office on the right side of the lobby. After closing the office door, he handed Arsen a backpack.

"This contains four C-4 bricks, detonator caps, and a timer. The target is a tunnel under the border in Socorro. The tunnel starts at an elementary school on the Mexican side of the border, crosses under the Rio Grande, and ends at a maintenance shack next to a playground at the Rio Bosque Park in Socorro. Aggressive bastards, huh?" Handing Arsen a piece of paper, Spencer continued. "Here, memorize the tunnel dimensions. Plant the C-4 about halfway down the tunnel on the Mexican side. Set it to detonate at midnight. Okay? I understand you're very familiar with C-4." Spencer raised an eyebrow.

"The C-4 will not be a problem. Where specifically is the park and where is the maintenance shack located in the park?"

Spencer communicated in bullet points. "Take the Southside Road exit off 375 and stay on it to Levee Road. Follow Levee all the way to the end, which is near the border. A gate to the park will be open. The maintenance shack is located about a hundred yards straight ahead. The door will be unlocked. A trap door is next to the wall under a stack of pallets. Got that?"

"Yep." Studying the paper for a few seconds, Arsen gave it back and said, "Just curious. I thought most of the tunnels were on the Arizona and California borders. Didn't realize there were any in the El Paso area."

Showing signs of a smile and elaborating for the first time, Spencer said, "El Paso is a city of secrets. There have been books and articles written about the supposed tunnel system under the city and it may have begun with the smuggling of illegal Chinese laborers to work on the railroads. The largest smuggling ring of Chinese in the world was created in Juarez. Some say there are tunnels under the Rio Grande from Juarez to El Paso and others say it would have been too difficult to dig those types of tunnels without being detected. Who knows? However, we do know about the tunnel in Socorro."

The two discussed additional details of how, when, and where the C-4 would be placed, with the timing of the operation being paramount.

After shaking hands, Arsen slung the backpack over his shoulder and turned toward the door.

He had dressed for the cookout and was wearing a pair of light blue pinstriped shorts and an Odessa Permian T-shirt.

Pointing at Arsen's arms, Spencer asked, "Hey, cowboy, you pump iron, or what?"

"No, just good genes." Arsen had a number of things on his mind, and muscle development wasn't one of them.

Arsen placed the backpack in the trunk of his Lexus, next to his golf bag. A pair of black cargo pants, a black shirt, and a pair of black boots were always in the corner of the trunk, along with a few other items of clothing.

It had been a long day, but it was far from over. After this evening's cook-out, Arsen had one more stop . . . the Seventh Avenue Lounge.

9

El Paso, Texas
Tuesday, July 4th

Jack, wearing only a pair of boxer shorts, opened the desk drawer and randomly took out one of his *burner* phones. He liked to call it a *burner*, since he had paid cash for the phone and didn't have to sign a contract, but in reality, it was simply a prepaid cell phone. The phone would be thrown away after the call to Carlos Delgado. The intrigue of being a big-time criminal was intoxicating to Jack. Almost as intoxicating as Robin, who now had placed her hand on the opening of his shorts and was starting their morning ritual, her fiery red locks cascading down Jack's chest.

"Yeah," Carlos answered in a low, guttural tone.

"Carlos, my friend, this is Jack. *Como estas?*"

"*Muy bien.* What's going on?"

"Are we still set for the first delivery this Friday morning?

Carlos hesitated before responding. "Yes. Why do you ask?"

Jack's voice went up an octave. "Oh, everything is fine here. We had to eliminate a couple of people at a potential distribution site yesterday. They wouldn't cooperate, so we got rid of 'em. We'll be ready by Friday. *No problema.*"

"Was it clean?"

"Absolutely. You know that I'm thorough."

"Yes, I know. Good work. Your reputation will expand and no one will fuck with you. That's why you're able to receive drug shipments on . . . let's say . . . consignment. You're the first person in the history of this business to have such a good arrangement. I owe you, but don't betray my trust. Okay?"

Jack knew what the subliminal message meant. It would be a deadly mistake to lose the trust of Carlos Delgado, friend or not. "I would never disappoint you, *mi amigo.* I'll be waiting for your man Friday morning. *Adios.*"

Jack had recently begun mixing Spanish phrases into his conversations with Carlos. He was disappointed that Carlos hadn't seemed more pleased with his conversational efforts.

Jack looked down at Robin and said, "Enough. Let's talk."

Standing, Robin, said, "What do you mean, *let's talk*? I wasn't finished!"

Jack was starting to hyperventilate. The pressure was starting to build on his new business venture, he'd forgotten to take his morning dose of Ritalin, and his long, blond hair was a mess. His thoughts were becoming completely random. As he ran his hands through his hair, he looked at his stomach and thought: *Too soft, too flabby. I'm totally going to shit.* Swallowing a pill, and chasing it with a drink of bottled water, he said, "We've got to get back on track. Do you have another potential distribution site for us to visit? I can't let Carlos down."

Robin was barefoot and wearing only a long red tee-shirt that extended half-way down her thighs.

"Well, sweetheart, I do indeed. I visited a store last week and it appears to be a solid possibility. The pharmacy we screwed-up yesterday was my first choice, but Barbie's Cards and Gifts on Cielo Vista Drive is high on my list and is in the same general area. It's strategically located to serve both the airport and Ft. Bliss ... just like the pharmacy."

"Are they open today, you know, on the Fourth of July?" The Ritalin had not completely taken effect yet.

Robin, in a barely audible voice, said, "No, my dear, I've not forgotten that today is the Fourth. They're not open today, but they'll be open tomorrow."

"How about the Rodriguez grocery store, Big City Grocery? When are you going to conduct training for them? Will they be ready on Friday when we supply them with produce?"

"The *training seminar* . . ." Robin had a self-satisfied look on her face as she teased Jack with one of her own business-like terms. ". . . will take place on Thursday. I'll take one of the boys with me."

Jack took a deep breath and slowly exhaled. "Robin, I appreciate your attention to detail, and tomorrow is fine. Actually, tomorrow is ideal. As you know, we're initiating a new member of the crew this afternoon, so we wouldn't have time to check out a new distribution site anyway." He was impulsively running his hands through his hair. "Since today is a holiday, we'll spend most of it celebrating. It'll be good for the crew's moral." *Jeez, all of a sudden, I'm way too calm. Maybe the twenty-milligram dose is too much.*

Robin asked quizzically, "Is this one of the guys I turned up from my Internet search?"

"Yeah, the guy on Craig's List that was looking for an investment to start some kind of a paint-ball park. Gus Fever. Real bad ass, but no police record. I'm going to call him Fiver, since he'll be the fifth member of the crew. Get it, Fiver ... Fever?" Jack was breathing easier, but still talking in clipped sentences.

Robin raised her eyebrows. "I hope we can afford him. The bar has start-up expenses in addition to the salaries you're paying these guys."

Jack said, "Well, as you know, the hundred grand I inherited from my father has kept us from sleeping under a bridge, so we're okay for now. The profits from our new business venture should be pouring in soon."

"Hope so."

"Back to our new-hire. I met with this Gus character, and I think he'll fit in just fine. No problem."

Robin shrugged. "Well, I hope he fits in with the rest of the crew. Actually, I don't think the rest of the crew *fits in* with each other."

"Don't be concerned, I'll handle these minor personality issues."

"Oh yeah. One of the *personality issues* murdered a pharmacist yesterday!"

"Have you looked on your phone for any news of what happened?"

Opening her palms and nodding, Robin said, "There's nothing in this morning's on-line *El Paso News*. Since today is a holiday, the bodies probably haven't been discovered yet."

"Jesus Christ! It could be several days before anyone gets suspicious! The bodies will ----"

"Nothing can connect us with what happened. My only concern is how Lester is handling it. The little marshmallow craves attention, but I think he'll be okay if we stroke him enough."

Jack continued with his attempts to smooth his too-long, swept back hair. "You're correct. Lester needs lots of attention to make up for his younger years. I doubt that he had any friends in high school, and probably never got laid until he could pay for it. I've got a good handle on his inner-needs and thoughts. He's just looking for an opportunity to make some big bucks so that he can go back to his next reunion and impress all the girls."

Jack was back, once again in charge of his actions, philosophical thoughts, and speech. With an awkward grin, he said, "I've never shared this with you before, Robin, but I think there's one underlying reason why you and I click. It has to do with the *shadow aspect* of our personalities. As Carl Jung wrote, everyone carries a *shadow* in their unconscious mind, and the less it's embodied in an individual's conscious life, the blacker and denser it is. He described it as being one's link to more primitive animal instincts and human darkness. What do you think?"

Robin slowly shook her head and said in a barely audible voice, "What the fuck are you talking about?"

Jack's inclination was to discuss more of Carl Jung's research, but instead pulled down his boxer shorts and said, "Take off your tee-shirt and sit in my lap. We'll make Carl turn over in his grave."

It was 6:00 p.m. and the initiation ceremony for Gus Fever had been completed in Jack's office. The Seventh Avenue Crew now had five members, only two shorts of a fully operational organization.

Gus Fever put on his shirt and looked at Burk. "Damn! You cut that seven a little too deep."

Grinning, Burk squeaked, "Hey, don't be a such a puss."

Chiming in, Lester added, "If you're whining about the little cut on your shoulder, I can't imagine how you reacted to the big slice someone put on your face!"

Gus had a six-inch scar that ran from the corner of his mouth to near his right ear. He was nearing forty, making him the oldest member of the crew. The scar, his shaved head, and his bushy eyebrows provided Gus with an intimidating look.

Even though Gus had known Lester for less than an hour, he quickly replied, "Look, *Plain Jane*, don't mess with me or else you may get a scar of your own."

Jack intervened. "Gentlemen, and lady, we're a team. And teams that work together in harmony are teams that win. Believe me, we're going to win, and win big. This is a once in a lifetime opportunity. Okay?"

Robin, rolling her eyes, offered a half-hearted response. "Let's be winners."

Jack decided to proceed with the "carrot" portion of his "carrot and stick" management style. "Since today is the Fourth of July, we're going to celebrate. Drinks are on me. Let's adjourn to the bar and create our own fireworks."

Shelly Jones, the lounge manager, was serving one of the eight customers sitting at the bar, in addition to three middle-aged ladies sitting at one of the tables. Shelly was what Jack called a "religious freak" because she was so straight and honest. She was the bartender, the janitor, kept the books, and worked with the beer and liquor distributors. Robin had known her before she became a Born-Again Christian, and she was perfect for the job. Shelly didn't have a clue as to what Jack was all about. They would hire more bar staff as business increased.

The pool table was silent, but the juke box was blaring a new-age rock song.

Jack stopped at the end of the bar while the rest of the crew made their way to the booth near the juke box.

"Shelly, how's business?" Jack was proud of his multi-tasking abilities.

Shelly was not beautiful, but attractive. In Jack's mind, her unbelievably large breasts more than made up for her overly religious attitude. Jack hoped the customers paid more attention to her physical characteristics than to her basic beliefs.

"Pretty good, Mr. Pope. The heat outside and the holiday have brought us more business than usual. I have a friend coming in this evening to work on a tips-only basis. Praise Jesus!"

Jack thought: *Jesus my ass! Just sell the alcohol!* But instead, he said, "Keep up the good word . . . I mean good work."

Jack took a chair from an empty table and placed it at the end of the booth. Shelly followed him and began taking drink orders from the crew. Robin and Jack ordered martinis, Burk and Gus ordered bourbon on the rocks, and Lester, after hesitating for a few seconds, finally ordered a Singapore Sling.

Burk struck first. "Singapore Sling! That's about the most girly drink I've ever heard a man order."

Robin, sitting next to Lester in the booth, rubbed her hand on his back and said, "Your bra strap seems a little tight. Maybe your Singapore Sling will loosen it up."

Jack observed his four employees and gave himself a positive stroke: *This is going to be a great team building exercise. The Seventh Avenue Crew is on the way to the top. With my leadership skills, we may become more well-known than Pablo Escobar ever was.*

"Say what you want," Lester said. "I'm the only one here who's made his bones. Right, boss?"

Robin raised her eyebrows and shrugged. Burk nodded.

Gus Fever cocked his head and frowned. "How did you *make your bones?*"

Jack further fortified Lester's ego by saying, "We had a little issue with a couple of potential distributors the other day and Lester solved the problem.

It was an accident, but at least Lester showed a little initiative. You'll be reading about it in the paper in a day or so. Enough said."

Shelly brought the drinks and the party was nearing lift-off.

"Shelly, honey, keep the juke box hot. We need to enhance the reputation of the Seventh Avenue Lounge. You know, a place to have a good time. Music and fun." Jack liked the feel of being an entrepreneur.

As Shelly walked away, Gus spoke for only the second time since sitting in the booth. "Does Shelly have a boyfriend?"

Burk sprang into action. "No, but she spends a lot of time staring at me. Keep your hands off."

After only two sips of his Sling, Lester commented on the discussion. "There's only two places I would like for my hands to be on Miss Shelly. And I think she would like it a lot."

"You couldn't pick up a whore if you had a fist full of hundred-dollar bills and two credit cards." Burk's high-pitched voice could be heard across the small lounge.

Lester downed most of his drink in a single gulp. "Oh yeah, see those three strays sitting at the table over there. I'll bet I can get one of them to dance with me. Come on, I'll bet you ten bucks!"

"Okay, you're on. It'll be worth ten bucks to get you out of the booth."

Lester demonstrated that he was more than just plain. "Stayin' Alive" was playing on the juke box as he strutted across the floor. One of the ladies took his hand and started dancing by the table. Lester, lacking even the most basic elements of rhythm, moved his hips and arms trying his best to look cool.

Burk shook his head and shrieked, "Looks like two frogs fucking in a blender!"

Jack glanced at Robin and mumbled, "I thought mild-mannered Burk didn't swear."

"He seems to have a difficult time holding his liquor."

The party continued for the next three hours. More patrons came into the lounge and the crew continued drinking. The martinis, bourbon, and Singapore Slings kept coming. Jack's team-building plan was becoming expensive, but worthwhile.

And the gentleman wearing the Scottish touring cap standing at the juke box went completely unnoticed.

10

Juarez, Mexico
Tuesday, July 4th

It was not quite noon, and Carlos Delgado and his right-hand man, Arturo Hernandez, were drinking beer on the patio of the compound's main house. Carlos's complex consisted of five acres with a ten thousand square foot residence, two smaller houses, and a bunk house that could sleep twenty men. The acreage was surrounded by a fifteen-foot stone wall. The entire wall was topped by rolled razor wire.

Carlos was leaning back in his chair, his feet on the glass table top. "I had a call from Jack Pope this morning."

"Jack Pope? You mean the bitch you met in college?"

"Yes, the bitch. As you know, I owe him a favor for what he did for me. I always repay my debts. I'm honor bound. Right?" Carlos was handsome by anyone's description. Not only was he handsome, he had a charismatic personality and a captivating smile. People who knew him relished his smile ... but never his frown. A serious frown from Carlos Delgado usually meant that either he or one of his men was going to kill, or seriously hurt someone.

"Right. Supplying him with drugs on consignment . . . already cut, already packaged . . . is a very gracious way to repay the debt. You always keep your word."

Carlos finished his beer and tossed the bottle into the swimming pool. Both of Carlos's young daughters, who were sitting on the far edge of the pool, immediately jumped into the water to retrieve the bottle.

Carlos continued with his analysis of Jack Pope. "He's such a dumbass, he wouldn't know what to do if we sent him uncut, unpackaged, raw product. I told you about his idiot attempt at being a bookie in college. Anyway, I owe him. Even though it's a longshot, maybe using small businesses as distribution sites will add to our profits. No one can say I don't pay my debts."

Arturo adjusted the red bandana he wore on his forehead and laughed. "I understand, boss."

49

Carlos was relaxed and reflective, which was unusual for him. "How long have you known me, Arturo?"

"Six years. We were just wet-behind-the-ears young men when we joined the cartel. You've progressed well, and I appreciate you taking me along for the ride."

"In all those years, you never mentioned my connection to El Chapo. You know he's my biological father. Right?"

"Yes, I know it to be true."

"You've never accused me of being in this leadership position because of my father. You've never called me a bastard." Carlos knew full well that if anyone should be so bold as to call him a bastard, he would have them skinned, chopped-up, and dumped in the desert.

After drinking half the beer in one swallow, Arturo said, "You have a good bloodline. You've earned your promotions and your position. And like I said, you've been good to me. We've accomplished a lot over the years in this very dangerous business."

"Yes, we have."

"I don't recall you ever mentioning your mother. Is she still in your life?"

"No, she passed away several years ago. She was a dancer in Mexico City when she got pregnant. Never married. She had me and lived off a monthly stipend from El Chapo for the rest of her life."

Arturo finished his beer and opened another one. "Was he in your life when you were a child?"

"I saw him occasionally, but he had another family. Oddly enough, most people didn't know who he was at the time. As you know, he's short and heavy set, while I'm tall and lean … due to my mother's genes. I took a lot of shit growing up until I finally put a stop to the teasing and harassment."

"How did you do that?"

"When I was fifteen, an older boy stole my lunch and called me a 'mommy's boy.' I followed him after school and cut his throat, cut off his ears, and cut out his eyes. There were no witnesses, so nothing came of it. For some reason, I was never picked-on again at school, or anywhere else for that matter."

Arturo, who was in the process of peeling the label off his beer bottle, looked up and said, "Well, you have to be a man in this life. You got everyone's attention."

Carlos's mood changed from sunny and bright to dark and foreboding in an instant. "Antonia will be delivering the drugs to Jack Pope on Friday.

You'll have the shipment ready. Am I correct?" As he spoke the last three words of his statement, his eyes narrowed.

"Absolutely. I'll have them packaged, boxed, and ready to go for her. She's a special young lady, very special, and everything will go smoothly. I'll arrange for her to cross the Santa Fe Street Bridge without any problems. No worry, boss."

"Oh, Arturo, my friend, I don't worry. Only people who fuck-up my plans need to worry."

11

El Paso, Texas
Tuesday, July 4th

Siri had been flawless in guiding Arsen to Jamie's parents' home on West Cliff Drive. It was located on a narrow street in a well-maintained, middle-class neighborhood. Arsen parked at the curb and made a closer observation. The split-level house was aesthetically pleasing with the second story above the garage, a simple roofline, and symmetrically spaced windows. The front yard consisted of desert-style landscaping on both sides of the driveway, where two cars were parked. Another was at the curb in front of Arsen. He assumed Jamie's two sisters would be attending the cookout.

Although the humidity was low, the afternoon temperature was close to a hundred degrees. The front door opened as Arsen reached the porch.

"I knew you would be on time. Come in and meet the rest of my family." Jamie was carrying a beer and smiled as he shook Arsen's hand. "Follow me. Everyone is outside by the pool."

As they exited the kitchen door onto the awning covered patio, Arsen stopped and stared for a moment. He wasn't looking at the swimming pool with the two children floating on colorful tubes, the smoking grill on the right, or Jamie's parents who were talking with a woman who was keeping watch on the kids. It was the young lady standing on the edge of the patio. She was wearing a white tank-top and white shorts that accentuated her tanned legs and jet black, shoulder length hair. Arsen was struck by her natural beauty.

"Hey everyone, this is the fellow I was talking about . . . Arsen." Jamie made the announcement with a flourish of his hands as if he were introducing a foreign dignitary to a convention audience.

The attractive young lady approached Arsen, extended her hand, and said with a smile, "Nice to meet you Mr. Arsen Arsen. My name is Kasie. Kasie with a K."

Arsen took her hand. "My pleasure, Kasie."

Her hands were soft, but her grip was firm . . . just like her brother's.

Jamie filled in the blanks. "Kasie graduated from UTEP in the spring and will start her accounting career with Ernst and Young next month. She's way smarter than I am."

"Oh sure, Doctor Rodriguez, I'm the smart one!" The sun was behind her, but there seemed to be a sparkle in Kasie's eyes as she expressed her modesty.

Arsen was trying to identify the intense feeling in the pit of his stomach.

Mr. and Mrs. Rodriguez shook hands with Arsen for the second time that day. Neither of them appeared old enough to have three grown children and two grandkids.

The woman with the two children shouted and waved from near the pool. "Hi. I'm Rosa. I'll see you guys when I get these two fish out of the water."

Jamie motioned toward the chairs under the patio awning and said, "Let's sit and have a drink. What's your pleasure?"

Arsen and Kasie both requested beer, and both parents asked for iced tea. The next hour consisted of small talk about the weather, Jamie's medical school grant, the grandchildren, and Arsen's military and private investigation experience. Rosa situated her two children in front of the TV inside the house, and then joined the group. Kasie was seated next to Arsen and touched his arm several times as they talked. His aesthetic senses were on overload.

High clouds in the west did their best to obscure the glare of the July sun, but it was still warm. The laughter of children and the barking of dogs could be heard coming from the street. The promise of a fireworks display later in the evening was the cause of the excitement. Jamie rotated between the patio and the outdoor grill, taking food and drink orders. The group ate, drank, and waited for the main topic of discussion.

Jamie initiated the conversation regarding his parents' traumatic experience at their grocery store. "Dad. Mom. I've given Arsen a summary of what happened at the store earlier in the week. Maybe you should fill him in on the details and then he can tell us what he found out about these guys."

Mr. Rodriguez spoke first, expressing his concern about the threats to his family. He described Jack Pope, both his physical appearance and his personality. He did the same regarding Robin, the woman with the iron fist. He hesitated when he came to Burk. "And then there's the guy that tore off my wife's blouse. I don't remember if they called him by name, but I'll never forget him. He's tall, skinny, and has a high, shrieky voice." Lowering his head, Mr. Rodriguez continued. "This is the one that carved the seven in my wife's shoulder, and then poured ink in the wound."

Mrs. Rodriguez had not spoken during the conversation. She had been sitting absolutely still with her eyes focused on Arsen. Her lips parted twice as if she wanted to speak, but she remained silent. Finally, lowering her head and looking at her shoes, she said, "He was holding me from behind, and kept rubbing his groin on me. It was worse than the cut on my shoulder."

Jamie was slowly shaking his head. His sisters appeared stunned.

Kasie stood, arms extended, palms up. "What exactly were the threats? Did they threaten to kill all of us, or what?"

Mr. Rodriguez pursed his lips and shrugged. "They just said they would harm us. Probably an empty threat. The leader of the gang said there would be some kind of training on Thursday, and then they would bring the drugs on Friday."

Arsen was taking mental notes. "He specifically said they would bring the drugs on *Friday?*"

"Yes."

Jamie gritted his teeth and frowned. "What do you think, Arsen? Were you able to find out anything about these people? Unless there's an immediate solution, I'll try to handle it myself."

Several thoughts were racing through Arsen's head. Jamie and his family had known him for only a short time, and for some reason, they seemed to be looking at him as a superhero type. *Where did that come from? Miguel Burbano referred Jamie to me. What did he tell the young man? Miguel has a good idea about my profession, but he doesn't know the details. The family is in a bind, they're afraid to go to the police, and they're grasping at straws.*

Arsen proceeded in a very deliberate manner. "Jack Pope *is* the name of the gang leader. This points to an inflated ego since he used his actual name. He has no criminal record and he has a college degree from New Mexico State. Unfortunately, he does have contacts within the Sinaloa Cartel. A friend of his from college is a lieutenant in the cartel. I've made a few assumptions based on what I know about the Pope gang, and based on my experience with the cartels."

The Rodriguez family was listening intently to Arsen's every word.

"This whole Jack Pope thing seems more like a favor being owed to him, as opposed to some big-time drug distribution scheme. Therefore, I don't think the cartel is, or will be, personally involved with anyone other than

Jack Pope on this side of the river. The cartels make their statements to the other cartels and don't want unnecessary exposure on this side of the border. That's the responsibility of the low-life drug dealers over here."

"So, you think this Jack Pope fellow is operating mostly on his own?" Jamie kept probing.

Arsen didn't mention the name of the bar Pope owned. The last thing he wanted was for Jamie to get involved right now. More information was needed.

"Yes. They probably get the drugs delivered from Juarez and distribute them over here. Which leads to another assumption . . . there must be other small businesses here in El Paso that are involved in the distribution." Looking at Mr. Rodriguez, Arsen said, "It wouldn't be possible for only one outlet of drugs to make it financially feasible to take such risks."

"What should we do?" Jamie said, with a questioning look.

"I'll be conducting additional due diligence this week. I'll stay in contact and let you know what I find out. In the meantime, we should keep the authorities out of this and maintain a low profile."

Jamie shrugged. "Okay."

A slight breeze arrived and seemed to punctuate the end of the troublesome conversation. The evening sun was beyond the two-story house next door, and the excitement was growing as evidenced by the children's voices in the neighborhood. The fireworks displays were at least an hour away, even though an occasional streak from a rocket could be seen.

Arsen believed his assumptions to be accurate regarding the cartel keeping to their side of the river ... at least ninety-five percent accurate. Jack Pope's leverage was in using the threat of the cartel taking revenge on the family at some time in the future, just like in the movies. The fact that Pope openly used his own name bothered Arsen. Either his threat was valid, or else he had an overwhelming egotistic, personality disorder.

I'll be alert, but I'm comfortable with the odds.

The two beers Arsen had consumed in the past two and a half hours should have relaxed him. Instead, his stomach . . . or was it his head . . . was churning. It had something to do with the young lady sitting next to him. He was having trouble getting his thoughts under control: *What is this? There's no such thing as love at first sight! I know the difference between love and lust, don't I? Bullshit. I don't know anything about her."*

Being so absorbed in his thoughts, Arsen barely heard Kasie speak. "I'm glad you're helping us. It gives me comfort."

Arsen said, "Yes . . . Yes, like I said, more information is needed. We have a few days before they return on Friday with the drugs. We're just getting started."

Jamie's sister, Rosa, and her mother, had gone into the house to check on the children. Mr. Rodriguez and Jamie were now standing next to the outdoor grill. Jamie had a wire brush in his hand.

In a light-hearted manner, Kasie said, "Jamie told me the story behind your double name. I like it. It's unique and cute."

Tilting his head and raising his eyebrows, Arsen said, "Well, as a kid, it was a little embarrassing, but I've been able to live with it." Smiling, he added, "But thanks."

"I mean it." Another touch on Arsen's arm.

Arsen asked, "What do you do in your spare time? Any hobbies or passions?" *Jeez, why would I use the word passion?*

"Well, since I graduated in June, I swim laps most every day, play tennis two or three times a week with my girlfriends, and eat out a lot."

"Any favorite restaurant?"

"One of my favorites is the Hoppy Monk. Great selection of beer, hence the name *Hoppy*. Teasingly, she added, "You know, like hops used in the brewing process."

Arsen nodded as if he'd just heard the secret formula for Coca Cola. "Got it."

"Anyway, great comfort food. Hamburgers and the like. Lots of UTEP students frequent the restaurant. If you have time this week, Jamie and I could introduce you to the Monk."

"How about tomorrow evening? I'll clear all other social obligations from my calendar." Arsen was trying his best to be clever and appealing.

Kasie nodded, and then motioned to her brother who was still standing at the grill. "Hey, Jamie. Want to go to the Monk with us tomorrow evening?"

Jamie strolled across the patio and took a seat. "I can't tomorrow. I told one of my high school buddies I'd go to his son's little league baseball game. Any other day would be okay."

With a hint of a smile, Kasie quickly said, "Never mind. You lose. I'll show Arsen the Monk." Touching his arm, she added, "Let's meet at six. We can have a beer and study the menu. Okay?"

A small sonic boom was followed by a dense, spherical burst of colored stars with multiple explosions in the center. Another loud bang resulted in trails of silver and gold strands producing a weeping willow effect. Several loud reports and white flashes covered the sky. Arsen wasn't sure if the fireworks display was real of if he was imagining the whole thing, but he knew he was tightly wrapped in the moment.

Regaining his composure, Arsen said, "Perfect. See you at six." And then thought: *Uhh oh, I have to blow up a tunnel late tomorrow night.*

Rosa, her mother, and the children returned to the patio. Arsen stood and vaguely referenced a report he needed to prepare for a client. During their initial meeting, he'd told Jamie he needed to visit El Paso to conduct business. And tonight, business it would be.

After saying his goodbyes, Arsen walked toward his car and looked at his watch. *Time to continue the party . . . at the Seventh Avenue Lounge.*

<hr/>

It was 9:00 p.m. when the black Lexus pulled into the parking lot adjoining the Seventh Avenue Lounge. Arsen noted the twelve cars and eight pickup trucks that had arrived before him. There was space for at least another ten vehicles near the street, but he chose to park at the back of the lot. A one-bulb light was attached to the side of the brick building, about ten feet from the ground and above a metal door. The door was located at the far end of the building near Arsen's car.

As he opened the trunk of his Lexus, Arsen realized it had been over twelve hours since he'd dropped off last night's date at J.D.'s After Dark. And here he was at another bar.

I've got to control my bad habits.

Reaching into the back corner of the trunk, he removed several items. He traded his shorts and T-shirt for a pair of black cargo pants and a black shirt. Within a few seconds, he was wearing a fake mustache, a fake goatee, and a pair of black-rimmed glasses. The Scottish touring cap completed his new look.

Arsen looked at the light bulb above the metal door and decided the five-iron in his golf bag would be adequate. He walked the short distance to the door, positioned himself, and smashed the bulb. After placing the golf club back in the bag, he removed a folded, plastic tarp from the bottom of the trunk and placed it, still folded, under the back of the Lexus. He left both Glocks in the golf bag, but attached the ankle holster containing the switchblade knife.

I need another drink.

Arsen paused as he entered the lounge. Typical interior: a bar being tended by a lady with large breasts, another female waitress waiting on the tables, numerous neon signs promoting various types of alcohol, a juke box playing loud music, and a pool table with drink glasses sitting on the rails. The feeble lighting came primarily from the glare of the neon signs over the bar. The quiet hum of voices blended nicely with the sound from the juke box.

No seats were available, so Arsen stood at the end of the bar. The patrons could have been transplanted from the bar he had visited the night before.

The dress code in all Texas bars must specify boots, tee-shirts, and baseball caps.

"What's your pleasure?" The bartender with the abundant chest was pleasant and polite.

"Tito's on the rocks. Lemon twist."

Looking at Arsen's Scottish touring cap and speaking over the ever-present din, she said, "I could tell you had class. Ordering the really good stuff, huh?"

Arsen smiled. "Hand crafted and distilled six times."

In few minutes, the bartender returned with the drink and said, "Enjoy."

Arsen pointed at the back of the bar and said casually, "Thanks. Say, I notice there's a one-way window on the wall. I suppose it's an easy way for the owner to keep tabs on the activity."

"I guess so, but he doesn't have to tonight. He and his team are over there in the corner booth next to the juke box."

"His team? Do they own other lounges?"

"Oh no. I think I was told they import precious stones. You should see the safe in his office. It would be easier to get into Fort Knox."

She's obviously not part of the distribution scheme. Or very bright.

Arsen turned, drink in hand, and leaned on the bar. A few patrons were going in and out of the door gawking at the fireworks in the night sky. The tiny dance floor between Arsen and the corner booth cleared when the music stopped. Based on Mr. Rodriguez's description, the gang was easy to identify. Jack Pope, with the long, blond hair, was sitting in a chair facing the booth. He seemed to be dominating the conversation with an animated style. A sexy, redhaired woman was sitting in the booth next to Jack's chair and had her hand on his thigh. A tall, skinny member of the group stood and walked to the juke box. Arsen did the same.

"What kind of music do you like?" Arsen leaned forward while studying the list of songs.

In a drunken, high-pitched voice, Burk said, "Hard rock. And don't even think about playing any of that goddamned country shit!"

This is the guy who carved the seven in Mrs. Rodriguez's shoulder.

After punching several buttons, Burk returned to the booth. Arsen remained a few minutes, having already memorized every song on the juke box. A mean looking member of the group slid out of the booth and headed for the restroom. The scar on his face was noticeably red. Jack Pope continued to talk and wave his hands. Arsen could only pick up bits and pieces of the monologue, but he thought he heard Freud's name mentioned several times.

The man with the scar returned to the booth and the tall, skinny one stood and said in a loud, shrill voice, "It's time to drain the *big dong*. Don't let those ladies at the table over there go anywhere. One of 'em is going to see *big daddy* tonight!"

Arsen walked toward the end of the bar and fell in step behind Burk.

This is way too easy!

Before the restroom door closed behind Burk, Arsen pushed through it.

"Hey, asshole, how about a little privacy!" Burk finished his sentence, but was too inebriated to duck.

The heel of Arsen's right hand connected squarely on the side of Burk's head, causing him to stagger against the outside of the restroom stall, his arms flailing, trying to maintain his balance. With his left hand, Arsen gripped the skin around Burk's Adam's apple and squeezed. Several undistinguishable squeaks emanated deep from within Burk's throat.

"Come with me."

Arsen put Burk's arm in a hammer-lock and pushed him out the restroom door. He continued pushing the semi-limp body down the short hallway to the metal door. The parking lot was mostly dark, lit only by the faint light from across the street. Arsen slammed Burk's head on the trunk of the Lexus, watching him slump to the gravel-covered surface. Reaching under the car, Arsen removed the plastic tarp and quickly unfolded it.

Burk was still whimpering as Arsen laid him on the tarp and sat on his chest. "What the fuck! What's going on?"

Arsen got straight to the point of the meeting. "I need one piece of information. Understand?"

Burk blinked his eyes several times in rapid succession before answering. "Information?"

"Is Jack Pope tied to the Sinaloa Cartel in Juarez?"

Burk didn't answer, so Arsen removed the switchblade from his ankle holster.

The sound of a switchblade being released from its base can be terrifying. Burk gasped, his body stiffening.

"Wait! Yes, Jack has a friend in Juarez." Regaining some of his senses, Burk attempted his tough-guy approach. "And Jack and his friends will kill your ass if you put a mark on me."

Arsen gripped Burk's left arm, stretched it out, and made a cut across the inside of his wrist, being careful to cut only veins, not the artery. "Bright red, oxygenated blood is now spurting out of your artery," he lied. "I figure you'll pass out in couple of minutes, or less, and then bleed to death. If you answer my questions, I'll put pressure on the wound and stop the bleeding. Understand?"

Burk dropped the manly tone, and asked with a whine, "What do you want?"

"How involved is the cartel? When do they deliver the drugs? Do they have any interface with the distributors you set up?"

"Stop the bleeding! They deliver here at the bar every Friday morning at six! That's all I know."

"Will they conduct long-term revenge on Jack Pope's enemies over here?" Arsen knew it was a ridiculous question, but he asked anyway.

"I don't know. I told you that Jack has a friend in the cartel. I don't know him. Stop the bleeding!"

A large fireworks display was taking place near downtown. A green and yellow splash exploded overhead creating the appearance of a little-leaf palo verde blooming in the spring. The parking lot was fully lighted, but only for an instant.

Arsen stood and pulled Burk to a standing position. "Did you enjoy carving the seven in Mrs. Rodriguez's shoulder? Did that make you feel like a real man?"

Burk used his right hand to reach into his back pocket, pulling out his carving knife. He lunged at Arsen, the knife slicing thin air. Arsen stepped to the side, wrapping his arm around Burk's neck. A violent twist caused a loud crunching sound that blended perfectly with the overhead explosions, and Burk crumpled to the ground, his body leaning one way, his head pointing in the opposite direction.

I should carve a seven in this asshole's forehead and leave him here, but I don't want to tip-off the rest of the gang just yet. Instead, I think I'll confuse them.

Arsen wrapped the body in the tarp and placed it in the trunk of the Lexus. He removed his cell phone from his pocket and from memory dialed the number of the transfer site.

"Yes." The answer came during the first ring.

"Put a log on the fire. I'm bringing you some business."

12

El Paso, Texas
Wednesday, July 5th

Lunch had come and gone. Jack was disturbed.

"Where the hell is Burk? Why did he run out on us last night without saying goodbye? Why isn't he on time for our meeting? Try his cell phone again." Jack had a mild hangover and was taking out his frustrations on anyone within shouting distance.

Robin was getting frustrated. "I've tried to call him three times this morning. I left messages, but he's not picking up."

Lester and Gus sat back in their chairs, watching the heated conversation between Jack and Robin unfold.

"Burk knows we're setting up another distribution outlet this afternoon . . . *Muffy's Gift Store* or whatever the fuck the name of the place is. We have to get them up and running." Putting his hand on his forehead, he exploded. "Shit, we have to do it today! The first shipment is coming Friday."

Robin exhaled, and said, "The name of the store is *Barbie's Cards and Gifts*. They close at five, so we need to be there a few minutes earlier. The store is owned by two spinster sisters, and I'm confident it will work out."

Jack swallowed a Ritalin tablet without water and said sarcastically, "Are you *confident* the training session scheduled for tomorrow at Big City Grocery will also go smoothly?"

"Yes, I *was* going to take Burk and Lester." Looking at Gus, she said, "If Burk doesn't show up by tomorrow, I guess I'll take Lester and Gus."

"Tell me again. What information will you give them in the session?" The Ritalin hadn't kicked-in and Jack was squirming in his chair, his hands and arms flailing back and forth.

Robin remained unflappable. "Three main things. First, I explain about the ten-thousand dollars in product they'll be receiving, and how they'll need to secure it. I'll give them a coded menu and pricing guidelines for the drugs. W for weed, M for meth, E for ecstasy and so forth. I'll explain that we'll be there each Friday morning to deliver the product and pick up the prior week's receipts. I guess you could add a fourth item, since I also explain how they get to keep five percent of the gross each week."

"Okay, okay. First things first. I'm not worried about the grocery store. The Rodriguez couple was definitely scared and they'll cooperate. How old are these sisters we're visiting today?"

"I'm guessing they're both in their forties." Robin crossed her arms, looked at the floor, and exhaled again.

"Without Burk, how are we going to carve the seven into their shoulders?"

Gus spoke for the first time. "I don't see the need for the seven. I think the one on my shoulder is infected. Dumb idea, if you ask me." The scar on his face had turned beet red.

Jack took a deep breath. "Okay, I'm open to new ideas from the crew. We'll skip the seven from now on. The threat of their entire family being butchered, including their pets, should be enough. Right?"

"Good idea." This was the full extent of Lester's input regarding the tattoo business. For no apparent reason, he added, "Man, I've got a major hangover. I can't remember most of what happened last night, and wish I could skip the entire day." He grinned as he looked at the other members of the crew, but no one responded.

Jack resumed his leadership role. "We have to find out what happened to Burk. His car is locked and still in the parking lot. He must have left with someone from the lounge. Are you sure you didn't see him leave?"

Robin offered a suggestion. "Why don't we ask Shelly? Maybe she saw something."

"You mean Shelly with the big bazooms?" Lester was making a comeback.

"Goddamn it, this is serious!" Jack returned to his most comfortable management style. Autocratic. "Robin, get her in here."

Looking through the one-way mirror, Jack could see three customers sitting at the bar. Shelly was talking to one of them, but she responded immediately to Robin's request.

Jack started talking before Shelly reached his desk. "Shelly, as you probably know, Burk left the party early last night and hasn't shown up since. Did you see him leave with a woman?"

"No, sir. I noticed him having a good time with you guys, but not with anyone else. Lester, here, was doing most of the mingling."

Lester moved his head in an "aw shucks" manner.

Gus tried to be of assistance. "Did he leave with a guy?"

Robin was quick to answer. "Burk is a perv, but not like that. He prefers young women, older women … any and all women. Period."

Shelly pursed her lips and said, "Come to think of it, I did see him talking to a fellow at the jukebox. Nice looking, young man with a dark mustache and goatee. He was wearing one of those foreign golf hats. But I didn't see them leave together."

Jack was staring directly at Shelly's breasts as he said, "Would you recognize this guy if you saw him again?"

With a girlish grin, Shelly said, "I would absolutely recognize him. He caused me to have impure thoughts."

Jack lowered his head and mumbled, "Praise Jesus." Looking up, he said, "Okay, Shelly, thanks for the input."

After Shelly left the office, Lester said, "Well, that was helpful."

Jack was back to business. "Everyone be back at four-fifteen. We're going to establish *Muffy's Gift Store* as one of our top distributors. Right?"

Robin shook her head and said quietly, *"Barbie's Cards and Gifts."*

The four members of the crew were unusually quiet during the trip to *Barbie's*. Jack sat in the passenger seat clenching and unclenching his hands. Burk was missing in action and the grand scheme was not progressing according to schedule. Jack was getting desperate.

Turning in the passenger seat of the van, he said, "Gus. Do you have any friends we could contact? You know, anyone who might make a good team member?"

"Funny you should ask. Two of my buddies asked me about my new job yesterday. They would damn sure be interested . . . and qualified."

"Do they have police records?"

"Not that I'm aware of. And either one of them could beat the shit out of Burk."

"Get 'em both to come in for tomorrow morning's meeting. Ten sharp. Okay?"

"They'll be there."

Robin parked the van directly in front of *Barbie's Cards and Gifts*. There were no other cars near the store. A barber shop was on the left, the storefront on the right had a "FOR LEASE" sign in the window, and a Burger King was across the street next to a busy parking lot. It was five minutes until closing time for *Barbie's,* and Jack had committed to memory Robin's notes regarding the two spinsters.

As the crew exited the van, two ladies emerged from the card shop and began locking the door. Both were dressed identically in red leather pants, white blouses and black tennis shoes, and both sported pixie-cut hair styles.

Lester tilted his head toward Jack and whispered, "They look like the fucking Bobbsey Twins."

Ignoring the comment, Jack approached the sisters and said in a pleasant voice, "Hey, it's not five yet. We need to do some business with you."

The middle-aged lady holding the key chain appeared delighted to assist the late arrivals. "I'm so glad you caught us. Please come in."

The interior of the store was larger than Jack expected. Shelves packed with small gifts and trinkets lined the walls, while the center portion contained four rows of greeting cards. Lester closed the door behind the group and immediately went to an aisle with birthday cards.

Jack craved the attention he received in small gatherings of employees . . . and victims. Pontification fueled his ego. As the sisters positioned themselves behind the counter, Jack proceeded. "This is your lucky day. We're here to offer you the business opportunity of a lifetime. Day after tomorrow, which is Friday, you're going to start distributing drugs for us. Oh, by the way, my name is Jack Pope and these folks are part of the Seventh Avenue Crew, of which I'm in charge."

The lady standing next to the cash register, seemed unimpressed with Jack's presentation and said, "Drugs? Please explain."

Jack proceeded straight to the intimidation part of his speech. "I know, I know. The first thought in your brain is to inform the police. Right?" Not giving them time for an answer, he continued. "We know that you live on a cul-de-sac on Cielo Vista Drive. We know that your parents live in an apartment in Phoenix and that your brother lives in Cloudcroft."

With a sigh, she unenthusiastically said, "Thorough. Now tell us about the drugs. We're in. What's our cut?"

Jack had expected a different response, and was completely caught off-guard, so he decided to skip the threatening segment of his presentation. "You're a very smart lady. Your cut is five percent of each week's take."

"Ten percent would be more to my liking." Looking at her sister who had remained quiet during the conversation, she said, "Bonnie, does ten percent seem reasonable to you?"

Jack was losing control of the negotiation. "Look, it's going to be five percent initially, but we can change it if you can generate enough volume. Okay?"

"We'll give it a try."

Robin and Gus were looking at each other with raised eyebrows. The scar on Gus's face was turning red once again.

"Robin, do you have a product menu handy? You can conduct the training session now." Jack was in full management mode.

While Robin went to the van to get a pricing menu, Jack continued to probe into the sisters' personal situation. Addressing the lady who seemed to be the main spokesman, he inquired, "So you're Barbie and your sister's name is Bonnie?"

"No, my name is Billie." Looking at her sister, she said, "This is Bonnie. Barbie is the name of our sister who died during childbirth."

Jack was speechless. *Too bad Shelly isn't here. She would really get into this weirdness!*

Robin returned with the menu and conducted the training session. The sisters appeared genuinely excited about the opportunity to make extra cash.

Lester continued to browse through the birthday cards. "Hey boss, look at this card!"

"Pay the ladies for the card and let's go. We have things to do."

The trip out of the parking lot was lively. The crew exchanged high-fives and fist bumps as they discussed how well the meeting had gone.

Lester beamed as he read the card he'd purchased at Barbie's. "Listen to this. The front of the card shows a birthday cake and it says, *You're Not Old*, and on the inside, it says, *You're Just Ugly*! Is that funny or what?"

Gus said flatly, "Not funny."

Jack ignored Lester's birthday-card comments and said, "Robin, there's been nothing on the news about the pharmacy. It's not that far out of the way, so why don't we drive by and see if there's any police tape."

"Good idea. Shouldn't take more than a few minutes to get there. I'll be careful."

No one in the crew noticed the black Lexus that had followed them to Barbie's. It continued following them as Robin turned left onto Montana Avenue.

13

Juarez, Mexico
Wednesday, July 5th

Carlos Delgado supported his body on his elbows and knees while he carefully removed himself from the woman underneath him. He remained in this awkward position as he leaned forward and kissed her neck and cheek. Sitting up, he admired the glistening, nude body. The woman was beautiful, young, and married . . . but not to him. Being a serial philanderer provided additional fuel for his power trip.

"Your body is shining with your wetness." Even though he tried, Carlos had never been known for his pillow talk.

"Carlos, my love, three times in two hours makes me perspire." Fluttering her eyelashes, she said, "Do you like what you see?"

"You know *I like*. Be here this Sunday at the same time."

"Why can't we go to a really fancy hotel? This is so ordinary."

"I know people at this hotel. They take care of me. It's safe and secure. Just be here Sunday at two." Although he had been seeing the young lady for almost a year, he couldn't get enough of her. If her schedule permitted, he would have the clandestine meetings seven days a week.

The Hotel del Rio was located in Juarez only two blocks from the Santa Fe Street Bridge. The hotel had twenty-five rooms, and a newly refurbished lobby bar. Everything about the hotel was a perfect fit for Carlos's personality.

"I know, you like the danger of meeting so close to the border. You've told me several times it's an aphrodisiac, it makes you hard."

"I'm in no mood to talk about anatomical functions. Get out of here and get home before your husband arrives. See you in a few days."

Arturo Hernandez, wearing his signature red bandana on his forehead, had been waiting downstairs for the past two hours. It was early afternoon and he was the only customer in the dimly lit lobby bar. Ten empty beer bottles were arranged like bowling pins in front of him. He had just taken his first drink from an additional bottle when Carlos approached the bar.

"No wonder you're so fat. You drink beer as if it's about to be rationed." Carlos didn't care how much beer Arturo drank, he admired the man's violent, ruthless nature.

"My weight stays at two hundred sixty pounds. Never varies."

"If our business ever falters, you should apply as a counselor for Jenny Craig."

Taking a long swig from his eleventh beer of the afternoon, Arturo burped. "Whatever. How was your woman today?" Belching again, he said, "Tell me, boss. Does she perform best on Wednesdays or Sundays?"

"Fantastic on both days. She knows more tricks than Lassie."

Carlos was married, had two daughters, and another child on the way. The doctor had been told not to divulge the gender of the upcoming birth because Carlos thought it would be bad luck. Good luck to him would be having a son, bad luck would be having another daughter. He secretly wished his mistress would get pregnant and deliver him a boy. Like father, like son. He knew he could kill her husband and take care of mother and child.

On the verge of slurring his words, Arturo said, "You've been meeting her here for the past year, and I've always wondered why you choose Wednesdays and Sundays?"

"It has to do with her husband's job. I'm trying to figure out a way to meet her more often. Don't worry about it."

Arturo was rubbing his fingers across the many scars on his face as he changed the subject. "Boss, I'm not entirely drunk, but I am a little confused. As you know, I'm sending one of our best men to Socorro tonight to meet-up with our *source*, as you call him. They're going to kill some guy named Arsen after he blows up a Juarez Cartel tunnel. Right?"

A slight frown crossed Carlos's brow as he said, "And why are you confused?"

"A couple of things. Why would we kill someone who's destroying a competitor's tunnel, and how did our source know about the tunnel in the first place?"

"Our *source* knows many things about our competition . . . and about the United States government's actions against the cartels. The Juarez Cartel has been using the tunnel in Socorro for several months to move a significant portion of their drugs. I told our source about the tunnel, he told his superiors, and his superiors got this Arsen guy to blow it up. Arsen, as it turns out, is one of our enemies, so our source and your man are going to kill him after he completes his job."

Shaking his head, Arturo asked, "How do we know this Arsen fellow is an enemy?"

"Remember a couple of years ago when two of our people were assassinated in Agua Prieta? The tunnel architect and one of our attorneys were killed and we thought it was another cartel that was responsible. Instead it was a contractor for the U.S. government. Our source told me about him. His name is Arsen, and tonight he dies."

"Brilliant." Arturo was not your typical yes-man. He was practical.

Carlos handed out a rare portion of praise. "That's why we pay our source, this double agent, so much. I predict he'll be worth his weight in gold as we continue our hold on the Juarez corridor. You've done an excellent job of interfacing with him over the past year. Keep up the good work."

Arturo laughed, and said, "We need to keep paying him well, because we can use his assistance in our war against the Juarez assholes. The newspapers are full of shit about what's going on here. They say the killings in Juarez are on the decline, down to a couple of hundred a year. Hell, my men have eliminated more than two hundred in the last week. We just burn them, bury them, or throw them in the sewers so they don't get counted. Kind of hurts my feelings."

"You are one of a kind, Arturo. One of a kind."

14

El Paso, Texas
Wednesday, July 5th

Wednesday had been uneventful by Arsen's standards. Uneventful, except for the fact he kept thinking about the young lady he had met last evening. Earlier in the day, he'd driven to Socorro on a dry run for tonight's tunnel activities. He knew exactly how long the trip would take and where to park.

It was now 5:30 in the afternoon as Arsen made a U-turn and followed the van leaving the parking space in front of *Barbie's Cards and Gifts*. He'd been parked on the opposite side of the street in a Burger King parking lot for the past half hour. His instincts told him to follow the van even though he was supposed to meet Kasie at 6:00.

Arsen was surprised when the van turned onto Montana Avenue, and then a mile later slowly pulled into a strip shopping center. Arsen parked across the street in front of a snow cone stand. The van hesitated in the parking lot and made a U-turn back onto the avenue.

Deciding to forget the van, Arsen got out of his car and observed the strip center. Nothing unusual. A jewelry store and a pharmacy were the only two businesses of any consequence.

Maybe this is their next target. Either business could distribute drugs.

Arsen looked at his watch. He'd have to think about it later. Time to meet Kasie.

It was exactly 6:00 p.m. when the Arsen arrived at the restaurant. He was surprised at how small and plain the Monk looked from the outside. The parking lot was also tiny, but because it was relatively early, several parking spaces were available. Arsen locked the car, aware that there was enough C-4 in the trunk to blow-up half of a city block. He wasn't concerned due to his knowledge of explosives, particularly his cargo.

Stuff's very stable, insensitive to most physical shocks, and can't be detonated by even a gunshot or by dropping it onto a hard surface. No worries.

As he walked toward the door of the Monk, Arsen's thoughts didn't include the C-4, the tunnel, or the Jack Pope gang. He was concentrating on how to act in Kasie's presence. For some unexplained reason, these thoughts were disconcerting. He'd been with numerous women over the years, he was still young, and he had his wits about him, but these unfamiliar feelings were tugging at him.

I must have an allergy or something.

"Hey, Arsen squared." The voice came from the parking lot.

Turning, Arsen couldn't keep the smile off his face. Kasie was wearing a pair of floral shorts and a white blouse. Her light brown, tanned skin seemed to glow as it reflected the rays of the evening sun.

Yep, she's one good-looking woman. "Well, if it isn't the young accountant."

Kasie put her hand on Arsen's arm and gently pulled him toward the Hoppy Monk entrance. "Are you thirsty, stranger?"

Trying his best at a John Wayne impression, Arsen said, "You betcha, pretty lady. I could use a shot of red-eye."

They both laughed as they entered the door. The interior was aesthetically pleasing with a matte black ceiling and warm lighting. The seating consisted mainly of wooden tables and chairs. Kasie chose a table for two at the back of the room.

"Despite what it looks like, this is one of the most popular pubs in the city. Kind of a 'gourmet dive bar.' The hamburgers are to die for and there are seventy craft beers at our disposal. No way you have any place this cool in *Odessa*." Kasie smiled as she emphasized the word Odessa.

"You know, we do have two Burger Kings in Odessa. We know how to live." Arsen returned the smile.

A waitress took their drink orders and later returned for their menu selections. The coming and going of the waitress, the wide selection of beer with strange names, and the hamburgers were just a blur to Arsen. His entire focus was on the conversation with the young lady sitting across from him.

Kasie began her playful interrogation. "So, what were you like in high school? Did you play sports, lots of girl-friends and all that stuff?"

"I ran track, but was too small to play football. I only weighed about one-sixty-five when I graduated and went to junior college. In the two years following high school, I grew four inches and added almost fifty pounds."

"No way!"

"Way." Arsen laughed. "I started lifting weights, working out and eating right. As far as dating, there was one girl I particularly liked, but she was going steady with one of the football players. So much for that romance. After junior college, I was so full of myself, I joined the army and applied for the special forces. That pretty well summarizes my life." Arsen was attempting to be vague in his comments, while at the same time trying to be as truthful as possible.

"Jamie said you got wounded in Syria. Was it bad?"

"It could have been, but a fellow soldier carried me for over a mile back to our post. I got hit in the side. Couple of broken ribs. I rehabbed for a few weeks, and then went back and finished my tour. It was the same fellow that referred Jamie to me."

"Jamie said something about you supporting a CIA operation while you were there. Must have been interesting."

"Yep. Met some good people."

Kasie kept firing questions, not giving Arsen time to inquire about any of her personal experiences. They covered his time in Dallas as a private investigator, and his likes and dislikes about living in a metropolitan city. The most difficult question to answer finally arrived.

"When you moved to Odessa and started your own investigation firm, was it hard to find clients? I mean, how did you market your expertise and services? Isn't Odessa kind of small for a private eye?" She was the Wolf Blitzer of dinner dates. Her questions were non-stop.

Arsen hesitated before answering the questions. "Well, actually, I don't do much business in Odessa. Most of what I do is out of town." He wanted to be completely honest with Kasie. He was ready to tell her where the gold was buried, and he didn't even have any gold. "The fact of the matter is, much of what I do is international in nature."

"How cool it must be to travel internationally. Who are some of your clients?"

"I really can't talk about most of my clients. Some of what we do is rather sensitive." This was the best answer Arsen could come up with for now.

In her teasing way, Kasie said, "Oh, I get it. You work for the CIA guys you met in the army."

Arsen rolled his eyes and saw an opening to change the topic of conversation. "Okay, tell me about your life. Please start when you were three years old."

They laughed and continued to poke fun at each other. The Monk was filled with noisy patrons, the craft beer was flowing. Arsen was surprised when he glanced at the clock behind the bar and noticed it was almost 9:30.

Time flies when you're having a damned good time.

He realized he would have to leave within the next hour in order to change clothes and drive to Socorro and for his tunnel job. He didn't want to blow up a tunnel; he wanted to stay and talk with Kasie until dawn.

The conversation continued for the next thirty minutes. They covered Kasie's high school years, her four years in college, and the young men that passed through her social life.

Arsen was surprised someone hadn't already latched on to her by now.

"As much as I regret it, I have to meet a client in a few minutes." The *regret* was evident in Arsen's voice.

Laughing, Kasie said, "See, I told you. You work for the CIA. Who else would have meetings this late!"

Even though she was smiling, Arsen detected a small amount of disappointment in her voice. *I think it was disappointment, wasn't it?*

After paying for the beer and burgers, Arsen walked Kasie to her car. He thought for a second that he had chill bumps, but there was not a breeze, and the night air was warm.

"Thanks for a great time, Kasie. We'll have to come back to the Monk again. Do you have any other favorite places to eat?" *Please say yes. Invite me out again tomorrow.*

Tilting her head, she smiled and said, "Well, if your CIA friends will let you off tomorrow evening, we could try Mi Piaci. It's an Italian restaurant with great food and a lovely dining patio. I can make the reservations."

In a surprising move, Kasie leaned forward, putting her arm on Arsen's shoulder and gave him a light kiss on the cheek.

Now, that was unexpected. "Tell me your address and I'll pick you up at six." *What's going on here!*

It was almost eleven when Arsen drove slowly past the gate on Levee Road, made a U-turn, and parked about a hundred yards away. The full moon highlighted both the gate and the maintenance building that was located another hundred yards beyond the fence. The night breeze felt good on his upper torso as he changed into the black cargo pants, a black shirt and black boots. He strapped on the ankle holsters containing the Glock 42 and the switchblade knife. The backpack with the C-4, the detonator caps, and the timer was heavier than it appeared. The evening with Kasie had been relaxing, but it was time for full focus on the tunnel project.

The gate to the park was open and the door to the maintenance shack was unlocked as promised. After closing the door, Arsen turned on his flashlight and noticed the windowless interior. He flipped a light switch and saw three large wooden pallets near the far wall. The air was heavy, the temperature over a hundred degrees as he easily moved the pallets and looked at the metal casing over the four-by-four opening in the floor. A wench and chain contraption hung on the ceiling above the tunnel entrance. Arsen removed the covering and observed the tunnel slanting down for seventy feet, just as Spencer's notes indicated. He was surprised at the series of light bulbs strung along the smooth sides of the hole. The aluminum ladder sparkled from the lighting.

Spencer had mentioned the sophistication of the tunnel, and had complimented the civil engineers responsible for its construction. This particular tunnel was over 800 feet in length and had probably cost two million dollars, but the investment would quickly be paid off from the smuggling profits.

Too bad their expertise couldn't have been put to better use.

The drop in temperature was noticeable as Arsen completed his descent down the ladder. The first thing he noticed was a high-capacity battery bank in the main tunnel that was connected to the strands of lights.

Spencer was right. The tunnel is about four feet wide, six feet tall and equipped with a rail system and ventilation. Heavy wooden beams are spaced every ten feet, both on the sides and the ceiling of the tunnel. How could Spencer know the facts about these dimensions?

The tunnel curved slightly to the left as Arsen counted his steps toward Mexico. Spencer's instructions indicated that one hundred-fifty paces west would be an approximate location to place the C-4.

Unbelievable! Under the Rio Grande River!

Arsen stooped slightly as he walked, causing his hamstring muscles to feel as if they were on fire by the time he arrived at his destination. It was 11:35 p.m. when he removed the backpack and carefully emptied the contents. Ten minutes later, the C-4 bricks were wrapped around one of the beams, the detonator caps were attached to the four bricks, and the timer was synced with his wrist watch. He had fifteen minutes to make his way back to the tunnel entrance.

No time to stumble.

Arsen glanced at his watch when he reached the base of the aluminum ladder. Exactly two minutes until the blast. He placed his right foot on the bottom rung and both hands on the rails as he began his ascent. Something wasn't right. He raised his head and saw that the metal covering was in place over the entrance.

Now what! I left the metal covering beside the hole. Someone is probably waiting for me to exit and I need to be out of the tunnel before the explosion. What if they put the pallets on top of the lid? Why can't life be easy? Shit!

He reached the top rung of the ladder and raised his pant leg to expose the ankle holster containing the Glock. Twenty seconds until the C-4 would be activated. Arsen was unsure of the damage the blast would cause at his end of the tunnel. At the very least, there would be a rush of hot air and dust. Worst case scenario, the entire tunnel would collapse and the Rio Grande would flood it.

Whatever happens, I need to haul-ass as soon as possible.

He decided on a *double surprise*. The idea came to him in a flash, maybe because he had absolutely no other options. He'd never been so calm in his life. He knew he would be facing trouble when he left the tunnel and he knew that if he didn't exit . . . even worse trouble. A simple mathematical calculation told him the power of the explosion would reach him within two seconds after the detonation.

So much for detonation pressure and explosive velocity, I need to get the hell out of here!

He firmly positioned his body and placed both hands on the metal cover. Immediately after the blast, he flung the cover into the air, and dropped down two steps on the ladder, still stooped over, but looking at the opening. The tunnel shook and hot air rapidly soared through the narrow entrance, followed by blinding dust particles. The first surprise was the metal cover flying three feet in the air inside the room. The second surprise was Arsen not being visible to whomever was waiting.

Several shots rang out from above as the metal lid bounced on the floor of the shack. Arsen looked through the fog of dust and saw two shadows standing by the opening with their hands over their eyes. He pulled the Glock from the holster and removed the safety in one quick motion. His first shot hit the closest shadow. The body lurched backward as Arsen trained his weapon on the second person and fired twice. The dust and smoke obscured the results of the shots. As he reflexively began rubbing his stinging eyes, the aluminum ladder shook and began slowly sliding down the shaft.

Arsen tossed his Glock through the darkness, and grabbed at the sides of the opening with both hands, fully expecting to be shot. The rumbling sound in the tunnel below told him which of his predictions had come to pass . . . the entire tunnel was collapsing. He was unsure if the Rio Grande would make an appearance.

He hung on the sides of the opening for a second, and then placed his foot on the wall for leverage, before flinging his body onto the floor of the shack. Choking and almost blinded, he swept his arm over the floor until he found the Glock.

Still alive. Maybe I got both of them. What if there were more?

Arsen crawled past one body and reached the open door. He rolled through the door and emerged in a half-standing position. The warm night air filled his lungs as he began coughing up dust and rubbing his eyes with the sleeve of his shirt. No one visible, only the full moon and a sky full of stars . . . and the sound of a car speeding through the gate on Levee Road with the lights off.

The dust was settling and Arsen could once again see the faint glow of the lights in the maintenance shed.

Definitely hooked to a different power source than the lights in the tunnel.

Walking in a crouch, looking in all directions, he reentered the shed. Dust particles glittered and drifted downward, trying their best to hide the body with the bloody neck wound.

Damn! Only one body!

Arsen knelt beside the body and listened to the short, gasping breaths. Blood was flowing from the wound and from the man's mouth.

"Who do you work for? Who was with you?" Arsen asked the questions, not expecting an answer.

A bloody gurgle emanated from the man. It was impossible to know what he said, but the response was in Spanish. They were the last words he would ever speak.

Something ain't right. Time to call Nils.

15

El Paso, Texas
Thursday, July 6th

Jack unlocked the door to his bar at 8:30 a.m. and was met by the smell of stale beer and several other odors he couldn't immediately identify. He switched on the lights and surveyed his small kingdom. Business was on the rise in the bar, and he was optimistic about the progress of his new drug distribution venture. The crew now had two distributors on line, the first shipment of drugs would arrive tomorrow morning, and Gus's two friends would be joining the crew in an hour and a half. Robin had decided to sleep-in this morning, but promised she wouldn't be late for the 10:00 a.m. meeting. Life was good, except for two unanswered questions: what happened to Burk, and when would the bodies at the pharmacy be discovered? The episode at the pharmacy happened two days ago and was somewhat unsettling to Jack. He was curious, but not overly concerned.

Burk's disappearance was the most difficult to understand. Burk had appeared to be a loyal employee who enjoyed his job and the financial potential. The fact that his car was still in the parking lot was also alarming. Even if he'd decided to get out of the drug business before it really got started, he wouldn't leave his car.

The second question was answered when Jack sat behind his desk and hit the local news app on his phone. The headline was to the point: **JIFFY PHARMACY OWNERS MURDERED**. The article gave details about the gunshot to the head of Bob Murphy, but was somewhat vague about the death of his wife, Alice. The El Paso police homicide division was on the case.

Jack was confident that no clues were left at the scene of the crime. Besides, if worse came to worse, he would blame Lester for the shooting.

I will take no responsibility! Lester did it goddammit!

Leaning forward, elbows on the desk, Jack began a mental evaluation of his new business venture: *Limited risk in obtaining the product; Carlos was a genius at getting drugs across the border. Unique distribution system. Minimal payout to the small businesses involved in the selling of the drugs. With the proper planning, the organization could be expanded state-wide, maybe nation-wide. Tremendous upside, manageable downside. God, I'm brilliant!*

Shelly entered the lounge and was walking toward the bar. Jack sat up straight and gawked at her through the one-way mirror. She was wearing a red, low-cut blouse and a white silk skirt. Jack had taken his morning dose of Ritalin, but he was anything but calm now. Shelly's breasts seemed to be rising and falling in slow motion as she walked. They were screaming at Jack. She was a gazelle being stalked by a hungry tiger, a red flag in front of a raging bull. Jack's deep-seated fantasies about Shelly were bubbling to the surface.

I'm in charge. I'm the man. When you're at the top of the heap, like me, you can do any damn thing you want.

Jack shouted through his open office door. "Shelly, come here for a minute."

I only want to look, not touch.

Removing a month-end statement from his desk drawer, he said, "Look at these numbers. I can't believe our utility costs are so high. Do you turn the lights off every night when you leave?"

Leaning over and looking at the paper, she said, "I know the electricity bill is high, but the lights are turned down during the day and completely off at night. Not sure what else we can do."

Jack looked up, his nose no more than a foot from the most desirable piece of real estate he had ever seen. His right hand involuntarily rose to the side of his head and smoothed back his hair. He placed his hand, very voluntarily, just below her neck and gently moved it downward. She flinched, but didn't resist.

He decided to be direct and in-charge, the way a successful executive would communicate. "Shelly, you're a beautiful woman and these are the finest breasts I've ever seen. I need you more than I've ever needed a woman. I'm as serious as I can be."

Her face was flushed, the tone of her voice unsure. "But...but...what about Robin? She's my friend. She's your woman, isn't she?"

Jack stood and towered over Shelly as he whispered, "You'll be helping me. This is a very stressful business. In a way, you'll also be helping Robin. Besides, she'll never know."

He took her by the arm and led her to the couch, shaking with an adrenaline surge and anticipation, raw lust. He had sunk to the lowest rung of Maslow's Hierarchy of Needs.

She wrapped her arms around his neck and initiated the clumsy tryst by pressing her body against his. With hurried moves, Jack removed her blouse and bra. She lay back on the couch and in a matter of seconds her silk skirt was up to her waist and her panties had been tossed on the floor.

As Jack removed his pants and underwear, Shelly began moaning, "I'm a sinner, I'm a sinner."

The chanting, the heavy breathing, and the excitement of the moment left the figure standing at the office door unnoticed. Robin stood motionless, calm, and seemingly unaffected by the floundering scene on the couch. She quietly walked to the bar and picked-up the carving knife used to cut lemons, limes and oranges for specialty drinks.

Jack's pale, white buttocks were glaring at Robin as she approached the two-person orgy. Shelly's legs were spread on both sides of the couch and her eyes were pressed closed while she continued asking for forgiveness. Jack was mumbling something about *Freud*.

Robin had several options at this point, all of which were inviting. She quickly analyzed the long-term and short-term consequences of her actions and made a decision. Looking at Shelly's outstretched leg and foot, Robin slowly placed the knife above the slot formed by the big toe and the index toe. She violently pulled the blade in a downward motion, cutting through muscular tendons and a fibular nerve before the inch-and-a-half deep slice ended against bone.

The scream sounded like something from a wounded animal. The anguished screams became louder as Shelly's body arched and both legs went straight up. Jack, still not aware of Robin's presence, was delighted, ecstatic, until he turned his head and saw Robin standing over him with the bloody knife. He was terrified. This was the closest Jack had ever come to passing out from shock and fear.

Robin casually picked-up Shelly's panties from the floor and used them to wiped the blood from the knife. Jack fell from the couch and was trying to get his pants on as quickly as possible. Shelly was still crying and asking for forgiveness from the Lord as Robin went to the bar and returned with a towel.

Handing the towel to Shelly, she said, "Here, wrap it up and take it to the emergency room before you bleed to death. Oh yeah, get back here as soon as possible because customers will be arriving soon. Okay?"

Still crying, her eyes as big as saucers, Shelly said, "Okay." Still looking at Robin, she added, "God forgive me. God forgive me."

Robin, as relaxed as someone chatting with a friend over tea, replied, "Well, I'm not God, and I don't forgive you. Just make sure it never happens again."

Jack was in awe as he witnessed the conversation between the two women. Now fully dressed, motioning with his hands and arms, he said, "It wasn't my idea. She led me into the whole thing. Swear!"

"I know, dear. It couldn't have been your fault. Remember though, you just used your "Get Out of Jail Free Card" . . . and I have an unused one."

Jack had watched Robin as she had cleaned the blood from the tile floor and had turned over the cushion on the couch. No traces of the morning activities remained. Lester, Robin and Gus sat on the couch, while the two new members stood next to Jack's desk. Robin had run background checks as best she could on Jimmy Patterson and Pat Melton, finding no history of arrests or run-ins with the law.

The first impressions of the two would have suggested otherwise. They made Gus look like a fashion model in comparison. It wasn't so much their clothes, as their overall general appearances. Patterson had a scraggly, patchy beard and beady, bloodshot eyes. Melton was close to six feet tall, a pimpled face, and looked like a lifelong body builder. This didn't bother Jack, because their scary looks would be good for the business. Jack was always planning ahead. The crew was now up to six members, only one short of a full drug gang.

After giving the basic orientation to the new members and answering a few questions about the drug operation, Jack said, "Okay now, you two new guys know how the crew is organized, tell us about yourselves. Melton, you first."

"Well, I grew up in a little town near Bakersfield, California. Place named Newhall. After I graduated from high school, I came to El Paso to participate in a bare-knuckles contest." Melton's distinct drawl was noticeable to everyone in the room.

Lester, in a friendly tone, couldn't help himself. "Bet you came in the back of a hay wagon, didn't ya."

Jack gave Lester a dirty look and said, "Bare knuckles?" He wasn't familiar with this type of event.

"Yep, that's where I met Jimmy and Gus. It's a non-publicized fist-fighting competition. None of us won, but we became good friends. For the last several years, I've been working at a feed lot on the other side of town. And I must say, Jack, I'm excited about this opportunity."

"How about you, Patterson?"

"I had a track scholarship to UTEP. I was a hurdler, but got hurt during my sophomore year and decided to quit school. I scraped by for a few years selling pots and pans. I've been selling used cars ever since. Like Melton said, we met at the bare knuckles event."

"Either of you married?"

Patterson shook his head and said, "Hell, no."

"Me neither. Tried it once, but it wasn't worth a damn." Melton didn't elaborate as to why it didn't work out.

"How many of you have concealed weapon permits?" Jack was back to basics.

Everyone but Robin raised their hands.

"That's fine and good, but you know by law that you can't bring a concealed weapon into a bar. Right?"

The gun owners all nodded in agreement.

Robin made a sarcastic comment to close the gun conversation. "Well, we certainly wouldn't want the crew to violate any laws, would we?"

Jack smiled, trying his best to get on Robin's good side.

Lester changed the conversation. "Hey, where's Shelly? How come her friend is tending bar today?"

Robin, glancing at Jack, said, "She hurt her foot this morning and had to go to the emergency room. She'll be back eventually."

The temporary lull in conversation was broken by Jack. He squinted his eyes and in a solemn tone said, "You're all members of the crew now. I think you know the consequences of leaving or causing us any problems. My friend Carlos doesn't want any unnecessary . . . issues. On the other hand, we don't want any problems from our distributors, do we?" It was a rhetorical question, and no one answered. "Two people tried to make trouble for us a few days ago, and now they're in the news headlines. They're dead, but in the headlines, nevertheless."

"Who? What happened?" Gus asked.

Jack liked the intimidation factor. He had read somewhere about using intimidation as a negative motivational factor for employees. "Check out the *pharmacy deaths* in the paper. That's how Lester made his bones. Enough said. We mean business. Everybody on board?"

Gus looked at his two friends, and then at Jack. "We're on board, boss."

Lester had a self-satisfying smirk on his face. Robin remained relaxed with a blank look.

"Okay, Robin is going to conduct a training session for Big City Grocery today. Robin, I think it would be a good idea for you to take all the boys with you. You know, for backup. It'll also further remind the owners how formidable our crew has become. I need to stay here and do some work on our finances. What do you think?"

"Good idea. Let's conduct the training session at Big City Grocery at 2:00 this afternoon. We'll need to leave here in the van at 1:45. Everyone got that?" Robin was starting to assert her authority as second-in-command. "Later this afternoon we're going to visit another potential distributor on North Mesa Drive. It's a gym by the name of Muscle Madness. The owner is a personal trainer and he operates his workout facility near UTEP."

The male members of the Seventh Avenue Crew all nodded. The Crew was on the road to success and Self Actualization.

16

El Paso, Texas
Thursday, July 6th

Arsen had a late breakfast in the Gardner coffee shop and returned to his room. He was excited about having dinner with Kasie this evening; he was concerned about the "ambush" he had encountered upon exiting the tunnel last night; he was curious about an article he had just read in the paper regarding a murder at the Jiffy Pharmacy. This was the same pharmacy the Pope gang had checked-out yesterday. He'd texted Nils after completion of the tunnel project, but now it was time to talk with him by phone.

As usual, Nils answered promptly. "Yes, Arsen, how can I be of assistance?"

"I was in a minor gun battle when I exited the tunnel last night. There were at least two people waiting for me. One of them won't be waiting for anyone again. He spoke a few words of Spanish before he died."

Nils was unusually quiet for a few seconds. "You're sure he was speaking Spanish?"

"Yep."

"You said there were at least two. Could there have been more?"

"I'm guessing there were only two of them. I fired a couple of shots at the second one when he was in the shed, but evidently missed. By the time I got out of the tunnel, a car with the lights out was hightailing it out of the park."

"Let me see what I can find out. However, you know how rampant bribes and coercion are in the drug business. I'm sure some of the maintenance workers employed by the park were involved in the tunnel smuggling operation. Hard to explain, though, how they would know your schedule? By the way, good job last night."

"Thanks, Nils. There's one more item. I mentioned to you the other day about a situation I'm working on for a friend. The guy I asked you about, Jack Pope, is part of the equation. He's trying to set up a drug distribution scheme using small, family-owned businesses as the distributors. He threatens them and their family members with serious consequences, either now or down the road, if they don't cooperate. You indicated that he's friends with Carlos Delgado, the Sinaloa lieutenant in Juarez. My question is this: how can I find out if Delgado's guys actually follow through with the long-term retribution thing?"

"You'll have to be very careful, my friend. Assuming the 'revenge equation' is in effect, you definitely don't want to hit Jack Pope at this time. It could set off the whole process. If you want to kill a snake, you have to cut off its head. In this case, Delgado is the snake, but it would be difficult to get to him. We've tried in the past. To answer your specific question, I would say that you need to get the answer from one of Delgado's men. Understand?"

"I understand."

"I'm *not* giving you the assignment to eliminate Delgado at this time, due to the slim chances of success and your own health and well-being, but if the opportunity should arise, your fee would be five hundred thousand dollars. Got to go. Stay safe."

Question answered. I need to meet the Sinaloa drug delivery man tomorrow morning. He'll be at Pope's bar at six. It'll be too early to have a drink, but maybe I can get some other type of satisfaction. Plus, Nils just planted a thought . . . probably on purpose. Five hundred big ones to nail Delgado. That's worth thinking about.

Arsen dialed another number and waited for an answer.

"Hello, Jamie here."

"Good morning, my friend. You missed out on an excellent hamburger at the Monk last night."

Chuckling, Jamie said, "Glad you enjoyed it."

"Let me give you an update. I realize how slow our progress has been, but based on what I've found out, we don't want to rush things at this point. Tell your parents to be patient and to cooperate with *Mr.* Pope for the time being. I have a few leads to follow, and hopefully I can come up with a plan within a couple of days. Okay?"

"You mean they should start peddling drugs out of their grocery store? You know that starting tomorrow the assholes will be giving my parents drugs to sell."

This was not the response Arsen was expecting.

"I understand, but we need to make sure there are no long-term consequences of taking action against Pope and his boys. We need to be calm for now. Seriously."

Jamie hesitated before responding and then said flatly, "I don't like it and they won't like it, but I'll convince them to cooperate for now. Please keep me posted."

"Will do."

I'll think twice before getting involved in anymore of this 'Good Samaritan' stuff. I could be home watching my tomatoes grow . . . although I am looking forward to having dinner tonight with Kasie.

Arsen was pacing the room, something was bothering him, a loose thread. Nils seemed surprised about the ambush in the park maintenance building. How would anyone know about the timing of the tunnel explosion? Was Spencer the only other person who knew about the operation? The dead shooter and his friend who got away were speaking Spanish.

At least one of them was speaking Spanish. What about the other one? Something's not right. Time to visit Spencer.

It was 11:30 a.m. when Arsen arrived at the empty parking lot in front of the Dunleavy Funeral Home and Crematorium. He opened his trunk and strapped on the Glock ankle holster. Entering the oak double doors, Arsen was met by an empty foyer and complete silence. The door to Spencer's office was closed, but a faint light was seeping through the crack at the bottom.

Arsen knocked three times.

"Ahh, yes."

Arsen interpreted the halting response as one of surprise, anxiousness, maybe alarm. Not waiting for an invitation, he opened the door and walked into the office. Spencer was standing behind his desk, wearing a pair of winkled army fatigues and a dark-green tee shirt. His eyes were bloodshot, he was unshaven and a large gauze bandage taped to the right side of his head showed blood stains. He was holding a plastic bottle of Advil.

"What do you need?" The tone of his voice indicated not surprise or alarm, but instead a sense of resignation.

Arsen immediately knew what had transpired. "It's not what I need, it's what you need. As you know, a bullet wound can get infected and cause serious health issues. Surely you know that, don't you?"

"What are you talking about?" Spencer said with a slight frown.

Arsen tilted his head and stared at the bandage.

"I slipped in my garage yesterday and hit my head on the wall." Spencer was making flimsy excuses. His facial features showed desperation. "Clumsy, huh."

Placing his left foot on the edge of Spencer's desk, Arsen lifted his pants leg to expose the ankle holster containing the Glock. The retention strap had been undone for a fast and silent draw.

"Take a seat, Spencer."

Spencer slowly sat down, looking at the holster, and then glancing at his middle desk drawer.

Arsen returned to his calm place. "Think about it, Spencer, I have essentially three moves to make: reach for my Glock, pull it from the holster, and fire. You, on the other hand, have five moves to make: reach for the drawer, open it, reach for your weapon, pull it out, and then fire. Because I'm so good at math, I know that five is more than three. Agreed?"

Spencer sank back in his chair, with a submissive look of despair.

Arsen continued to rest his foot on the desk. "Tell me all about it." It was more than a request, it was a subtle demand.

Spencer took a deep breath and appeared to relax for the first time since Arsen arrived. "You and your kind get the big money, the bonuses, the glory. I get a measly fucking salary and have to take out the trash. Figure it out."

"So, you're working for the Sinaloa Cartel?"

"The tunnel was built by the Barrio Azteca arm of the Juarez Cartel. The boys at Sinaloa don't like competition. They don't like you either. They know about you killing a couple of their men in Agua Prieta a few years ago. They don't forget."

"I get it. The old *two birds with one stone* thing, huh?" Continuing with a facetious tone to his voice, Arsen said, "How in the world did they find out I was the one who killed their two men in Agua Prieta?"

Ignoring the question, Spencer leaned forward slightly in his chair and said, "We could work together and make a shit-pot full of cash from these two cartels. You know, work both sides of the street. They would never know."

"How does Sinaloa get their drugs across the border? Do they have their own tunnels in this area?"

Spencer placed his elbows on his desk and continued. "Are you kidding me! They don't need to rely on tunnels because they've bribed so many border guards on the bridges. Driving across a bridge is a hell of a lot easier than going underground. When your drug operations earn over two hundred million profit per week, you can afford all kinds of payoffs. That's where you and I could make a fortune."

"Do you know Jack Pope?"

"Who?" Spencer didn't seem to recognize the name. He continued pleading for his life. "What do you think about working together and making the big bucks? Huh, what do you think?"

Arsen's foot still rested on the edge of the desk, elbow on his knee, thumb on his chin. Narrowing his eyes, he whispered, "What do I think? I think you're a piece of slime-bag shit. Open your desk drawer." *Bring it on home.*

The color drained from Spencer's face. He managed to open the desk drawer, but before his hand could reach his weapon, two bullet holes were in his forehead . . . one above each eyebrow. His body lurched backwards in the chair, the chair hit the wall, and he spilled out of the chair onto the floor.

Arsen picked up the two shell casings and a cell phone he noticed lying on the desk, put them in his pocket, and stood over the body.

Now, I have to take out the trash.

Arsen left Spencer's office, crossed the lobby and followed a hall to the back of the building. The door to the crematorium was unlocked, and as he entered, Arsen could feel the heat from the furnace. He had been in this very room two nights ago when he'd brought Burk's body for disposal. He walked across the room and looked at the instrumentation on the single-chamber furnace. The temperature gage showed 1800 degrees Fahrenheit.

Looks as if the oven has been preheated. I wonder who Spencer was planning on roasting today?

After removing two white bed sheets from a closet in the room, Arsen returned to Spencer's office. He wrapped Spencer's head in one of the sheets and removed most of the blood from the floor. He folded the other sheet in half and rolled the body onto it. Spencer was a large man and the arduous task of sliding the sheet down the hall to the crematorium took several minutes. Arsen placed the body on the feeding system and watched as the automatic door to the roaring furnace opened, the extreme heat stinging his eyes.

He would need to call Nils and tell him what had happened, so that he could send a replacement for the funeral home.

As the door closed, Arsen decided to lower his head and say a few appropriate last words for Spencer.

"Burn in hell, motherfucker."

17

Juarez, Mexico
Thursday, July 6th

Carlos was in the kitchen of his main residence drinking coffee. Even though the windows were bullet-proof, made with glass-clad polycarbonate costing $100 per square foot, he could hear the sounds of children playing in the yard. Outside, it was a pleasant morning. Rays of sun gleamed through the tall oaks on the east side of the compound. It was an idyllic life . . . for everyone except Carlos.

"Where is our goddamned *source*! You said you left Spencer two messages this morning about the tunnel in Socorro. Here it is almost noon and he still hasn't called back. Why can't we trust anyone!"

"You can trust me, boss. Spencer will call me back." Arturo was drinking beer and seemed considerably less agitated than his leader.

"Fuck Spencer! Have you tried to call your man you sent last night? Did he and Spencer make it to the tunnel?"

Carlos was on the verge of one of his meltdowns.

Arturo sat up straight and said, "He called me from Spencer's car when they arrived at the park last night. He said everything was on schedule. I've tried to call him this morning, but no answer. I suppose it's possible that things ain't right."

"Did you call his wife? Did you check with the other men? Have they heard from him?"

"I've called everyone who would know anything about his whereabouts. Nothing, but I'll keep trying."

Sitting back in his chair and taking a deep breath, Carlos tried to calm himself. "Call one of your contacts in the Juarez police department. Ask if they're aware of any tunnel activity near Socorro last night."

"On it." Arturo had his phone in his hand before Carlos finished his request.

After pressing a speed dial number and the speaker button, Arturo only had to wait a few seconds. "Anything happen last night I should be aware of?"

The voice on the call sounded nervous and whispered in short, rapid sentences. "A Juarez Cartel tunnel was blown up last night. Around midnight. The tunnel crossed over to Socorro. They lost five men in the explosion. Totally destroyed. Got to go."

Carlos sipped his coffee, frowning. "The tunnel's gone. That's good, but what happened to Spencer and our man? *They* lost five men in the explosion? Who's *they*? Was Spencer one of the five? Was our man one of the five? Goddamn it, what's going on? You've been responsible for coordinating with Spencer. Get me some answers!"

When Carlos got out of control, he had a tendency to blame anyone within hearing distance for a botched operation.

Arturo blanched. "Spencer mentioned something about going to a hot nightclub in El Paso to celebrate. He said it in passing and I didn't pay much attention. I'm sure he took our man with him. They probably got drunk, and right now they're sleeping it off with a couple of those El Paso chicks."

"Keep calling."

Arturo sat up straight in his chair. "I have a feeling they carried out their assignment. The government guy is most certainly dead."

Feelings can occasionally be completely wrong.

18

El Paso, Texas
Thursday, July 6th

It was 1:30 p.m., and in spite of the early July temperature, it was relatively cool inside the Seventh Avenue Lounge. A few customers were seated in the booths or standing at the pool table, but the male members of the crew, with the exception of Jack Pope, were all seated at the bar. Gus Fever was flanked by Lester on his right and the two newest members of the crew on his left.

Melton was leaning back on his bar stool, elbows tucked to his side, as he said to Patterson, "This is the technique I use to bench press my body weight. Pretty cool, huh?"

Patterson was showing little interest in weight lifting techniques, and instead was eyeing Debbie, the temporary bartender. He was trying his best to start a conversation with her.

Gus, who was on his second beer, said to no one in particular, "What do you think the boss and Miss Robin are doing in his office? They can see us through the damn window, but we can't see them."

Lester was quick to respond. "Now, I don't know this for a fact, but I would guess that they're back there doing things that a couple of rabbits would do. Just sayin'."

"What makes you think that?" Gus's facial features indicated he was not so much asking a question as encouraging additional sordid details.

Lester downed the last of his beer and said, "I've seen them come out of the office all mussed up and fuddled . . . several times. You don't have to be an FBI agent to figure it out. Hell, the boss-bitch is so hot I wish I was the one banging her."

"Yeah, I'd like to grab her red hair with both hands. I'll bet I could get her to give me an Alabama Slurpee." Gus didn't appear to be joking.

"A what?"

"You heard me. An Alabama Slurpee."

Lester, never to be outdone, whispered loudly, "I think the heat and the

90

alcohol have affected the few brain cells you have left. By the way, you never mentioned how you got that scar on your face. What happened?"

"Got in a hoe fight when I was twelve." Gus ran his finger down the side of his face.

Lester sat up straight on his bar stool. "You got into a fight with a whore when you were twelve!"

Debbie shook her head, and left to tend to the two men playing pool.

"No dumbass, it was a H . . . O . . . E, not a whore. Anyway, the other kid lost an ear. Guess it was a fair exchange. You know all my secrets, so tell me about the two people at the pharmacy. I read the article in the paper today at lunch."

Lester pondered the question for a few seconds before answering. "Let's just say that the two people in the pharmacy got out of control and I did what was required to straighten 'em out. They ended up with their names in the obituaries and I'm sitting here drinking beer. Jack Pope appreciates decisive people who take decisive action."

"Damn! I guess that makes you King of the Hill . . . for now." Gus nodded his head in approval.

"Heck, Gus, you're the one that has it made. The bald head, the bushy eyebrows, and the scar makes you a natural for this business. No one even notices me."

Gus casually leaned away from Lester. "Well, as much as I appreciate this bonding experience, I don't want you to feel like we're going steady."

As Lester was rolling his eyes, Robin emerged from the office. She was wearing a floral dress gathered at the waist that showed off her long, shapely legs. She was running her fingers through her unruly hair.

Lester and Gus glanced at each other and both nodded.

Robin put her hand on Lester's shoulder and said quietly to the group, "Okay, boys. It's time to leave for the training program at Big City Grocery."

As they left the bar and walked toward the van, Gus said, "Just a minute. I need to get something out of my car."

Lester put his hand on the passenger side door handle and yelled, "Holy shit! I'll probably have a scar on my hand. Feels like someone pointed a flame thrower at this side of the van."

"If you're too big a pussy to handle a little heat . . . move. Why don't you relocate to Duluth?" Melton looked at Patterson and they both laughed.

Lester examined the palm of his hand and said, "Yeah, why don't you move back to Newballs, dickhead?"

"It's Newhall, you ignorant hick. Newhall, California. And don't forget it."

"Boys! Get in the van. We don't want to be late." Robin smiled at the banter.

"Wait for me." Gus wiped sweat from his forehead as he approached his friends.

Lester sat in the front seat next to Robin who was driving. The other three men sat in the back. While Robin and Lester discussed the quickest route to the grocery store, Gus surreptitiously lifted his shirt to show the exposed handle of his pistol to Melton. The only response from Melton was a disinterested shrug.

The van pulled into the Big City Grocery's parking lot at precisely 2:00 p.m. Only one car was parked at the back of the small lot. The curb in front of the store was not occupied and there was little activity on the street. The excessive July heat seemed to be keeping the locals inside.

Robin led the pack as she and her four companions entered the front door. Lester pulled the shade on the door and changed the "open" sign to "closed," just as he had been instructed. Mr. Rodriguez was behind the counter working on some paperwork and frowned when he saw the five members of the crew. Mrs. Rodriguez emerged from a room in back and hesitated at the sight of Robin.

Robin got straight to business. "Greetings to you both. We're going to have a short training session this afternoon, since the first shipment of . . . ahh . . . produce will be arriving tomorrow morning. You'll need to be prepared because customers have been notified and will be arriving at all times of the day." Hesitating for a moment, she said, "You're still on board with the program, aren't you?"

Mr. Rodriguez glanced at his wife and nodded.

Handing a piece of paper to Mr. Rodriguez, Robin said, "Good. Take this list and memorize it. It specifies the type of merchandise you'll have in stock, and the unit pricing. I'll call you occasionally and confirm the amount of sales you've had and the amount of inventory remaining. We can bring whatever you need on short notice, although we would prefer to replenish the stock each Friday morning. Okay?"

Mr. Rodriguez nodded again and Robin went over the contents of the list, how to keep track of sales, and suggestions for storing the drugs and the cash. Lester remained stationed at the front door and Melton and Patterson wandered toward the storeroom. Gus stood near the counter with his hands in his pockets.

A silhouette on the door's shade went unnoticed. The silhouette didn't move for several seconds, followed by the door opening with considerable force. Lester was startled and reacted by raising his hands.

Bursting through the door, Jamie saw a woman standing next to the counter who matched the description his father had given. A man standing near the door had his hands raised in a threatening manner. Jamie's reaction was swift. His right fist connected squarely on the side of Lester's nose, making a cracking sound. Lester's body hit the wall and he struggled to maintain his balance before sliding to the floor.

Gus's reaction was also rapid. He pulled the .38 Special from his pants pocket and aimed it at Jamie, who was only twenty feet away. Jamie lurched toward the counter as Gus fired his weapon. Jamie spun and fell to his knees. Jamie's parents started screaming and rushed toward their son.

"My boy, my boy!" Mrs. Rodriguez was clearly panicking as she reached Jamie.

Mr. Rodriguez shouted as he ran past Gus. "You son-of-a-bitch. You'll pay for this!"

Melton and Patterson were frozen in place, while Robin remained as calm as if she were sitting at home watching a low-budget movie.

Jamie was grimacing, but his eyes were open. The white tee shirt he was wearing showed only a small amount of blood. Mr. Rodriguez had instructed his wife to get a towel and was now bending over his son, putting pressure on the wound.

Robin walked to where Jamie was lying and said, "Based on my experience, it doesn't appear that this young man is critically wounded, so listen up. This is an example of what happens when you mess with the Seventh Avenue Crew. We'll be delivering the drugs to you in the morning, so be ready. Once again, don't involve the police. Tell them a guy wearing a mask came into the store and shot this fellow while attempting a robbery. Like we told you before, if the police get into this, we'll kill your two daughters and the grandkids. That's a promise. It may take a few months, but it'll happen. You're going to start doing business with us tomorrow. Period!"

Walking toward the door, Robin told Gus to take care of Lester, who was sitting-up with his hand over his bloody nose. She turned and looked at Mr. Rodriguez. "Better get the young man to the hospital. He's looking a little pale."

An awkward silence accompanied the crew on the drive back to the bar. Robin told Melton to remove his shirt so that Lester could hold it on his bleeding nose. Blood had soaked his shirt and the front of his pants.

Gus finally spoke, concern in his voice. "I'm not so sure about this role as an enforcer. I must admit that I was a little envious of Lester's role in the pharmacy shooting, but now I'm worried about going to prison . . . or worse."

Robin lowered her voice. "Now, now, Gus. Take it easy. That kid could have caused us serious damage. I didn't realize they had a son. Isn't that what the old lady called him? My research turned up the two daughters and the grandchildren, but not a son. Fucking internet." The red-rimmed sun glasses masked her eyes as they narrowed. "This is not over. We need to make a solid statement to the Rodriguez family. They're going to be a distributor whether they like it or not."

Lester went straight to the men's room after the crew entered the bar. Melton strutted bare-chested across the floor, since his shirt was being used on Lester's nose. The few customers at the tables didn't seem to notice or care. It was hot outside and the drinks inside were cold. Debby shrugged at the sight and continued mixing drinks.

Jack was sitting at his desk when Robin and the three men entered the office. "Where's Lester? Where's your shirt, Melton?"

Robin had organized her thoughts and was ready for Jack's questions and concerns. "Keep your seat and let me explain what happened."

After hearing Robin's detailed description of the events at Big City Grocery, Jack said, "You did the right thing, Gus. We're in the drug business and we might as well face the fact that there'll be some collateral damage. Robin, you're sure the kid isn't gonna die?"

"I looked at him as we left the store. I've seen serious gun-shot wounds and I think he'll be okay. Just guessing."

Gus nodded in agreement and breathed a sigh of relief as he seated himself on the couch.

Robin wasn't finished. She spoke in a very deliberate manner. "I have a plan that well make Carlos Delgado and the entire cartel proud of the crew. I recommend we put an exclamation point on our visit to the grocery store today. I'm sick and tired of the old man's belligerent attitude. The Rodriguez couple have two daughters. Right? We need to grab the young one who lives at the Royal Palms apartment complex. We can hold her for a day or two to show the old couple we're serious. That should get their attention and keep them in line. What do you think?"

Jack thought about the proposal for a few seconds and said, "Not a bad idea, but where will we keep her?"

There was a knock on the office door and Lester entered carrying Melton's tee shirt. He handed the shirt to Melton and sat on the corner of the couch, an embarrassed look on his face.

Robin surveyed the damage to Lester's nose, shook her head, and continued with the plan. "We can blindfold her and keep her in our spare bedroom. After we grab her, we can drive around for a while and she'll never know where she is. We'll let her go in a couple of days. It'll be a hell of a warning shot."

"When do you want to do it?"

Looking at her watch and then the crew, Robin said, "I think we should snatch the girl tomorrow afternoon. It's three-thirty now, and we have another potential distributor to visit this afternoon. Remember me telling you about the gym called Muscle Madness? The owner's name is Bill Hayes and he runs the place by himself. He closes at six, so let's leave here at five-thirty."

Jack was feeling left out of the planning process. He was the boss and needed to regain control. "Yeah, snatching the girl tomorrow afternoon will be perfect. I have to be here at six in the morning to meet Delgado's guy with the first shipment. It shouldn't take more than forty-five minutes or so. Everyone be here at seven-fifteen and we'll all leave together in the van. We'll deliver the drugs to Big City Grocery when they open, and we should arrive at Barbie's Cards and Gifts at about eight when they open." Jack was sure the crew was impressed with his mastery of the timeline. "Plus, we can take a load of product to the Muscle Madness guy if the visit to his place works out this afternoon."

Holding a wet paper towel on his nose, Lester snorted, "Darn good plan, boss."

"Works for me," Gus said loudly. He was becoming as much a sycophant as Lester.

Feeling the adulation, Jack decided to continue with his management expertise. "I propose that we grab the girl tomorrow afternoon at her apartment. Let's say at five. She'll probably be getting ready for a night out on the town." Looking at Robin, he added, "Where did you say she lives?"

"Royal Palms. Not far from here . . . on Park Street. The good news is that she lives in a first-floor apartment. Her back patio is next to the parking lot."

"Excellent. I have an idea. We'll come back here this evening after we finish up at Muscle Madness and put the finishing touches on the *girl grab* plan." Jack was feeling good about his ability to come up with catchy phrases. "Drinks on me."

Robin was all business. "Okay. Drinks are on the boss when we return."

The crew filed out of the office and was met by the smell of stale beer and music blaring from the jukebox. Gus and Lester sat at the bar and began talking about the similarities of their .38 Specials, the benefits of a two-handed grip, kneeling versus standing positions, and the new slant to Lester's nose.

Gus was focused on Lester's face. "Hey, my friend, I've got some friendly advice. You know, with that manly knot on your nose, you should grow a mustache and a goatee. You'd be able to attract all kinds of tail."

"Thanks for the suggestion, partner. I may do that."

Melton and Patterson headed for the front door. Patterson, who had been quiet most of the afternoon, said matter-of-factly, "I suppose things could be worse. So far, we're only facing murder, attempted murder, drug dealing, and soon-to-be kidnapping charges."

"We're officially outlaws. Live with it."

19

El Paso, Texas
Thursday, July 6th

It was early afternoon when Arsen returned to his room from the funeral home. Sitting on the edge of the bed, he dialed Nils for the second time that day.

"We're spending a fair amount of time on the phone, Arsen." Nils had his customary neutral tone, he didn't sound critical or overly friendly.

"Yes, I'm aware, but you need to know about a recent loss. One of your employees." Arsen was interested in how Nils would respond.

The reply was immediate, with an element of surprise. "Who?" Quickly followed by another short question. "Spencer?"

"Yep. He was the other person in the maintenance shed. I acted on a hunch and made a visit to the funeral home this morning.

Arsen detailed the encounter and related Spencer's suggestion that they work together with the cartels.

"I assume you used the transfer site for its intended purpose."

"I did. How soon will you have a replacement? The furnace will need a thorough cleaning."

"Late this afternoon. Arsen, surely you won't be needing the facilities before then. Correct?" Nils was being mildly sarcastic.

"I can't promise anything. What's the person's name and what's his phone number?"

Nil's sarcasm continued. "The person's name is Leela. And be nice to *her* or she'll kick your ass. She'll have the same phone number as Spencer, except that the last digit is an eight instead of a two."

Arsen walked to the window in his room and stood staring at nothing. He didn't have an appetite due to his recent experience at the funeral home. This bothered Arsen. He liked the idea of "delivering justice to the deserving," but deep down there was a hint of regret. He wondered if Spencer had a family, friends, or even a dog.

These are stupid thoughts. Hell, Spencer knew the risks . . . and he was deserving.

Arsen was also having thoughts about life in general . . . his in particular. In the past two days, he had killed Burk, blown up a tunnel, killed a man in the maintenance shed, and killed Spencer. A lot of death and destruction in such a short time. He had plenty of cash from his past exploits, so retirement was a distinct possibility.

I don't like these kinds of thoughts. Dangerous. If this is what happens every time I meet a good-looking woman, I'm in trouble. I need to make a decision about my social life one way or the other. Soon. It's risky having doubts in this business.

After closing the window curtains, Arsen removed his shoes and stretched out on the bed, trying to eliminate the questions and negative feelings flowing through his mind. He was tired from lack of sufficient sleep. His thoughts drifted back to the night he spent with the lady he met at the bar in Odessa, the drive to El Paso, the late night at the parking lot next to the Seventh Avenue Lounge, and then the close encounter at the tunnel.

How long has it been since I've had a deep, uninterrupted sleep? Seems like forever.

And a deep sleep arrived . . . for twenty minutes. The sound of the cell phone on the bed-side table ended the healing process.

Arsen answered with a sluggish, "Yes."

"Arsen, Jamie's been shot!" Kasie was sobbing as she spoke.

Still not fully awake, Arsen said, "What? When? Where are you?"

"On my way to El Paso General Hospital. Mother just called and said that Jamie has been shot and is being prepped for surgery."

"I'll meet you there. Where exactly is the hospital located?"

"Oregon and El Paso."

"Okay."

Thirty minutes had passed by the time Arsen arrived at the facility. He was met by the unmistakable disinfectant odor of all hospitals, mixed with the smell of sadness, concern, and fear. The sparkling white marble floor of the lobby echoed the soft murmurs of the fifteen or so visitors. Kasie and her parents were seated in chairs against the far wall. Based on his last conversation with Jamie, Arsen was concerned about the reception he would receive from the family members.

He was relieved when Kasie, wearing a light blue blouse and tennis shorts, walked toward him and took his hand. Even is this environment, under these circumstances, he felt a spark of excitement, but he still didn't want to admit it.

Arsen spoke softly to the family. "How's Jamie?"

Mrs. Rodriguez was first to reply. "We don't know yet."

"What happened?"

Mr. Rodriguez appeared to be composed, but his voice cracked when he said, "The gang came into the store and gave us a list of the drugs we're supposed to sell."

"They didn't bring the drugs, did they?" Arsen already had a plan and he wanted to insure the timing was correct.

Mr. Rodriguez began talking in short, hurried sentences. "No, just a list. The drugs will come in the morning. Jamie came in and hit the man guarding the door. A man with a big scar shot Jamie. They warned us not to tell the police. They'll kill our daughters. They said to tell the police it was a masked robber."

Arsen's eyes narrowed as he slowly repeated what he had just heard. "The drugs will be delivered in the morning?"

"Yes."

"You said the man that shot Jamie had a scar on his face. Was it on the right side?" Arsen drew a line with his finger from the corner of his mouth to his ear.

"Yes. Do you know him?"

"I think I've seen him."

The conversation was interrupted as two serious looking men wearing sports coats approached from the front desk. The taller of the two was the first to speak.

"Hello. I'm Detective Mottern and this is Detective Arnett. I understand that you're the family of the gunshot victim who was brought in earlier."

Mr. Rodriguez stood and answered in a clipped, uncertain tone. "Yes, we're the family. Our son was shot."

"Were there any witnesses?"

Pointing at his wife, who was also standing, Mr. Rodriguez said, "My wife and I were in our store with our son and a robber wearing a mask came in and shot Jamie." His voice trailed off with the last few words.

"Was anyone else present?"

"No."

Looking at the couple, the detective said, "Could you and your wife have a seat and answer a few more questions?"

With a heavy sigh, Mr. Rodriguez mumbled, "Okay."

Before they could begin, a doctor wearing a surgical mask hanging around his neck approached the group. He had a pleasant smile on his face as he said, "I take it you're Jamie Rodriguez's family?"

Mrs. Rodriguez was first to speak, her concern evident. "Yes. Is our boy going to be okay?"

"Don't worry. He'll be fine. He's a strong young man and he didn't lose much blood. The bullet grazed his side and clipped a rib, but there wasn't any internal damage. We'll keep him in intensive care overnight and hopefully he can be released within a day or so."

Arsen was taking mental notes: *Sounds almost like the wound I received in Syria. Someday we can compare scars.*

While the two detectives and Jamie's parents continued to talk, Arsen and Kasie began walking slowly toward the main entrance of the hospital.

Kasie was relieved after receiving the doctor's report and said, "I'll stay here and take care of my parents. As you can tell, they're very upset over this whole mess."

"I know. I'm sorry it turned out this way, but tell them to cooperate for a few more days. I think I'm close to finding out some critical information. I should know more by tomorrow."

"Do you still want to have dinner this evening?"

Arsen had not forgotten about their dinner plans. "Well, maybe we could have dinner and then stop by here afterwards and see if they'll let us visit Jamie. What do you think?"

"Good idea. I made reservations at Mi Piaci for six-thirty, so you can pick me up at my apartment at six. Let me give you directions."

Kasie explained how to get to the patio door of her apartment by parking at the corner of the parking lot. Arsen filed away the instructions.

My appetite is returning!

On the drive back to the hotel, Arsen started another recap of his recent activities, but stopped in mid-thought: *Screw it. I need to think about the problems in front of me. The past is the past. Anyway, I'll be with Kasie in a couple of hours. Later this evening I'll visit the guy with the big scar.*

The van containing the Seventh Avenue Crew parked in front of Muscle Madness at a few minutes before 6:00 p.m. The gym was located in a small building at the front of an otherwise empty lot. The surrounding area was only sparsely developed, and traffic was at a minimum. A red, hand-painted sign over the front door identified the business.

Lester offered his observation. "This is just a cut above a dirt-ball dude selling drugs on the corner."

Patterson poked Melton in the ribs with his elbow and said, "Hey Arnold, maybe you can pump iron while the rest of us get a little work done."

Melton silently mouthed, "Screw you."

Jack, always the entrepreneur, said, "Get serious. I like the looks of this place. We need to make it happen. Right, Robin?"

Robin slowly nodded. Lester also nodded as if he had been the one addressed.

As the six members of the crew entered the front door, a large, figure emerged from a restroom in the back. His tank top and shorts could barely contain his well-developed body.

The reflection of light from his dark eyes complimented the whiteness of his teeth when he smiled and said, "I'm about to close for the day, but I would be happy to sign all of you up for a twelve-month membership."

Robin was transfixed on Bill Hayes's physical appearance, his baritone voice, the sparkle of his deep, dark eyes. An involuntary shudder ran through her entire body.

Despite the physical presence of the man on the other side of the counter, Jack proceeded with his intimidation speech, knowing he was being backed up by five members of the crew, most of whom were armed. "No, I'm not going to sign up, but I think *you* will after you hear my proposal."

Other than his address, Robin had not been able to discover any personal information about the owner, so Jack was going to use simple personal threats.

"I know that your name is Bill Hayes and I know where you live. My name is Jack Pope and we're known as the Seventh Avenue Crew. You're going to sell drugs for us, right here out of your ugly, little gym. And you'll make some cash doing it."

"How much cash?"

"Depends on how much you sell."

The gym owner violently slammed his fist on the counter, scattering pencils, brochures and a small weight lifting trophy. Gus instinctively jerked his gun from his back pocket; the rest of the crew were temporarily stunned.

The owner bellowed, "It's about time! I've been working my ass off for over a year without a break. Maybe this is it!"

Jack breathed a sigh of relief and proceeded to explain the business model to his newest distributor. The owner listened intently as Jack spoke, but his eyes were focused on Robin.

Jack finished his sales pitch and said, "Robin, do you have a product list with you?"

"Yes, it's in the van."

"Go get it and you can conduct the training session for Mr. Hayes right now. He'll be receiving his first delivery tomorrow."

The training session was over in fifteen minutes and Jack finished with his standard warning about not contacting the authorities. He told Hayes to expect the first shipment of product at 8:30 the following morning.

It had been an active day for the crew and everyone was in an ebullient mood on the drive back to the bar. Even Gus, who had shot and wounded, or maybe killed, someone earlier in the afternoon, was starting to act like a big-time gangster.

"Hey, anyone have any news on their cell phones about the shooting at the grocery store?" Gus sounded curious, but not concerned.

Jack's voice was flat. "Not yet. Like I said, collateral damage happens in this business."

Patterson couldn't contain his amusement. "You know, I think Melton and Lester both pissed themselves when the big guy at the gym pounded the counter."

Even Robin chimed in. "Yeah, I was afraid he would make us mop the floor. Jeez, did you see his shoulders and biceps? He looked like an NFL linebacker."

Not to be outdone, Lester said, "It would have been easy for Melton and me to have taken him down. Steroid heads like that guy are just big, not strong."

"He could have thrown both of you through the goddamn wall!" Patterson wouldn't relent.

Jack was quiet, but satisfied. The crew was starting to coalesce into a functioning organization.

My leadership has provided the motivation and direction for this team. I knew I could make it work.

"Well, we've had an excellent day. Drinks are on me when we get back to the bar."

Lester had the last word. "I wonder what the heck happened to Burk?"

20

Juarez, Mexico
Thursday, July 6th

Carlos and his six direct reports were sitting around the large table in his library. Bookshelves covered three walls, all packed with various types of literature: law, philosophy, religion, fiction, and economics. He had majored in economics at New Mexico State and all of his college text books were on display.

Carlos had been in a bad mood all day and the news that Arturo had just relayed to him didn't help matters. "Arturo, tell them what you just found out."

"Sanchez is dead." The news brought groans from the other members of the gathering. "We sent him on a mission last night, and I was informed by our contact at police headquarters that he was found shot dead at a maintenance shed in Socorro this morning."

Carlos was entering his unpredictable, dark place. A change appeared in his facial features and in the pitch of his voice. "This is what happens when you don't pay attention to your job!" What Carlos lacked in sympathy, he made up for in pragmatism. "Arturo, did you tell him it was dangerous? Did you tell him to be careful? He worked for you, and you didn't take care of him."

Surprise showed on Arturo's face. This was the first time he had been reprimanded in the presence of the other team members. "I told him as much as I could about the details of the operation. I told him to be alert and to take care of himself. He was a good man."

"No more goddamned excuses! From now on, all of you need to get your heads out of your asses. Understand?"

All six men nodded in unison. It was no secret that Carlos was experiencing pressure due to the Juarez Cartel's efforts to regain a foothold in the Juarez-El Paso corridor.

Carlos wasn't through with Arturo. "Antonia is delivering the first drug shipment to Jack Pope in the morning. It had better go smoothly, Arturo. Smoothly. Do you understand?"

With a cowed expression, Arturo responded timidly, "There will be no problems. I'll go with her."

"No! She needs to learn the business on her own. Just make sure everything is arranged so that she gets across the bridge without any delays. Okay? Besides, you'll be busy tomorrow helping Jack Pope."

"Jack Pope. How am I going to be helping him?"

Carlos leaned back in his chair and glared at his men. "Most of you know about the experimental distribution program we're trying out in El Paso. Jack Pope, a college acquaintance of mine, is in charge of it. The owners of one of the businesses in the program, a grocery store, seem to be having difficulty following orders. Pope thinks it would be a good idea to kidnap one of the owners' daughters in order to make a statement. I agree. Arturo will assist them in getting the girl and bringing her to Juarez. I'll spend some . . . *personal time* . . . with her and then let her go back to her parents with the message that we mean business." A sly smile accompanied the conclusion of his statement.

Arturo managed a smile after hearing about his new assignment. "Good idea. What's my part in the kidnapping?"

"I'm going to Mexico City on business this evening and will return around four on Saturday afternoon. You'll need to have the young lady at the Hotel Azetca Aeropuerto when I arrive. Call Jack Pope and get the details of the operation . . . and don't fuck-up this one."

Arturo, still trying to placate his boss, said. "I'll have the young lady at the Hotel Azetca Aeropuerto. She'll be ready for you." Looking at the book lying next to Carlos's drink, he continued his efforts to get back on his good side. "What book are you reading, boss?"

Carlos's sour mood suddenly changed and he answered the question in an amiable manner. "I'm glad you asked. The name of the novel is *Doublewide*. It was written by some obscure author in California and it gave me an idea for another way to expand our distribution system. The story alternates between a trailer park in Dallas, Texas, and the Hotel Zone in Cancun. A statistic in the book caught my attention. Did you know that over nineteen million passengers travel through the Cancun airport each year? There must be ways and methods of having a few of those passengers take some of our product back to their home countries. Or . . . we could distribute sample drugs to the tourists, you know, like salting a gold mine. Anyway, we need to think outside the box." Addressing his number two man, he said, "Santiago, I want you to take this idea and expand on it. Okay?"

"Sure thing, boss. I'll get on it."

Carlos waved his hand as if he were being bothered by a swarm of mosquitos, and all the men at the table hurriedly left the room.

21

El Paso, Texas
Thursday, July 6th

Arsen was able to park in the side lot near Kasie's patio. The sun was still visible in the west, but the evening temperature was bearable. He could hear children's voices and water splashing nearby. As he rounded the corner of the apartment building, he could see several youngsters standing on a diving platform. The water was not in view due to a well-trimmed hedge.

Kasie was standing on her patio talking to another woman, both holding glasses of wine. Waving, she motioned to Arsen to join them. "Arsen, this is my friend, Diane. She lives two doors down. Kasie placed her hand on Arsen's arm as she completed the introduction."

An electric charge surged through his body at the feel of her touch. *What's happening to me?*

"Kasie tells me that you live in Odessa. I've heard it's a beautiful city." Diane was about Kasie's age, but had short blond hair and fair skin.

Smiling, Arsen said, "Well, you must have heard it from someone who works at the Chamber of Commerce. That's not exactly the description you would hear from someone who lives there."

The light conversation continued for a few minutes before Kasie said, "We need to get going if we're going to make our six-thirty reservation at Mi Piaci."

Using the wireless remote, Arsen unlocked the doors to the Lexus when they were ten yards away. He surprised himself when he walked with Kasie to the passenger door and opened it.

This is the first time in ten years that I've opened a car door for a lady.

"Tell me, Miss Kasie, how do we get to Mi Piaci from here?"

"Turn left out of the parking lot and turn right when we come to Mesa Street. It's not far."

"Have you heard anything from your parents about Jamie?"

"No, but it's only been an hour and a half since we were at the hospital.

The doctor didn't seem to think it was all that serious. They'll let me know if anything changes. I'll call them after dinner."

The interior of the Italian restaurant had the ambiance and charm Arsen expected: dark wood paneling, soft lighting, white table cloths, and a well-stocked bar. Soon after they were seated, a waiter appeared and took their drink orders. Kasie asked for a house cabernet and Arsen took a moment to consider what he should drink due to his plans for later in the evening.

"I'll have a Tito's straight up with a couple of olives." *Maybe a martini will get me motivated to find the guy with the big scar on his face.*

"Is Tito's a vodka?" Kasie looked confused.

"Yes, it is. Distilled six times in Austin, Texas. One of the finest vodkas ever made. Do you know where the name Tito's came from?" Arsen was enjoying flaunting his knowledge of vodka in general, and Tito's in particular.

"No, I haven't, but I get the feeling I'm about to find out."

"That's the founder and CEO's first name. You'll never guess what his last name is."

"I give up."

"Beveridge. Can you believe it . . . Tito Beveridge."

Smiling, Kasie said, "Arsen, you're just one big surprise after another."

"I've been meaning to ask you about your sister, Rosa. Where was her husband the other evening at the cookout?"

"The family doesn't talk about it, but Rosa's husband left her last year. She and her kids drove to Albuquerque yesterday to visit friends for a few days. I called and told her about Jamie."

The drinks arrived, dinner was ordered, and the conversation continued. Arsen would have been happy to sit at the table with Kasie until morning. The warmth of the moment erased the low buzz created by the other patrons in the restaurant. Arsen was barely aware of eating his grilled tilapia. All of his attention was on Kasie.

Getting serious, Kasie said, "Arsen, tell me again about your profession. You've been somewhat evasive in explaining exactly what you do."

Arsen danced around the question, not getting much closer to the truth. "The companies I work for have reputations to uphold, even though they sometimes have to resort to extreme measures to protect their patents and their properties. These companies have international businesses, international customers, and international problems of various kinds. I guess you could say that I'm a go-between. I assist with international problems."

"Please don't take this the wrong way, but is everything you do legal?"

"It depends on how you define legal. What's legal in one culture, may be on the edge in another."

"Is it sometimes dangerous?"

Now it was time for an outright lie. "Oh no, sometimes strenuous, but not dangerous."

Arsen was certain the discussion was leading to Kasie's next question.

"Arsen, can you tell me if my parents' problem can be solved? Can you solve it? Can anyone solve it? Are we all in danger? Look what happened to Jamie."

Without skipping a beat, Arsen leaned forward and said with a calm certainty, "Yes, I can solve your parents' problem. And I will. I'll know by tomorrow the amount of risk involved."

"What's happening tomorrow?"

It could have been the effects of the martini, the dimly lighted room, or maybe just being in Kasie's presence, but Arsen decided to share a few items of information with her.

"I don't want you to repeat what I'm about to tell you. Especially to Jamie." He hesitated before proceeding. "As you know, the leader of the drug gang is a fellow by the name of Jack Pope. Your father told us that bit of information. I've followed up on a few leads, and I know that Pope owns a bar on Seventh Avenue . . . near the Santa Fe Street Bridge. I've been there. I've seen his so-called gang."

"Really!"

"You won't have to worry about the gang member that cut your mother's shoulder. He's out of the picture." Arsen's tone and the look in his eyes didn't encourage further questions about the fellow with the high-pitched voice. "I plan to visit the bar again later tonight and try to meet the guy with the scar. He may have some input about the questions you asked."

"Do you think he'll know about the threat of long-term revenge to our entire family?"

"Maybe." Pausing, as if to weigh the impact of his next statement, Arsen leaned forward, lowering his voice. "Remember me telling your parents about Carlos Delgado, the cartel lieutenant in Juarez? The answer to your question lies within the cartel. I'm also, for lack of a better word, *engaging* with one of their guys tomorrow morning. He'll be delivering the drugs to the Pope gang at six o' clock. He and I need to have a little chat."

Kasie had one final inquiry for her mysterious date. "Do you consider yourself a gentleman?"

Taken by surprise, Arsen paused and carefully answered, "Well, that term can have various connotations. From a social standpoint, I try to be aware of other people's feelings and I've never been overly aggressive with women. As a matter of fact, I'm probably a little shy when it comes to the opposite sex. I'm not perfect, but on the other hand, I'm not the biggest jerk in town."

As soon as they reached the car in the Mi Piaci parking lot, Kasie called her mother.

"Mom, how's Jamie doing?"

Arsen could only hear one side of the conversation, but he could tell from Kasie's reaction that Jamie was doing fine.

"Well, the doctor is positive that Jamie will be released from the hospital within the next two days. Mother says Jamie is still sedated and that they are going home in about ten minutes. I'll visit him in the morning."

"Good news. It could've been much worse."

The drive to Kasie's apartment was in an awkward silence. Arsen wondered what she was thinking, even though he was sure it had something to do with her brother or the safety of her family. After parking, Arsen walked Kasie to her patio. The sun had set, but the excited sound of children could still be heard coming from the swimming pool.

"Those kids are going to look like prunes from being in the water all day." Arsen was trying his best to be pleasant.

Stepping up onto the patio, Kasie turned around, facing Arsen, and said, "Well, as you can tell, I'm worried sick about my brother and all that's going on. Arsen, you're the only reason I'm not having a nervous breakdown."

Arsen, still standing in the grass, was about the same height as Kasie. Their eyes met, followed by their bodies. They reached for each other at the same time and embraced. The kiss that followed was soft, intense, lingering, only as a first kiss can be.

Kasie gently pulled back and whispered, "Arsen, we're moving awfully fast. Maybe we should slow down and think about what we're doing."

Arsen stepped onto the patio and looked down at Kasie. "As much as I hate to say it . . . you're probably right. However, you're all I've been thinking about since we met." His voice trailed off as he said, "This is an unusual feeling for me."

"Same here, but it feels good."

Kasie stepped forward and rested her head on Arsen's chest. He could barely hear her voice as she murmured, "Call me tomorrow. I'm going to the hospital to see Jamie around nine in the morning. Okay?"

"Don't worry. I'll call. As a matter of fact, I may see you at the hospital."

"And be careful tonight. Please."

"Oh, don't worry. I'm only thinking about having a beer and a nice conversation with Scarface."

———————————•————————————

The Seventh Avenue Lounge was unusually busy for a Thursday night. All the tables and booths were occupied, as were the eight stools at the bar. Jack and the crew were being generally loud and obnoxious in the corner booth near the jukebox. Four rowdy customers were playing pool, while three couples had created their own dance floor between the tables and the bar. Debbie, the temporary bartender, was overwhelmed with drink requests, but paid particular attention to the corner booth.

Jack was conducting a one-man, spirited recital for his crew. "I must say, I'm elated that the night club portion of our business is doing so well. Look at all these customers! Tomorrow, the rubber meets the road, when we officially kick off our main venture. Right?" He had already taken his third dose of Ritalin for the day, but nonetheless was close to being hyper. The gin and tonic, mixed with the Ritalin and his super-charged enthusiasm, made Jack pontificate more than usual. "Freud considered dreams to be the royal road to the unconsciousness, since it's in dreams that the ego's defenses are lowered." Jack enjoyed quoting from his college text books.

Robin, who was on her second martini, shook her head and rolled her eyes. "Here we go again. I think Freud had small hands and a little dick."

Everyone laughed except Jack. Drinks were on the house.

Jack was still wound up. "There's so much I could teach you folks, but I just don't have the time or patience. I did, however, have another excellent idea on the drive back from the muscle-what's-the-fuck-gym this afternoon. Lean in and listen up." He finally had everyone's attention. "I called my friend, Carlos Delgado, and told him about the little problem we had at Big City Grocery. He likes our plan to kidnap the daughter in order to make a statement. As a matter of fact, he liked the plan so much, he wants to send one of his men to participate in the grab tomorrow afternoon."

Jack explained the conversation and the plan in detail. The entire crew nodded in agreement. He was feeling totally in charge . . . powerful.

Lester changed the topic. "When's Shelly coming back? I miss looking at her . . ." He glanced at Robin before completing the thought. "You know, her finer assets."

Gus shook his head and said, "Lester, my man, like I told you, you need to finish growing a mustache and goatee before you even consider approaching a real woman. The tape on your broken nose is helping, but the hair I see growing on your face makes you look more like a child molester than a movie star."

There was hearty laughter all around the table. Even Jack, who usually didn't laugh at anyone else's jokes, tried to smile at the banter.

"She'll be back tomorrow," Robin said without emotion.

Lester wouldn't let it go. "What happened to her foot? See, I have concerns about all of her body parts, not just her tig ol' bitties."

Completely ignoring the essence of Lester's comment, Robin replied, "She cut it. Got something in her . . . foot . . . that shouldn't have been there."

Melton raised his glass. "Lester, what you lack in looks, you make up for with your questionable sense of humor."

It was 10:00 p.m. and the activity in the lounge was starting to slow down. Jack stood as he downed the last of his drink, hinting for the rest of the crew to do the same.

"Okay, as we discussed, everyone be here at seven-fifteen in the morning and we'll officially kick-off our little business venture. You'll benefit from this endeavor. Believe me."

Arsen watched the four male members of the crew walk out of the bar together. Although he was standing only ten feet away, appearing to be gazing at something across the street, none of the crew paid the slightest attention to him. His black jeans and black tee shirt blended with the warm, still night. Even if they had looked closely, they could not have seen the slight bulge around his left ankle. Out of the corner of his eye, Arsen could see them high-five, say their inebriated good-byes, and walk toward their respective cars.

The figure dressed in black followed the man with the long, red scar on his face . . . the man who had shot Jamie.

Gus pulled out of the parking lot and turned right on Seventh Avenue. After a short drive on Campbell Street, he made another right turn on Paisano Drive. The traffic was light at this hour of the night and Arsen stayed a considerable distance behind Gus's white Ford pickup.

A few flashes of heat lightning could be seen in the west, but the moon had made its presence known in the opposite direction. The pickup exited

Paisano and turned on San Marcial Street and continued for a block before parking in the driveway of a small stucco house, which appeared not to have a garage. Arsen parked at the curb, two houses away, and was able to see Gus exit his pickup, walk across the porch, and enter the front door.

The street was deserted as Arsen slowly made his way toward the house. The porch light exposed surface cracking, deterioration, and peeling on the front walls of the stucco structure. His initial impression was that the neighborhood consisted primarily of inexpensive and not well-maintained homes.

Arsen stopped in the darkness of a Live Oak growing next to the driveway. Gus had turned off the porch light and turned on a light in the front room. He was clearly visible standing in the room, taking off his shirt. As Arsen removed the Glock from his ankle holster, and slowly walked across the yard, he could see a woman enter the room carrying a baby. Gus took the baby and cradled it in his arms.

Hmmm, this complicates things.

A flurry of thoughts swept through Arsen's mind in a flash: the two men he had killed in Agua Prieta, Jamie rushing toward Gus in the grocery store, Kasie, Nils. He continued looking at the scene unfolding before him. The woman kissed Gus on the cheek and left the room, Gus continued to hold the baby, gently rocking it in his arms.

Turning and walking back to his car, Arsen thought: *That dick-wad is still not off the hot-seat. Besides, I need to get some shut-eye. Going to have a busy day tomorrow.*

And a busy day it would be.

22

El Paso, Texas
Friday, July 7ᵗʰ

Jack was standing outside the front door of the Seventh Avenue Lounge at 5:45 a.m. He'd been there for twenty minutes and was trying to calm himself with various breathing exercises. The morning air had a fresh, salty smell, even though the nearest ocean was five hundred miles away.

This was an important day in Jack's fledgling criminal career, a test of his leadership and execution skills. The first shipment of drugs would be arriving at any moment, and later in the day he would be involved in a kidnapping. He felt as if his rapidly beating heart was about to exit his chest and bounce on the concrete slab by the door. He normally took his first dose of Ritalin at 8:00 a.m., but he wasn't sure if he could wait another two hours.

Random thoughts were skimming through Jack's mind like flat rocks on a smooth lake surface. *Why is Robin avoiding my sexual advances? The thing with Shelly wasn't my fault. She started it. Besides, real men don't ever admit mistakes. It's a sign of weakness.*

These thoughts came to an abrupt halt when a white, panel truck slowly pulled into the parking lot. Due to the early morning dimness, combined with the vehicle's heavily tinted windows, Jack had to lean forward and strain to see the occupants. The lettering on the side of the truck gradually came into view----**PRETTY FLOWERS**----accompanied by a picture of a red rose.

There are probably three or four of the meanest motherfuckers alive delivering the stash.

Jack had an overwhelming need to urinate as the panel truck parked next to his van. He involuntarily stood straight, arms at his side, eyes fixated on the driver's side door as it opened. An unexpected sight met his eyes. The young woman, barely in her twenties, was wearing a halter print dress and wedge sandals. Her black hair was cut short and had a classy, girlish look. And she spoke perfect, flawless English.

"Sir, you must be Mr. Pope."

"Yes, yes, I am."

She approached Jack with hand extended. "Carlos gives you his regards. I'm pleased that we can conduct business together. Oh, by the way, my name is Antonia."

"Who else is with you?" Jack felt stupid the minute the words left his mouth, but it was all he could think to say.

"Oh, I'm alone. Except for the three boxes of goods in the van. You know, boxes of flowers." Antonia displayed an impish grin when she said the word *flowers*.

Jack was beginning to return to the real world as he asked, "Why don't you pull around to the side door and we can unload the *flowers* there. I'll go inside and open the door."

The cardboard boxes were small, and Antonia took all three of them to Jack's office with a small hand-dolly. Jack had opened the standing safe and proudly recited the description of its size and weight.

Antonia opened the boxes and displayed their contents. "This is exactly what you ordered." Removing a piece of paper from one of the boxes, she continued, "This is an invoice and a description of the contents. You're very lucky to have such a good friend as Carlos. I've never seen anyone else get to sell these goods on a consignment basis."

This is what Jack liked to hear. He was a special person and he thrived on compliments such as these. "Well, Carlos and I go way back. He's a really, really great person and I'm very fortunate to have such a good friend."

"Yes, I agree. Oh, I forgot to mention that Carlos is my brother."

The pitch of Jack's voice rose a notch as he expressed his surprise. "Really! I've known him for almost ten years and I didn't even know he had a sister."

"I'm the youngest in the family . . . and speaking of Carlos, he asked me to give you a message."

"And what would that be?" Jack was expecting more compliments from the young lady.

"He said for you *not* to fuck-up this opportunity."

Antonia returned to the panel truck and drove out of the parking lot, turning left on Seventh Avenue. The morning traffic had increased significantly, and the rising sun was causing a glare in the windows of the on-coming cars and trucks. Four minutes into the trip, Arsen rose from the back floorboard and quickly slipped a piano wire garrote over Antonia's head, using the wooden dowels to pull it firmly into her neck.

"Stay calm my friend and turn left into Armijo Park." Arsen's voice was as serene as a late-night, classical music deejay.

Antonia turned into the deserted park and drove for about a hundred feet.

"Park by the curb." Arsen was specific.

"What do you want? I don't have much money. Honest. Only a few dollars in my handbag." The wire was digging into her throat.

"Settle down, missy. I don't want your money, only a little information. Okay?"

Antonia's voice cracked as she gasped, "Tell me what you want."

Releasing the pressure somewhat, Arsen said, "Listen closely. I'm late for breakfast and I don't want any bullshit. Understand?"

"I understand."

"Where does Carlos Delgado live in Juarez?"

"It's not a secret. He lives in a compound that backs up to a park like this one. It's at the intersection of Avenida Vincente Guerrero and Ignacio Ramirez." Antonia's voice had taken on a more relaxed tone. "However, it would be difficult, if not impossible, for you to enter the compound. Sorry."

"And why is that?"

"The walls are high and the guards are many."

"How long have you worked for Carlos?"

"All my life. He's my brother."

Even though Arsen was mildly startled by the new revelation, he continued his line of questioning. "How long have you known Jack Pope, the fellow you delivered the drugs to this morning?"

"Twenty minutes. This was the first time I met him."

"You seem like a reasonable person and I think you and I could be good friends. So, tell me, how involved is your brother with Pope? Does he have Pope's back? Will he seek revenge from Pope's enemies over the long haul?"

An angry tone emerged with Antonia's next statement. "No one is safe from Carlos if he feels threatened or if someone harms one of his friends or his family."

Antonia rapidly twisted her shoulders and head to the right, a sudden move that caught Arsen off-guard. The small 9 mm Ruger in her right hand was instantly pointed over her shoulder as Arsen involuntarily jerked the garrote wire.

Antonio's hands flew upward, her body arched backward, and the gun discharged causing a bullet hole to appear in the roof of the truck. Simultaneously she began making gurgling sounds as the wire cut through her larynx and trachea. Unconscientious and death quickly followed.

Arsen was stunned as he loosened his grip. *Shit! This wasn't in the plan. What now?*

Arsen exited the back door of the panel truck carrying a furniture pad that had been covering the boxes of drugs. He opened the driver's door and pushed Antonia's body across the seat onto the floorboard. He placed the pad on the seat to cover the blood and mess caused by the ligature strangulation. The Ruger and the handbag were lying in the passenger seat. Dropping the gun in the handbag, he noticed a wallet, a package of tissues, and a pink cell phone.

During the drive to the Dunleavy Funeral Home and Crematorium, Arsen dialed the new phone number he had received from Nils. It was similar to the number for Spencer, except for the last digit which had been changed. Nils had indicated it was the number for a woman named Leela.

"Yes."

"Is this Leela?"

"This must be Arsen. Your reputation precedes you."

Without asking about his reputation, he said, "I have business for you. Can you meet me at the side door to the crematorium in ten minutes?"

"The door will be open."

It was 7:15 a.m. when Arsen parked the truck. He removed the body wrapped in the furniture pad and carried it through the open door to the furnace conveyer belt, the handbag dangling from his hand. The furnace was roaring, the room seemed hotter than it did during his last visit.

He turned and looked at the lady standing next to the door. The first thing he noticed was her flawless, smooth ebony skin. She appeared to be about five-seven with a symmetrical face, high cheek bones, and long black hair pulled back into a pony tail. The white pantsuit she was wearing displayed her shapely body.

"I understand that you're the reason for my promotion." Leela had a pleasant smile, a friendly demeanor.

"This has not been a good week for drug dealers. I'm glad it's at least furthered your career." Turning completely serious, he hesitated before saying, "This one didn't go according to plan. I'm not proud of the outcome, but there was nothing I could have done to avoid it." He knew he was back to rationalizing his actions.

Leela was in the process of putting on a long, canvas apron, a pair of gloves, and plastic safety glasses. As she walked toward the body on the conveyor belt, she said in a light-hearted manner, "I suppose your purse is a huge distraction to all of your adversaries. Help me undress your friend. You made a mess with the last one that you burned on your own."

Disregarding the purse comment, Arsen said, "I thought the furnace took care of the body, clothes, and all."

Shaking her head as she unwrapped the body, Leela sighed. "Just help. I don't have time for a full training class . . . Christ! This is a young one!"

"This is Carlos Delgado's sister. She was delivering drugs this morning. I don't have time to tell you the full story. Okay?"

As they removed Antonia's shoes, clothes, and jewelry, Arsen said absently, "Say, have you ever met Nils in person?"

"Who's Nils? Never heard of him. Are all of you *contractors* delusional?"

Rolling his eyes, Arsen ignored Lella's obvious facetiousness. "Okay, answer this. Nils, or what-ever-his-name is, said not to mess with you. His specific terminology was that you could kick my ass. Since this implies that you've had some training, why are you assigned to funeral home duty?"

"You're very astute. Let me put it this way. About a year ago I was called back from my post in Algeria because of what was termed 'the use of excessive force' against a certain government official. I was riding a desk until this job came along, so at least it's a step in the right direction. No more questions."

"Got it. I need to get back to my car. I parked it a block away from the bar where all this started."

Leela was a step ahead in the process. "Yeah, I know. You carjacked Delgado's sister at the Seventh Avenue Lounge. Right?"

"Jeez!"

After initiating the cremation process, the two new associates drove the panel truck to Seventh Avenue, parked on a side street, and walked leisurely to Arsen's Lexus. Leela continued to stonewall him regarding any questions about their mutual employer, and Arsen didn't offer additional details about his morning's activities.

After returning to the funeral home, Arsen had one last question. "How long do you anticipate being in this assignment?"

"Depends on how busy you keep me."

Extending his hand, he said, "I'm sure we'll meet again. Probably sooner than later."

With a firm grip, and a smile, Leela responded, "Just call. I'll be in the neighborhood."

Arsen was uncharacteristically confused and depressed on the drive to the hospital. He was accustomed to unexpected surprises, and twists and turns in his line of work, but not like this. He was beginning to doubt his moral compass, question his personal direction, and wonder about the constant rationalization of his belief-system.

Why am I suddenly thinking about these things? Yes, Antonia seemed like a nice enough young lady, but she was a fucking drug mule, a cartel member. All of this is because of Kasie. I'm getting soft! I should be back in Odessa growing tomatoes.

After checking at the front desk, Arsen finally arrived at Jamie's room and gently tapped on the closed door. Kasie greeted him with a hug and Jamie's parents waved from chairs near the bed. Jamie was sitting up with a tube in his arm connected to a hanging bag of clear substance.

Jamie managed a smile and said, "My friend. Did your shot to the ribs hurt as badly as mine?"

Arsen grinned and walked to the bed, placing his hand on Jamie's arm. "I was thinking that we could compare scars after you've had a chance to heal."

"Getting shot was my own fault. You told me a couple of times to be cool and to stay out of it, but I just lost it when I saw those guys in the store. I screwed up."

"Don't worry about it. The good news is that you're going to be okay."

Jamie's mother got out of her chair and put her arms around Arsen. "We thank you for getting involved. We appreciate your help."

Jamie frowned, and said. "Where are we on this whole thing?"

Arsen glanced at the closed door, and then back at Jamie. His voice was low, his tone serious as he spoke. "I've . . . I've met with a couple of the players in this game and received only limited information. There's a key person I need to confront before I have a complete answer for you. It will be soon. I promise."

Before the sentence was completed, an idea flickered like a neon sign in need of repair. It started as a sensation and then morphed into a coherent thought. Segments of reality and pieces of logic, mixed with pure determination, flashed through Arsen's brain. And then the solution came into view.

He repeated, "I promise."

Kasie wrapped her arm through his as they left the hospital room. The hall was empty, the disinfectant odor was persistent.

"What do you think about me fixing dinner for you this evening? I know that you're experiencing considerable stress because of my family's situation."

"Tell me what time. I'll be there."

"Why don't you come over around five? No, make it five-thirty and I'll prepare something special for you."

"See you at five-thirty."

Kasie was about to discover how important thirty minutes can be in one's life.

23

Juarez, Mexico
Friday, July 7th

Arturo lived in one of the two smaller houses in the compound. It was only 1200 square feet, but it was private. This was one of the benefits of being second-in-command to Carlos Delgado. He could drink and bring women to his house whenever he wanted. Unlike the men in the bunkhouse, he enjoyed complete privacy.

He looked at the cell phone on the table, next to a nearly empty bottle of beer, expecting it to ring on demand. He'd left several messages for Antonia to call him. He wanted to make sure she'd made it across the bridge without incident.

What if she was arrested for having three boxes of drugs in the van? What if there was a raid at the Pope bar? Why doesn't she return my call?

Several other disturbing thoughts were running through Arturo's mind. He knew he was fat. He knew his scarred face was a mess. He'd been teased and ridiculed all his life, but that had never bothered him. What did bother him were the comments Carlos had made during the meeting the previous day. Carlos had criticized him in front of the other men. Those comments hurt.

Why would Carlos talk to me that way? I've risked my life for him and his father over the years.

Arturo had been engaged in the war against the Juarez Cartel since 2009. He had no idea of how many men and women he'd killed and maimed in the ensuing years. Guns, knives, small explosives. They were just tools of the trade. He was a loyal soldier. Besides, after each killing, he crossed himself and said a short prayer asking for forgiveness. God understood that he was just doing his job. His conscious was clear. He was a major asset to the Sinaloa Cartel.

Finishing the beer, Arturo's thoughts returned to Antonia: *I offered to go with her, but noooo, Carlos thought she needed the experience. Fuck the experience . . . she's a young girl! She'll call. I know she'll call. She probably stayed over in El Paso to do some shopping. That's it. She's either shopping, or fucking some gringo in El Paso.*

24

El Paso, Texas
Friday, July 7th

It was 6:35 a.m. and Jack was sitting alone at the bar staring at the blue and yellow Modelo Especial sign that was casting a ghostly, colored haze throughout the dimly lit lounge. He'd made a pot of coffee, but even the caffeine didn't offer any assistance to his depressed state. It wasn't because of the stale beer odor seeping from the walls of the lounge, or the initials someone had carved into the bar, or even the recent problems he'd encountered with Robin. The comment made an hour ago by Antonia Delgado was the cause of his consternation.

Don't fuck it up! Why would Carlos say that? We're friends. She probably made it up. Bitch!

Random thoughts raced through Jack's mind. He wondered why anyone would hang out at a bar like this. What attracted people to bars? Loneliness? Weirdness? Horniness? He managed a tight smile as he congratulated himself for coming up with such a profound theory. And then the disconsolate feeling returned, along with mental images of Carlos attacking him with a knife. Or was it the knife that almost cut off Shelly's toe? Or was it due to the killing of the Jiffy Pharmacy owner followed by the shooting of the young man at the grocery store?

Jack was saved from his own terrifying thoughts when Robin, Lester, and Gus walked through the front door of the lounge.

"Hey, boss. Are you having a shot of bourbon for breakfast?" Lester smiled. He had a fresh strip of tape over the bridge of his broken nose.

Even Gus appeared to be in a good mood. "You're a real man. I never start drinking until at least eight o' clock."

Completely ignoring their attempts at levity, Jack looked at Robin and said, "Where are Melton and Patterson?"

No sooner had the words left his mouth, than the other two members of the crew arrived.

"Good morning, boys and girls." Melton tipped his new white Fedora hat.

"You look like a goddamned pimp with that stupid looking thing on your head!" Lester was on a roll.

Melton flexed his pectoral muscles and said, "Shut the fuck up or I'll break your pussy nose again."

Robin looked at Patterson, rolling her eyes.

The banter helped, but didn't completely lift the cloud from Jack's brain. "I'm glad to see that you guys are in such a positive place, even though I don't understand why."

Robin said coolly, "The business officially starts today. The boys are excited about the prospect of making some big bucks." Joining the rest of the crew in their attempt at cleverness, she added, "Plus, our first kidnapping of the season will take place this afternoon at five. Will that be fun or what!"

The slight smile on Robin's lips helped rectify Jack's gloomy state of mind. Standing, and leaning on the bar, he said, "Everyone pull up a chair or a bar stool. Since we don't open for a few hours, we'll have our meeting here." Waiting until the scraping of chairs ceased, he continued. "The first shipment of product arrived this morning at six." It was important for everyone to know that he was missing a little sleep for the good of the team. "As discussed, we'll deliver the goods to Big City Grocery first, Barbie's Cards and Gifts next, and then to our newest distributor, Muscle Madness. And speaking of Big City Grocery, the news hit the wire about the shooting that took place yesterday. Congratulations, we're out of the woods. The cops think it was a masked man, and a robbery gone bad."

Gus breathed a sigh of relief, as he uttered, "Good."

Patterson, who had been quiet since entering the bar, said, "Leave your gun at home from now on." He didn't appear to be joking.

Jack was quick to move the conversation forward. "Okay, team, let's get on with it. Robin, back the van to the side door and we can load the product. Lester . . . you, Patterson, and Gus get the boxes out of my office. The product has been broken down into three separate batches, so there's not much to do. Oh, Robin, have I missed anything?"

"Only that Shelly Jones will be back on the job today. She'll open at ten."

Jack was silent as he led the boys to his office.

The excitement continued during the trip to the grocery store. Robin was quiet, but the rest of the crew tried to outdo each other regarding the spending of their upcoming wealth.

Patterson had a definite plan. "I'm going to retire at forty-five and buy a plantation in Hawaii. Grass skirts, booze, and sunny beaches."

Lester announced his own ideas about spending money. "Yeah, well I'm going to by a villa on the French Riviera and have hot and cold running babes surrounding me."

"With your fucking nose, you may be able to attract a cold one, but the hot ones will be running away as fast as they can!" Melton was still on the nose theme.

The grocery store parking lot was empty and there were no cars parked on the street. Robin backed the van into the space closest to the front door.

Jack once again assumed his leadership position with some actual logic. "Gus, stay in the van and keep watch. It wouldn't be a good idea for you to be seen, since you shot the owners' son yesterday. Okay? Melton, you have the big muscles, so you can bring in the box. Let's go. We're making history here."

Mr. Rodriguez was alone in the store when the crew entered. With a slight frown, he pointed Melton to the back room. Robin followed, once again explaining to Mr. Rodriguez how the menu aligned with the contents of the box. Melton was instructed to place the box and its contents into another larger box labeled onions.

Robin frowned at the old man's surly attitude and said in a toneless voice, "Any further questions?"

Mr. Rodriguez shook his head.

"I'll call you every day to see how things are progressing. You know what happens if we have any problems from you."

"I'm sure things will be fine." Mr. Rodriguez sounded less than enthusiastic.

The deliveries to Barbie's and to Muscle Madness were smooth and fast. Jack was feeling much better about the entire operation, despite the earlier comment from Carlos's sister. He knew he could make it work. The crew could barely contain their excitement about the financial upside to the drug business. And to make it even more exciting, they were more or less a subsidiary of one of the largest drug cartels in the entire world.

After arriving back at the bar and exiting the van, Jack said to the crew, "Let's meet in my office and go over the plan one more time for this afternoon's endeavor. Carlos and I cooked it up perfectly."

Jack spotted Shelly's car the minute he stepped out of the van. *Oh, no!*

He avoided looking at Robin as they entered the bar, hoping the couch debacle would soon be forgotten. The cool, dim interior was a welcome change to the July heat and it took Jack's eyes several seconds to adjust. Shelly was standing behind the bar watching the crew arrive.

Lester was the first to speak. "Hey, Shelly, good to see you back." Leaning over the bar, he observed the walking boot she was wearing. "How in the heck did you cut your foot? Huh?"

"I stepped on a knife," she said, swallowing the last word.

Gus chimed in. "How do you step on a knife?"

With her head down, as if apologizing to her foot, she said, "It was an accident and I'm so sorry it happened."

Robin mumbled a few unintelligible words under her breath and headed for the office. The rest of the crew followed. The kidnapping plan Jack was about to describe again was simple, but at the same time elaborate.

Jack was at his best when the odds were heavily in his favor.

<hr>

Arsen dialed Leela's number while walking to his car in the hospital lot. This was the first time in four days that he felt he could have an impact on the outcome of the Rodriguez dilemma. In the far recesses of his mind, he was envisioning an additional benefit . . . the elimination of Carlos Delgado.

"Yes, Arsen."

Always seems to be a step ahead of me. "Do you still have the handbag?"

"Are you talking about the purse you were carrying this morning?" Leela asked.

She seems to enjoy yanking my chain. Skipping the profanities that initially came to mind, he spoke bluntly. "Yes or no?" Arsen considered this to be a very important question.

"Yes."

"Excellent. I was afraid you might have incinerated it along with . . . everything else."

"I'm holding it in my hands at this very moment."

"Is her cell phone still there?"

"Yes, sir."

Smart-ass. "Great. I'm on my way over. Okay if we meet in your office? The back room is starting to freak me out."

"I'll be waiting."

The drive to the funeral home took less than ten minutes. Arsen's mind was spinning, calculating, traveling a hundred miles an hour. He had the beginning of a plan . . . and Leela would be a key ingredient.

The office door was open, and Leela was sitting behind the desk, holding Antonia's cell phone. "I take it that pink is your favorite color."

Does she ever slow down? "We can talk about that later. I have a proposition for you. Want to hear it?"

"I'm all ears."

"Nils, the boss we share, knows generally about what I'm doing in El Paso. And I have the feeling that you know something about it as well."

Arsen proceeded to fill in the blanks, including how he and Jamie Rodriguez were introduced, as well as the specifics of Spencer's demise. Leela nodded several times as Arsen laid out the story and told her that Spencer was working with both the Sinaloa Cartel and the Juarez Cartel.

"Now, that brings us to crunch time. I have a feeling that you sort of miss being in the field. I mean *really* being in the field, not running some funeral parlor."

"Do I have to pay for this psychological evaluation?"

"No, but this *psychological evaluation* may be worth your while. With your help, I think I can get the answers I need for the Rodriguez family, stop this little drug distribution scheme by Jack Pope, and maybe, just maybe, have a big payday for both of us at Carlos Delgado's expense. It'll be risky, but . . . life's risky. What do you think?"

"If you won't mention it to our boss, I won't. Let's do it."

Arsen reached into his pocket and displayed Spencer's cell phone. "Okay, give me a pen and something to write on and I'll list the numbers and times of Spencer's recent calls. You do the same with the pink one and then we can compare numbers to see if any of them correspond. I'm looking for Carlos Delgado's number."

"Makes sense to me."

After fifteen minutes, Arsen said, "Have you found anything interesting?"

"Yes. The number she called most frequently has the six-five-six Juarez area code." Handing her list of calls to Arsen, she continued, "Any of Spencer's calls match this number?"

"Bingo. Spencer called the same number twelve times in the last two weeks. It has to be Carlos's number, or someone very close to him."

"What do we do now? Call and tell him that you whacked his kid sister?"

Arsen spoke in a somber, deliberate tone. "You're going to call him and explain how you took Spencer's place at the funeral home and that you want in on the action."

Leela was a quick study. "I'll tell him that my boss found out about Spencer's activities and sent me here to eliminate him. As a matter of fact, I'll call on Spencer's cell phone. They'll be surprised when they hear a greedy, conniving female asking to be part of their organization."

"I like the idea of you calling on Spencer's phone. You'll need to be prepared for any questions he might have about his sister, even though he has no reason to believe that you would know anything about her. For that matter, he has no reason to believe that you know anything about the Pope gang. Correct?"

"Correct on both counts. However, if he bites on my request to get on his payroll, the first thing he'll want to do is meet with me." Feigning anger, she rolled her eyes and made exaggerated hand movements. "Now I see why you need me! You need a little girl to do your work."

Shaking his head, Arsen said slowly, "You *are* a piece of work."

"When do you want me to call the number?"

"I'm tied up tonight, but I'll be back here in the morning around nine and you can make the call then. In the meantime, let's go over the details, okay?"

"You're the boss."

Arsen removed the battery from the pink cell phone, and the newly formed partnership discussed the specifics of the scheme: suggested meeting locations, response to various questions, and details about Spencer's plan to work for both the Sinaloa and the Juarez cartels.

Leela had two more questions. "It's only been a few hours since Carlos's sister went off the air. What's he thinking? What's his next move?"

Raising his eyebrows and shrugging, Arsen said, "Jack Pope will have some explaining to do."

25

El Paso, Texas
Friday, July 7th

Jack's plan was in motion. Carlos Delgado's number two man, Arturo, arrived at the Seventh Avenue Lounge at 4:30 p.m.

Meeting him at the door with an overly zealous handshake, Jack said, "Very nice to meet you, Arturo. Carlos speaks highly of you."

Arturo grunted and pointed at the bar where Robin and the rest of the crew were seated. "How about a beer. It's a long goddamned drive over here."

"Sure, sure. You can meet my gang." Rather than using the term "crew," Jack decided to use a term Arturo would understand.

Arturo ordered two beers and downed the first one within thirty seconds. Mixing words with a loud belch, he said, "Did Antonia deliver the stuff on time this morning?"

Jack nodded and forced a smile. "Oh yeah. Absolutely. She was on time and seemed very knowledgeable about her job. It was a pleasure working with her. I look forward to seeing her next Friday morning."

Arturo took a long drink from his second beer and murmured, "Good."

Jack gestured toward each member of the crew as he introduced them. Arturo showed more interest in his beer bottle than in his new acquaintances, never extending his hand.

Robin displayed a frown, and said to Arturo, "Do we need to go over the details of the plan?"

Finishing the beer, Arturo said, "I don't need any fucking details. I know what to do. Show me the way."

Jack led the group to the parking lot where they spent a few minutes gawking at the new $96,000 S-Class Mercedes sedan Arturo was driving. Jack got into the Mercedes with Arturo, while Robin and the rest of the crew piled into the van and led the way to Kasie's apartment.

"Arturo looks like a killer. Only killers wear red bandanas during the day." Lester was wide-eyed as he fidgeted in the passenger seat next to Robin.

Melton offered his observation. "I've never seen so many scars on one man's face. Shit, it makes your scar look like a pimple, Gus."

Even Patterson had a comment. "I'm not sure whether the scars outnumbered the tattoos, or the other way around. He's one scary looking son-of-a-bitch. On top of that, he has absolutely no respect for us."

"Yeah, but he drives a nice car," Robin said.

Lester summarized the kidnapping plan, adding a few questions. "Correct me if I'm wrong, but as I understand it, Arturo has a knockout drug he's going to administer to the girl, and then we're going to put her in his trunk. You know it's over a hundred degrees today. What if he screws up the shot? What if she suffocates in the trunk on the drive to Juarez? What if he stops along the way and rapes and kills her? I know Jack thinks the plan is foolproof, but a lot could go wrong."

Patterson shrugged and said, "I'm fairly sure these expensive cars have air-conditioning in their trunks. This Arturo guy probably kidnaps people every day. Quit worrying about the small stuff."

Robin exhaled and raised her voice. "I've said it before and I'll say it again. You're all a bunch of pussies. We're in the drug dealing business, for Christ's sake, so grow some balls. We need a reputation of being tough; our distributors need to know that we mean what we say."

Lester agreed. "Yeah, the tougher we are, the more our reputation will spread. You know, like Billy the Kid, or Clint Eastwood."

"Lester, sometimes I wonder about the shit crawling around in your brain. Clint Eastwood? Give me a break." Disgust showed on Patterson's face.

"All I'm saying is that I agree with Robin. The grocery store folks need a hint as to who's boss."

Gus, who had been quiet during the conversation, said, "I thought that I already gave them a reminder when I shot their son. I guess some people need more than one hint. Huh?"

There was silence for the remainder of the short trip.

Arriving at the apartment complex, Robin offered a reminder. "They're not going to physically harm her. It'll only be a warning shot across the bow, and it will keep the Rodriguez family in line. I'll call the old man tomorrow and let him know that we mean business. If they shape up, she'll be released in a couple of days."

Even though several vehicles were parked in the side lot, Robin found two open spaces. Arturo, who had been following, parked next to the van.

Arturo was a large man. Much of the weight was in his stomach, but his arms and neck gave him the appearance of being extremely strong. After checking his pocket for the syringe, he grunted, "What are we waiting for? Let's go."

The plan was for Jack to get into the van and stay out of sight. No need for the boss to be at risk. Arturo and the crew walked the short distance to the corner of the building. Patterson's job was to remain there and keep watch for potential trouble. Robin and the others casually walked to Kasie's patio. The four men stood to the side while Robin, after looking in both directions, knocked on the door. A few seconds later, Kasie opened the door, a surprised look on her face as she stared at the attractive woman wearing only one glove.

"Oh, hello, I was expecting someone else." She tilted her head and frowned in a questioning manner.

Before any realizations could reach a conclusion, Robin violently pushed the door open knocking Kasie backward. Robin quickly moved forward and slapped the side of Kasie's head with the metal-padded glove. Kasie fell against a side table, her long black hair swirling around her face, a ceramic statue of a horse smashed on the hardwood floor. As she fell to her knees, Robin grabbed a handful of hair and put a choke hold on the stunned victim. Arturo entered the open door with the syringe already in his hand. Gus and Lester held both of Kasie's arms while the shot was administered. Kasie's body went limp within seconds.

Robin leaned out the door and received Patterson's "all clear" sign. Gus and Lester placed each of Kasie's arms over their shoulders and maneuvered their way through the door and across the patio. Squealing children and the slap of the diving board masked the sound of Kasie's shoes dragging on the concrete. The entire operation had taken less than ten minutes from the time the crew and their accomplice had arrived at the apartment complex.

Arturo pressed the wireless trunk release on his key chain and the lid opened in slow motion. There was still no activity in the parking lot as they laid Kasie in the trunk of the Mercedes and applied duct tape to her hands and feet. A final strip was placed across her mouth before the trunk lid hummed to a close.

Arturo turned and faced the crew, spittle on his lips, combined with an unctuous grin. "We'll drop her off a block from the Juarez side of the Santa Fe Street Bridge day-after-tomorrow. Let her family worry until then. They'll know we're serious."

Arturo drove out of the parking lot at 5:20 p.m.

26

El Paso, Texas
Friday, July 7th

Arsen arrived at the side parking area near Kasie's apartment five minutes early. Not wanting to look overly eager, he decided to sit in the car for a few minutes. After ten seconds, he decided that he had waited long enough.

As he walked the short distance to Kasie's patio, Arsen could hear the familiar sounds in the swimming pool. Three boys were evidently cannon-balling the other swimmers from the diving board. The two-foot green hedge that surrounded the fenced pool prevented Arsen from seeing the sources of the squeals and cheers coming from the water.

Since the door to the apartment was partially open, Arsen knocked politely. He knocked again a few seconds later with the same result . . . nothing. An odd, unexplained feeling came over him as he glanced at his watch and saw that it was exactly 5:30.

"Hey, mister, you're too late. They got the drunk lady and left." The loud, shrieking voice laughed loudly as did the other two boys on the diving platform.

Arsen opened the door and called loudly, "Kasie. Are you here?" Entering the living room and seeing the broken statue on the floor, Arsen walked quickly to the bedroom, and then the bathroom. A bottle of unopened red wine was sitting on the kitchen counter, along with a box of pasta and several peeled garlic cloves.

Arsen instantly knew that something was seriously wrong. *Goddammit, this is my fault! I've been asleep at the switch.*

Trying to keep from panicking, Arsen jogged to the hedge nearest the diving board. "Son, did I hear you say that someone left with a drunk lady?"

The tallest of the three boys, replied, "Yeah, she looked drunk to me. I ain't old enough to drink, but I know one when I see one."

One of the boys jumped into the water, laughing as the splash hit several girls sitting on the edge of the pool.

131

"How many people were with the drunk lady?" Arsen's brow was damp, sweat was running down the middle of his back.

The youngest of the cannonballers, spoke up. "I saw 'em and I would say there were eleven or nine."

The tall youngster was more precise. "Darell, you're an idiot! There were three men and one lady with red hair. One of the guys was really fat and had a red scarfy thing on his head. They took her around the corner to the parking lot. I think there was another guy standing by the corner."

"How long ago did this happen?" Arsen was losing patience, he didn't want to waste any more time.

"Maybe ten minutes."

"Could you see what kind of vehicle they were in?"

"Nope. Not from here."

"Thanks for your help," Arsen said over his shoulder as he sprinted for the parking lot.

The tires on the car squealed as Arsen sped out of the parking lot and headed for the Seventh Avenue Lounge. The Friday evening traffic wasn't sympathetic to Arsen's sense of urgency. His customary ultra-calm bearing completely disappeared at the first red traffic light. The car in front of Arsen didn't move when the light turned green. It appeared the driver was looking at something he was holding in his hand. Arsen leaned on his horn and held it for several seconds until the car began to move. The rest of the short trip seemed like an eternity, a grueling exercise in restraint and self-control, road rage barely contained.

The number of vehicles in the lot indicated the Seventh Avenue Lounge was busy. After a hard week in the trenches, a cold beer or a strong drink provided the slow release of tensions that had built-up in the bar's clientele. Arsen parked beside the white van near the side of the building, got out of the car, and opened the trunk. He was wearing shorts, so the ankle holster was out of the question. He put the switch blade knife in his pocket and quickly walked to the door.

As Arsen's eyes adjusted to the cool darkness of the bar's interior, he spotted Jack and his gang sitting in their booth by the jukebox. The well-endowed bartender was talking to one of the customers at the crowded bar while another waitress, working the tables, happened to see Arsen as he entered.

Waving, with a big smile on her face, she approached Arsen and said cheerily, "Honey, all the chairs and booths are taken, but I can bring you a drink if you don't mind standing for a while."

"I'll wait for a seat, and then call you," Arsen said bluntly. He was in no mood for conversation and pleasantries.

Looking him up and down, she smiled as she said, "I'll be waiting for your call."

The music was loud. The customers were loud. And the group in the corner booth was extra loud as Arsen made his way to the jukebox and pretended to study the options. The only words he could pick up from the conversation were "bitch," "ugly motherfucker," and "payout." His primal instincts were to throw the jukebox across the room, charge the booth, and kill everyone sitting there. His better judgement told him to wait, just as he did three nights ago, and follow one of the gang to the restroom.

It's still light outside, so I'll have to conduct my interview in a tiny room.

"Hey, are you going to make a selection, or just stand there all night?" The irritated voice came from a middle-aged man wearing shorts and a tank top, his tattooed arms waving in the air.

Arsen turned slowly and stared directly at the man. No words were spoken, only the stare.

The man flinched as he turned to walk away. "Hell, I need some change before I can play this thing anyway."

One of the crew members rose from the booth and said something to the others that Arsen couldn't hear. Several comments were made by the others still seated.

"Oh, poor Pattie has to tinkle." The pale skinned female with the sun-kissed red hair was holding a beer bottle in her hand. "Be careful and don't pee-pee on your hand."

Jack Pope smiled at the raucous behavior of his crew. The occupants in the booth laughed and hollered more comments at Patterson as he walked toward the restroom.

Arsen immediately followed, brushing against chairs and tables as he hurried to catch up with the slender gang member. He arrived at the restroom at the same time Patterson put his hand on the door knob. An aggressive shove propelled Patterson through the door, hurling him against the urinal. Arsen had him by the throat with his left hand and slammed his head against the ceramic tile on the wall. Patterson was stunned, but the sickening sound of the switch blade opening made him gasp."

"Wha---" The partial word was all he could manage.

Arsen placed the tip of the knife about a quarter-inch into Patterson's right nostril. Without warning, without threat, Arsen pulled the sharp point viciously upward, splitting the nostril in half. Blood started flowing rapidly into Patterson's mouth and down the side of his chin. In unison with the scream, Arsen grabbed him by the hair, kicked open the stall door, and pushed his head into the toilet bowl. After a few seconds, he lifted Patterson to his feet and slammed his head against the wall again.

"What happened to the girl?" Arsen screamed. "Where is she?"

Blood was still pouring from the slice in Patterson's nose as he coughed and spit water. He was obviously terrified, and started talking in short, fast bursts. "A cartel guy named Arturo took her to Juarez. In his Mercedes. Ugly guy with scars on his face. Wearing a red bandana on his head. She's in the trunk. They'll let her go in a couple of days. Let me---"

The sentence was not completed. Arsen unleashed his right fist directly to the side of Patterson's jaw, knocking him to the floor next to the toilet. This was the only payout the slender man would receive tonight.

After washing the blood from his hands and the knife, Arsen opened the restroom door, expecting to see a line of anxious customers. Instead, he was met by the loud, harsh sounds of a typical Friday night at the Seventh Avenue Lounge . . . and Gus approaching the short hall leading to the restrooms.

Their eyes met briefly, their shoulders barely touched, and Arsen commented, "There's a pile of crap in the restroom. Someone needs to clean it up."

The violence temporarily dulled the panic Arsen had been experiencing, but not for long.

What now! A cartel guy named Arturo in a Mercedes with at least an hour head start. He's got Kasie. Got to get it together.

A hot evening breeze stirred dust from the asphalt surface in the crowded parking lot. Before opening his car door, Arsen glanced back at the bar and was surprised he wasn't being followed by the big guy with the scar and the rest of his gang. The bilious feeling in the pit of his stomach was getting stronger. Kasie was missing and his options were limited.

Only one option. Need to move fast.

The tires on the Lexus squealed as Arsen turned out of the parking lot onto Seventh Avenue. He dialed Leela's number, barely making it through a yellow traffic light.

"Yes."

"I have an emergency. Can we meet in your office in five minutes?"

"I'll be there."

Leela was sitting on the edge of the desk when Arsen arrived. She was wearing a wine-colored cocktail dress with a V-neck and spaghetti straps. The mid-thigh hem with a side slit flattered her long legs.

"I'm sorry if I interrupted your weekend plans, but something's come up." Arsen was visibly agitated.

"Not a problem. How can I help?"

Arsen briefed Leela on the events of the past hour, explaining his version of his relationship with Kasie.

In a soft and measured tone, Leela said, "Arsen, Arsen, Arsen. Do you realized the carnage you've caused since arriving in El Paso? You've wasted how many . . . four? Jeez, two in the past twelve hours."

"The guy tonight only has a broken jaw. And maybe a broken arm. If and when I want a sermon, I'll go to church."

"Yeah, I can see that happening really soon." Leela was back to her sarcastic self.

Arsen knew he was running short on time. "Are you sure you want to help, or would you rather sit this one out? I propose we move up the call to Delgado right now, instead of in the morning."

"I've already told you that I'm all in."

Arsen was confident that under Leela's smart-ass façade, she was tough as nails. Taking a deep breath, he said, "Okay, here are my assumptions. Carlos Delgado had no reason to believe that Spencer, your predecessor, had any knowledge about Jack Pope and his gang. Therefore, if you contact Carlos, and ask to get in on the same gravy train that Spencer was on, he won't associate you with Pope either. Correct me if I'm wrong."

"I think you're correct."

"I have no idea how close Delgado and his sister are. I guess I should say . . . were. Anyway, following my logic trail, I don't think he'll link you and his missing sister when you call him."

"Once again, I agree. However, she's been missing all day. I wonder if she was heading back to Juarez when she met you? Was she supposed to check-in after delivering the drugs to Pope, or what? But, as you say, I don't think there will be any connection between her disappearance and my phone call."

"Let's get on with it. Remember, try to set up the meeting either tonight or tomorrow morning. The sooner, the better."

Leela cocked her head and looked quizzingly at Arsen. "Now, how exactly is this supposed to help you get your girlfriend back?"

Nervously placing his hand on his chin, Arsen said, "I'm grasping for straws. Maybe he'll ask you about his sister, or try to connect the dots to his sister's disappearance and the Pope gang. Maybe he'll bring up the kidnapping." Arsen was feeling the pressure. "Fuck! I don't know what'll happen. One way or the other, I'm going over there tonight. I know where Delgado's compound is located."

Looking at a piece of paper on her desk, Leela entered the number into her phone that both Spencer and Delgado's sister had called most often. "Here's hoping."

There was an answer on the first ring. "Yeah."

"Is this Carlos Delgado?"

The line was silent for several seconds and finally Leela said, "My name is Leela. I was brought to El Paso to kill Spencer and take his place . . . which I did. But guess what? I also want to take his place as an informant working with the Sinaloa Cartel. I want to be paid the same as he was paid. Exactly the same."

"Where did you get this phone number?" The voice was detached, but suspicious.

"From Spencer's phone."

"Why should I believe you?"

"You should believe me because I love money more than I love my job. I place money above loyalty, motherhood, and apple pie. Oh, by the way, I'll bet you didn't know that Spencer was also working with the Juarez Cartel. If you treat me right, I'll only work for you."

"I'll need to meet you in person."

"When?"

"Tonight. Three hours."

"Where?" Leela asked.

"Hotel Azetca Aeropuerto. What do you look like? Describe yourself."

After giving a brief description of herself and how she would be dressed, she ended by saying, "The airport is too far. How about---" Leela stopped in mid-sentence when she heard the dial tone.

Looking at Arsen, she shrugged and said, "We're meeting at the Hotel Azetca Aeropuerto in three hours." Looking at her watch, she uttered, "About nine forty-five."

"Do you think that was Carlos Delgado you were talking to?"

"I have no fucking idea."

"It'll take forty-five minutes to get to the Juarez airport from here. And that's assuming there's no delay on the bridge." Arsen took a deep breath and continued. "There are photos of Delgado on the internet. Let's print one out and you can take it with you."

"What about you? Are you going with me?"

Arsen was focused, his words clear, concise. "Let's go in separate cars. Don't worry, I'll be there. We don't have much time. Find the picture, print it, and let's quickly discuss the meeting strategy."

"Will do. I have the distinct feeling that some asses are about to be kicked."

27

El Paso, Texas
Friday, July 7th

Jack Pope had never felt better in his entire life. Robin had smiled at him several times during the evening, the kidnapping had gone exactly to plan, his initial distribution sites were up and running, and the Seventh Avenue Lounge was conducting a booming business. In addition, his crew was showing him the respect he deserved.

Shelly Jones was limping from one end of the bar to the other taking care of customers and preparing drinks. Debbie, the temp, was serving the tables and booths. The jukebox was blaring a song that could barely be heard over the racket created by the Friday evening crowd.

Melton was on his third shot of bourbon since the festivities had begun, and two additional shot glasses were on the table in front of him. "Damn, Robin, you must have knocked the living do-wop out of the girl in the apartment. She was limp as a rag when Arturo gave her the needle."

Lester weighed in. "She's a good-looking young lady. I'm pretty sure I could do a lot better job of taking care of her needs than Arturo what's-his-name." He sat upright and looked around the table.

"Your mix of observation and braggadocio is overwhelming, Lester. Yeah, you're just a big hunk of man-meat." Robin appeared more relaxed than usual. She took one of the shot glasses sitting on the table, and in one swift movement gulped it down. "You know, that mustache and goatee you're trying to grow, along with the tape on your nose, makes you almost irresistible. Almost, being the key word."

Jack, as usual, was concentrating only on his own needs and desires, paying little attention to the conversation going on around him. His hand was under the table on Robin's thigh, and he was starting to get aroused as he moved it under her skirt. Robin leaned back slightly, took Jack's hand, and helped guide it slowly up her thigh. His kinky thoughts were fueled by his vodka-Ritalin cocktail: *I'm the boss and I can do any goddamn thing I please.*

The orgy-in-the-making was interrupted when Gus pushed his way to the table, a sound of alarm in his voice. "Someone beat the living shit out of Patterson. I called for an ambulance. Should be here any minute."

This was not the kind of news Jack wanted to hear. "Where? What happened!"

Gus was talking rapidly, out of breath. "I found him in the restroom stall. His face is a mess. There's so much blood it looked like a car hit him. I'm sure his jaw's broken, and when I tried to lift him he screamed like hell. His arm or shoulder may be busted, too."

"Who could have done it?" Jack was starting to panic as he slid out of the booth. "First Burk disappears and now this!"

"A guy came out of the restroom just before I went in. He said something about the place being dirty. Maybe he was talking about Patterson. It had to have been him."

Lester's face turned pale as he said, "Oh shit." And then he vomited on the table top.

Robin quickly slid out of the booth, trying to avoid the splatter. "What did he look like? Had you seen him before?"

"No, but I would recognize him if I saw him again. Big guy, nice looking, serious eyes."

Jack was trying his best to gain control of the situation. "Serious eyes! What the hell does that mean? Come on, follow me. Let's see if we can get anything out of Patterson before the ambulance arrives. Is he still in the restroom?"

The hall to the restrooms was packed with curious on-lookers. Jack, and what remained of the crew, managed to shove their way to the door.

An elderly man wearing overalls was kneeling over Patterson, holding a handful of bloody, wet paper towels. Looking up at Jack, he said, "Man, this guy's in bad shape. I'm sure he has a concussion and who knows what else."

Jack leaned over and said in a loud voice, "Patterson, can you hear me?"

Patterson opened his eyes, but there was no response.

Shelly had opened the back door at the end of the hall and was directing the paramedics.

Jack moved back into the hall and addressed Gus and Melton. "Take one of your cars and go with Patterson to the hospital. Try to find out who did this to him. Where's that pussy Lester? Tell him to go home and sleep it off."

Walking back into the bar area, Jack stopped and tried to make sense of recent events. First good news and then not-so-good news. The ups and downs of the drug business were coming from all directions. An irrational thought popped into his head: *Maybe some wild sex would clear my mind and make everything right again. Even if it's only for a short while, I've got to disassociate myself from reality. That's what Freud would do.*

He spotted Robin and motioned with a nod for her to follow him. He led her to the office, locked the door, and turned off the light. A soft glow floated through the one-way mirrored glass, silhouetting Robin's tall, slender body as in an 1840 Arthur Rackham pencil drawing.

Jack put his hands on her waist and directed her to the desk. His movements and speech were characterized by abrupt starts and stops. They were awkward and jerky, but practiced.

"You're . . . you're going to get the . . . the fucking of your life."

Standing behind her, he raised her silk skirt to the middle of her back and in a spasmodic move pulled down her G-string. She stepped out of her flimsy underwear as Jack was taking off his pants.

Pressing against her buttocks, he rapidly began moving his hips and pelvis for several seconds before saying, "I'm . . . something's wrong. What the . . ." The combination of vodka, Ritalin, and stress had taken its toll. His mind wanted only one thing, but his body refused to cooperate.

Robin raised her head and turned, barely able to see the outline of his face, and exhaled two short sentences. "What's the matter, dear? Is this your version of "deflate gate?" Her tone was flat, unsympathetic.

Jack's cell phone rang, sparing him the embarrassment of explaining his performance failure. He found his pants, removed the phone, and turned on the light. Robin was leaning back on the desk, totally nude, legs slightly spread. She had a taunting half-smile on her lips as she looked at Jack standing in the middle of the room wearing only a shirt.

"Yes." Few people had the number for this phone, and Jack was concerned when it buzzed. He pushed the speaker button for Robin's benefit.

There was no greeting, no pleasantries, only a hardened voice. "Where's my sister?"

It was Carlos Delgado.

Jack was caught completely off guard, stuttering and stammering a confused reply. "This morning . . . she . . . all the product in the boxes . . . what do you mean?"

"She didn't return to the compound. I'm in Mexico City and I've been trying to reach her. You're saying she delivered the drugs this morning as planned?"

"Yes, Carlos. She was right on time at six. She was only here for about twenty minutes and left in the white panel truck. You're in Mexico City now? When do you get back to Juarez?"

"Tomorrow afternoon. If she's on your side of the river, find her. Understand? I'll call you tomorrow."

"Yes. I'll get right on it." Jack heard the dial tone before he finished the sentence.

"What was that all about?" Robin was in the process of putting her clothes on.

Jack shook his head, unable to speak. He removed one of his spare Ritalin bottles from the desk and swallowed two pills without water. The emotional roller coaster he was on paused at the top of the track, and then began a steep downhill free-fall. The room was spinning, the muted noise from the bar was getting louder, and Jack's legs were unable to support the rest of his body.

He tumbled to the floor in a heap of soft, white flesh.

Robin shrugged. "Fuck the luck."

Jack had only been unconscious for a matter of seconds when he opened his eyes. He blinked a few times and experienced the unique sensation of returning from pure nothingness. It seemed as if time didn't exist. He felt refreshed, even though he was drenched in sweat.

Still confused, he managed to say, "What happened?"

Robin was standing over him with her hands on her hips. "Well dear, take your pick . . . dehydration, low blood pressure, alcohol poisoning, or drug overdose. Or, it could have been a result of neurological syncope. I'm not sure what the last one is, but I heard it onetime on *Grey's Anatomy* and never forgot it."

Uninterested in her medical diagnosis, Jack murmured, "Where are my clothes?"

"Here," Robin said as she tossed him his underwear and pants. "Let me help you to the couch."

Jack got dressed and sat on the couch. The party in the bar area was still going strong, the Friday night crowd showing no sign of slowing down.

Robin eased Jack's head down and lifted his legs onto the couch. "Lie here for a while. I'll go to the hospital and check on the boys. Okay?"

"I'll be okay. I'm feeling better. Don't worry."

The beginning of a smile was on Robin's lips as she walked through the bar, out the door, and to her car. She had put the three distributor's numbers in her cell phone. She called one of them.

"Bill Hayes at your service." The owner of Muscle Madness answered promptly.

"Mr. Hayes, this is Robin. Just checking to see if you need any more inventory?"

"As you are well aware, it was only this morning that I received the first shipment. Unfortunately, I've had no customers today."

"Well, something must be wrong. Maybe I could meet you at your gym and we could conduct additional training."

"I can be there in less than ten minutes."

"Me too. See you there."

In the ensuing hour, Robin used more than one *"Get Out of Jail Free Card."*

28

Juarez, Mexico
Friday, July 7th

The only light in the hotel suite was from a bedside lamp. Arturo was sitting on the couch in partial darkness. He had just taken a phone call from a female named Leela who he assumed to be a U.S. government agent. He was pondering what to do next: *She said she'd killed Spencer. That's why Carlos couldn't reach him yesterday. She said Spencer was also working with the Juarez Cartel. And she sounded serious about wanting to hook-up with the Sinaloa gravy train.*

Holding his phone with one hand, he rubbed his forehead with the other: *Agreed to meet this Leela bitch tonight. What if it's a goddammed trap? No possible way, but I can't afford to screw this up. Carlos won't be back until tomorrow afternoon. Need to call him.*

Carlos answered with his customary grunt and a short question. "What is it?"

"Boss, I have some information that'll blow your mind." For some reason, Arturo was speaking rapidly and having trouble organizing his thoughts. "A woman called and said she killed Spencer. I'm meeting her tonight."

"What the fuck are you talking about? What woman? Meeting her where? Did you kidnap the grocery store girl?" Carlos was a detailed oriented person, and he wanted details from Arturo.

"Yeah, yeah. The girl is tied up on the bed. I'm looking at her."

"Good. Save her for me. Understand?" Not waiting for an answer, he said, "What did you say about someone killing Spencer? Who are you meeting tonight?"

"A female just called me. She said she was sent to El Paso to kill Spencer. Then she said that she killed him and now she wants to take his place with us."

"Did she say who she worked for?"

Stammering, Arturo said, "I didn't ask her, but I'm guessing she works for the U.S. government, same as Spencer did."

"And you're meeting her tonight?"

"Yes. Here at the hotel. That's why I called you. If it's a trap, which I don't think it is, at least you won't be here."

"Well, *at least* you have half a brain. Okay, here's what we can do. Detain her at the hotel until I arrive tomorrow afternoon. It'll be easy enough to determine if she's on the level."

Arturo sounded confused. "You mean tie her up?"

Lowering his voice, Carlos said, "You can tie her up or nail her feet to the floor. I don't care how you do it, just have her there when I arrive."

"She'll be here. Maybe we can party with both of them."

Ignoring the *party* comment, Carlos continued firing questions in his search for details. "Did Antonia deliver the product to Jack Pope? Did you talk to her?"

Arturo placed his hand over his rapidly beating heart, his face was flushed. He seemed to be entering an altered state of consciousness and awareness. Maybe it was from dehydration brought on by his excessive use of alcohol. Maybe it was from lack of sleep. Whatever the cause, his next statement was a slight detour from the truth.

"Yes, boss. She delivered the product with no problems. Pope was pleased with her service. I called her and she's just fine. Just fine, boss."

"When did you call her?"'

"Uhh, this morning just before the delivery." Arturo was stammering. "Oh yeah, oh yeah, I saw Pope when we kidnapped the girl. He said there were no problems with the delivery."

Carlos was irritated as he said, "I've tried to call her twice this afternoon and she doesn't answer or return my calls. Have you tried to reach her in the past couple of hours?"

"I'll get on it. I'm positive she's okay."

"She goddamned better be okay. I'll be back around four tomorrow afternoon. Meet me at the airport." Carlos abruptly ended the call.

Arturo walked to the bed, cocked his head, and studied the lovely young lady lying on her back, a quarter-inch cotton rope binding her wrists to the slatted headboard, the last two buttons of her blouse missing. The ropes attached to each ankle were tied to opposite ends of the footboard. It appeared as if she were about to be interrogated on a fifteenth century medieval English rack. An eight-inch strip of duct tape was covering her mouth.

Arturo unbuckled his belt, unzipped his pants, and slowly removed his pants and underwear. This was as sexually excited as he had ever been in his entire life. Placing his palms on the edge of the bed, he leaned over and pressed his nose into Kasie's partly exposed midriff. His wet tongue moved toward the waist of her shorts and for several seconds explored her navel, filling it with saliva. Kasie's eyes were squeezed shut, tears silently sliding down both cheeks onto the bedspread. For no reason, or for maybe a good reason, Carlos's words flooded into Arturo's cloudy brain over and over: *Save her for me. Understand? Save her for me. Understand? Save her for me. Understand?*

Carlos was sitting in a chair in his Mexico City hotel room sipping from a glass of tequila. He was tired . . . and worried. Tired from the day-long meeting he had attended with the leaders of the Sinaloa Cartel, worried about his sister. He'd been given a direct order to step up the war against the Juarez Cartel. They appeared to be making inroads in the drug trafficking business in the Juarez-El Paso corridor. That was unacceptable.

He had just completed phone calls with Arturo and Jack Pope. Neither had brought peace of mind, only more questions. The first call was from Arturo, who was vague and scattered, as usual. Arturo said that he had talked to a woman who had killed Spencer, and now she wanted to take his place as an informant for the cartel.

Arturo will keep her at the hotel until I arrive tomorrow afternoon. I'll determine if she's telling the truth . . . or not.

The call to Jack Pope was more troubling. Pope had seemed nervous when he tried to explain how smoothly the drug delivery had gone with Antonia that morning. Carlos had left several messages on Antonia's phone and none had been returned.

Somethings not right. She always returns my calls. Fucking Pope! He always thought he was a woman's man. What if he did something to her? Cocksucker!

The three nude blondes on the bed were completely entangled. The sight reminded Carlos of a large pretzel. A king-sized pretzel on a king-sized bed. He was concerned about his sister and the Juarez Cartel, but the show unfolding before him had his complete attention for now. He leaned back, with his eyes on the blondes. The stress of the day contributed to his one-track mind: *I can take care of at least two of these blondes tonight, and then the grocery store girl and Spencer's replacement tomorrow afternoon. Four babes all within twenty-four hours. I'm invincible, nothing can stop me. Fucking invincible.*

29

El Paso, Texas
Friday, July 7th

Arsen opened the trunk of his car in the funeral home parking lot, quickly changed clothes, and strapped on both ankle holsters. He put the Glock 17 with the threaded barrel for the silencer in one of the holsters and the switch-blade knife in the other. He placed the silencer and an extra seventeen round-clip in his pockets.

A feeling of mild panic was new to him as he made his way to Stanton Street. The first sign he noticed warned against taking any weapons into Mexico. He wasn't concerned about the Glock or the knife. He knew that the odds of his car being searched were minimal, and even less that he would be frisked. The wait in the vehicle line took less time than expected, and within a few minutes he was no longer on U. S. soil.

After taking an immediate left on Avenida Ignacio Rafael, he weaved his way through moderately heavy traffic for fifteen minutes parallel to the Rio Grande and then merged onto Mexico 45. Only twenty minutes to go. He'd been up since 5:00 a.m. in order to confront the drug mule. The unfortunate ending to Antonia Delgado's life was troubling, but not as much as Kasie's kidnapping. Arsen was back to rationalizing his priorities and their outcomes.

His mind was racing: *No matter what, I'll call Kasie's parents tomorrow morning. Why are we meeting Delgado, or whoever it is, at a hotel near the Juarez airport? His compound is on the other side of Juarez, at least six or seven miles from this particular hotel. The guy I beat-up in the restroom bar said they would let Kasie go in a couple of days. What kind of shape will she be in? How many of Delgado's men will be at the hotel? I've got to find Kasie!*

After merging onto Mexico 45, a four-lane thoroughfare, the view changed dramatically, and so did the speed of the Lexus. The fading late evening sunlight allowed Arsen to see that the vista of the mountains in the distance was offset by a sea of low income, stucco houses and apartments. The barrio extended beyond sight on both sides of the highway.

Zoning was non-existent. Poverty-stricken neighborhoods contrasted with well-lighted business centers containing a combination of Mexican and American businesses: Oxxo, Wendy's, Pemex, Home Depot, Yazbek, Applebee's. It was all a blur to Arsen as he continued to run the same questions through his mind: *Why the airport? Was Leela speaking to Delgado? Did they take Kasie to the compound or somewhere else? I've got to find out where Kasie is being held from the guy we're meeting, whether or not it's Delgado. How many of these assholes will be at the hotel?*

It was 8:15 p.m. when the Hotel Azetca Aeropuerto came into view. At first glance, it looked as if the inventor of Lego's had been the architect of the hotel. The helter-skelter, nine story structure boasted multiple colors: sandstone brown, mustard yellow, off-red, and bright blue. The bottom half of the hotel was yellow, highlighted by a large portico covering the entrance. An outside fire escape on the side of the hotel was surrounded by a blue border extending to the top floor.

Arsen was surprised to see the parking area in front of the hotel filled to capacity with motorcycles, cars and pickup trucks. Slowly driving by the portico, he could see two hand-painted signs over the sliding glass doors... *Matrimonio de Alegria y Recepcion* and *Bikers Internacional*. People were streaming in from the parking lot and a crowd had gathered under the portico. The entrance appeared to be packed with a mix of well-dressed guests along with the stereotypical black leather garb of the bikers.

Arsen continued around the hotel and parked in one of the few available spaces. Another fire escape encased in a raised blue border was located at the back corner of the building. An emergency exit door next to the fire escape was painted a brilliant red.

Are they expecting a major fire, or what?

Arsen joined several families on the short journey to the front of the hotel. As he entered the packed lobby, he was certain that his black jeans and tee-shirt would fit in well with at least half of the milling masses. The better dressed segment of the crowd was drifting toward a meeting room located at the back of the lobby. A large sign directed the *Bikers Internacional* conventioneers down a hallway leading to the ballroom. A clock over the reception desk indicated Arsen was a little over an hour early for the meeting between Leela and the cartel member.

Arsen still had questions: *Where will this guy want to meet Leela? How many men will he have with him? Where will they be located? What if he wants to meet in a hotel room?*

A blue neon sign identified the lounge on the left side of the lobby. Based on the appearance and loudness of the occupants, Arsen assumed it was occupied by the biker contingent. He was not surprised that many of the revelers were women, all dressed similarly to the men.

Arsen managed his way toward the bar while continuing to observe the hotel interior. A wide set of stairs at the far end of the lobby led to a bank of elevators. Several people were sitting on the stairs and a young couple was leaning on the rail.

Good location for a lookout.

The neon theme continued inside the bar area with all brands of alcoholic beverages boasting their multi-colored blinking signs and logos, trying their best to pierce the dimness of the cavernous room. The noise could only be described as overwhelming. Everyone in the bar appeared to be either drunk or high, and they were all trying to talk or yell over the barely controlled mayhem. The colored walls, the flashing lights, and the booming fragments of music emboldened the out-of-control bikers.

A long, curving bar was complimented by numerous tables and booths. A private room at the back of the bar, with a couch, four upholstered arm chairs, and a long, rectangular coffee table, caught Arsen's attention. A serious looking fellow with an obvious lump under his jacket stood by the door. A sign taped to the wall indicated a private meeting was taking place, even though the room was currently empty.

This could be the meeting place. Maybe I should ask the guy if he belongs to the Sinaloa Cartel.

Two attendees of the biker convention, both wearing the Mongols emblem on their black leather jackets, spun their empty beer bottles on the bar top and walked over to one of the tables to continue their debauchery. Arsen sat at one of the vacated bar stools, the location giving him a good line-of-site to the private room. After finally getting the attention of one of the bartenders, he ordered a vodka on the rocks and began the wait.

Less than an hour until Leela arrives. I hope my eardrums don't completely blow-out before she gets here.

Arsen recognized most of the club names on the various jackets: Pagans, Outlaws, Mongols, Bandidos, Vagos, Warlocks, and the Hells Angels. All had been turned down for the Good Housekeeping Seal of Approval due to their drug smuggling, racketeering, and general violence. Other support clubs were represented with unrecognizable logos. Every section of the United States and Mexico was represented in this two-thousand square foot room.

This is a fucking chaotic situation and none of these assholes cares. I wish Nils would call and give me ten dollars a head to kill every goddamn one of them.

It was difficult for Arsen to sit still. Kasie was missing and he was in the middle of unfriendly territory. He couldn't decide who it was he disliked most . . . the cartel or the bikers. Arsen was familiar with this type of scene and had been involved in numerous interactions with these kinds of gang members. He was disciplined to a fault, they weren't. He had a military background, they probably didn't. He knew he over generalized their behavior, but couldn't help it.

I know I'm not perfect, but I still don't like these ignorant, low-rent pigs. If they spent as much money on dental work as they do on tattoos, maybe I would change my opinion. Probably not.

The next thirty minutes dragged by like a really bad movie. Arsen tried to concentrate on a plan of action, but he was constantly interrupted and annoyed by conversions taking place around him. He felt as if he had picked up enough information to build a Harley for himself...drive trains, air intake, transmissions, fuel systems, and staggered exhaust pipes. Nevertheless, a plan was formulating.

Leela and I discussed a general strategy, realizing we would have to play some of it by ear, but without a lot of luck, this could be the last plan I ever execute.

A scuffle broke out at one of the booths. Two women were throwing punches and pulling hair while a crowd gathered around them. Arsen put a napkin over his drink glass and quickly walked to the entrance of the lounge. He was not interested in the fight, but he was interested in taking another look at the elevator bank at the top of the short staircase. Logic told him that one or more lookouts would be positioned there if Carlos Delgado was anywhere in the hotel.

No one there. Even the stairs had been vacated.

Arsen returned to his seat at the bar. The fight had ended and the two women were standing next to the booth hugging. Despite the way he was dressed, he knew he looked out-of-place. No leather jacket, no chains hanging from his pockets, and no long dirty hair.

The Bandido sitting next to him leaned over and literally screamed, "Who the fuck you with?"

Arsen had more important things on his mind than fighting with a drunk biker. He smiled and said loud enough to be heard, "I'm the bouncer, so you'd better behave."

The biker sat back on the bar stool and thought about what Arsen had said for several seconds before he started laughing. "That's a good one! Really a good one!"

Fifteen minutes until Leela arrives. This waiting is driving me nuts.

Two hell raisers sitting on the other side of Arsen started arguing about the relative merits of the Harley versus the Suzuki. As they stood, arms waving, the view of the determined looking fellow with the lump under his jacket was temporarily blocked.

Arsen waved at the bartender, gave him a twenty-dollar bill, and moved to get a better view of the private room. The sentry was talking on a cell phone and at the same time seemed to be surveilling the bar area. Arsen glanced back over his shoulder just as one of the elevators doors at the top of the short stair case opened. Two men exited and took their time looking at the crowded hotel lobby. One of the men was slender and bald, the other was heavy set and was wearing a red bandana.

The words of the young boy on the diving board at Kasie's apartment complex immediately came to Arsen: *One of the guys was really fat and had a red scarfy thingy on his head.*

The overweight character descended the stairs and slowly headed in the direction of the private room, his partner remained near the elevators, taking in the scene. Suddenly, the bald one hurried down the stairs and pushed his way through the crowd toward the front entrance of the hotel. As Arsen expected, Leela had just entered the door. She had changed clothes and was now wearing a dark pantsuit and a white short-sleeved blouse. Her shiny dark hair and caramel complexion caused her to stand out from the masses gathered in the lobby.

The slender, bald gang member intercepted Leela near the door, talked to her for a few seconds, and then guided her by the arm to the private meeting room. The shades had been drawn and the door closed as soon as she and her escort entered. Arsen assumed that one of the cartel members was enjoying his task of frisking Leela.

Without being obvious, Arsen positioned himself as close to the door as possible. He turned facing the wall, removed the Glock 17 from the ankle holster, lifted the silencer from his pocket, and quickly assembled it before sliding it into the waist of his jeans, his shirt covering the weapon.

After fifteen minutes, the door opened and Leela and the three men emerged, walking in the direction of the elevators. Leela didn't appear to be in any stress, so Arsen followed at a safe distance. The noise had not subsided, although it appeared some of the crowd had moved to the reception room or to the main ballroom.

Arsen casually walked up the staircase as the elevator door opened and the foursome entered. Just as the door started to close, he rushed forward and stuck his hand between the metal jaws.

Managing a smile, Arsen walked into the crowded space and inquired, "Hey, mind if I ride up with you?"

Taken aback, the lookout wearing the jacket said, "Get the fuck out. Now!"

Leela responded by pressing the lighted button that had been previously selected. As the door started to close again, she placed her left foot forward and then exploded off her back foot, her right knee hitting the fat guy in the groin. As his head involuntarily came forward, she violently swung the point of her elbow into his temple. The entire elevator cage shook when he bounced on the floor, the red bandana lying beside the limp body.

Arsen had already removed the Glock from his pocket, and with only the hissing sound a silencer makes, shot both of the bodyguards in the forehead; the back of their heads exploding on the shiny surface of the elevator car. In another lightning fast motion, he slammed the butt of the gun against the side of the fat man's head. Leela placed her foot on his stomach as if posing with a big game trophy.

Leela was first to speak as she removed the guns from the two bodyguards, and then leaned down to wipe splattered blood from her arm using the red bandana. "Haven't seen you in a while. How ya doin'?"

Arsen was in no mood for lighthearted banter. "What happened in the meeting?" Looking at the elevator panel, he added, "What's on the ninth floor?"

"Slow down, cowboy. Actually, I'm glad you were on your toes. Arturo, who's resting here at my feet, wanted to continue our interview in his room. Not sure how that would have gone. According to him, he's Carlos Delgado's number one man. He calls himself an *operations manager*." Taking a closer look at his face, she added, "Nice complexion, huh?"

Arsen had retrieved the hotel room key from Arturo's pants pocket by the time the elevator doors opened. The short hallway led to what appeared to be two top floor suites . . . 900 and 901.

Looking down the hall, Arsen said, "Hold the doors open for a few seconds until I get back."

He returned with a cylindrical trash receptacle and placed it between the elevator doors. "This will keep the doors open while we get the bodies in the room. The key is to room 901."

"What about the blood and gore on the walls and floor?"

"I'll bring a bedspread and some wet towels. We can place the bodies in the bedspread and drag them to the room one at a time. We can use the towels to clean up the elevator so as not to alert the staff."

They moved the three bodies into the room and placed the two dead men in a closet. The fat man, sans bandana, was starting to moan. Arsen started to pull a light cord from a lamp to use as a restraint, when he noticed two rolls of duct tape on the living area couch.

"Something tells me this tape was meant for you. What do you think?"

"Gosh, I wish you hadn't showed up so soon."

Shaking his head, Arsen took off Arturo's shoes and tightly wrapped the duct tape around his ankles and lower legs.

"Help me lift him so I can tape his hands behind his back." Arsen seemed to be practiced at this type of activity.

"I'm for shooting him right here and now." Leela was enjoying herself.

"Get his feet and let's get him on the bed. I think he'll be wanting to talk with us."

Arturo was fully conscious and was starting to struggle, even though he had nowhere to go. Arsen propped the fat man against the slatted headboard and placed several pillows behind his back. He finished the preparations by wrapping several layers of duct tape across the man's forehead and attaching the tape to the headboard slats, his head held firmly in place.

Satisfied with the tape job, Arsen pointed to an ice bucket in the living room and said, "Open those two bottles of Champaign and save the corks. I need to get something out of my car. I'll be right back. Okay?"

"Whatever you say, boss."

Arsen returned within ten minutes and stood over Arturo, who was lying wide-eyed on the bed. He removed the hand-held dental drill from his pocket and checked the lithium-ion battery by turning the switch to the ON position. A low whine emanated from the five-ounce, high torque, Micromax drill.

Turning the drill off, Arsen laid it on the bed and said in a tone that a dentist would use when talking to an assistant, "Give me the two corks, please."

Handing the corks to Arsen, Leela said, "I think I see where this is going."

30

Juarez, Mexico
Friday, July 7th

Arsen was in a hurry. His initial instinct was to use his knife to hurry along Arturo's questioning. Instead, he tried to remain as calm as possible and to proceed with his plan.

After taking the Champaign corks from Leela, he pinched Arturo's nose closed. Arturo's mouth opened instinctively and Arsen placed one of the corks between his back teeth and then placed the other cork upright in the center of his mouth.

"Sir, I hope you're comfortable." Leela was unrelenting.

Arsen pushed the ON button and the unnerving, low whine of the drill pierced the otherwise quiet of the bedroom. Without any preamble, without any questions, he placed the 1.6 mm drill bit against one of Arturo's lateral incisors and gently pressed.

Arturo's eyes widened due to the high-torque squeal of metal against tooth.

Observing the procedure, Leela murmured, "This brings back memories of my first dental visit as a child: the crying, the screaming, the pain. Unfortunately, my friend, there'll be no ice cream or candy after this experience."

Arsen removed the drill bit from the tooth, and calmly said, "What's your name?"

"Arturo, asshole." His voice became high-pitched as he tried to maintain his manly persona.

Leela couldn't resist. "Arturo Asshole. That's an odd name."

Arsen was only interested in one thing. "Where's the girl?"

Arturo winced, but didn't answer.

Leela shook her head.

Arsen forcefully pressed the bit against the tooth and Arturo shrieked, his face turning red, his body uncontrollably convulsing against the duct tape, an animal sound coming from deep within his throat.

Arsen again removed the drill bit and held it in front of Arturo's face.

Arturo was sweating profusely, a clear mucus running from his nose to his upper lip, but he still refused to talk.

Arsen shrugged and placed the bit in the small indention that had been created in the tooth . . . and pushed. The drill bit penetrated the enamel, the dentin, and then the inner nerve pulp.

Arturo's body convulsed wildly before he passed out. Within twenty seconds he opened his eyes, only to see Arsen holding the spinning, whining drill bit.

Seeing that Arturo's attitude had changed about talking, Arsen turned off the drill and removed both corks from his mouth.

Arturo was whimpering, almost crying. "She's in the next suite, goddammit! The next suite."

Leela began looking for a connecting door, but stopped when Arturo volunteered in a breathy moan, "The other room is down the hall, the key's over there in the dresser drawer." The air generated in his mouth when he talked further aggravated the damaged tooth.

While Leela retrieved the key, Arsen removed a cell phone from Arturo's pocket and headed for the door. Hesitating for a moment, he went back to the bed and pressed another strip of duct tape across Arturo's mouth.

"She'd better be there and she'd better be okay."

Arsen's heart was beating rapidly, but he kept his senses about him as he said to Leela, "Follow me and be careful."

"Got it."

After walking the short distance to suite 900, they stopped at the door, Arsen holding his Glock and Leela gripping one of the body guard's revolvers.

Arsen inserted the key, and quietly pushed through the door, going to one knee. No one was present in the large living room. Leela pointed her weapon at one of the bedroom doors and cautiously moved in that direction. Arsen did the same on the opposite side of the room. Opening the door, he saw Kasie lying bound, hand and foot, on the large king size bed, her eyes full of fear and surprise.

Gently removing the duct tape covering her mouth, his voice cracked as he said, "Kasie, are you okay?"

She sobbed, unable to speak.

Using the knife from his ankle holster, he cut the rope from her hands and feet. He threw his arms around her and they embraced. It was the first time in five hours that Arsen had totally relaxed.

Breathing a sigh of relief, Arsen whispered, "It's okay now."

Kasie was crying. Tears running down her cheeks. She tried to talk but couldn't. Rubbing her wrists, she finally said, "Arsen, I can't believe you found me."

Leela stood near the bed, arms crossed. "Well, if this isn't the couple of the month."

"Kasie, this is Leela. I'll explain later, but she's our best friend. Absolutely our best friend."

"Aww, that's so sweet." Leela was trying to bring a touch of levity to a tense situation.

Arsen had unfinished business. "I'll let you two get acquainted while I take care of some unfinished business in the next suite." Looking at Leela, he said, "We need information on two things. The first has to do with the long-term revenge threat directed at Kasie's parents. The other has to do with Carlos Delgado. If the guy in the other room invited you here to be an informant, surely Carlos would want to meet with you also. Right?

"Well, your dental work did wonders for the man's memory. Why don't you ask him some more questions?"

Arsen was wearing a scowl as he walked down the hall. He knew he was close to being completely out of control . . . and he didn't care. Even though he was relieved to have found Kasie, his hatred for the cartel was at an all-time high.

Arturo was struggling against his restraints on the king-sized bed. He resembled a beached whale trying to get back into the water. Arsen jerked the tape from the big man's mouth and watched as blood poured down his chin.

"Where's Carlos Delgado?" He didn't waste words.

"Mexico City." It was apparent he didn't want more dental work.

"When does he return?"

"Tomorrow afternoon at four."

Picking up the dental drill from the bed, Arsen's voice hardened as he spoke. "Think before you try to bullshit me on this next question, otherwise I'll drill your tooth by going through your upper lip. Where's he going after he lands?"

Arturo didn't need to think. "He's coming here to the hotel to have a little party with the girl in the other suite. I'm supposed to pick him up. Six or seven of his bodyguards will be meeting me at the airport when Carlos arrives in his private jet."

Clenching his teeth and scowling, Arsen continued. "Has he got Jack Pope's back? Are Jack's enemies his enemies?"

Trying to force a laugh, in spite of the pain, he said, "Carlos thinks Jack Pope is a pompous dumbass, but he has some kind of debt to repay to the man. That means Carlos is honor bound. He hasn't given me any instructions about Pope. Just the kidnapping."

Crossing his arms, with the drill still in his right hand, Arsen asked a straightforward question, not necessarily expecting a straight answer. "Does Carlos ever go anyplace alone, or with a minimum of protection?"

Arsen was sure that this was a defining moment for Arturo. The tears sliding down his cheeks made it apparent that he was in pain and that his mind was foggy. "Think about it, asshole, if anything happens to Carlos, since you're number two, maybe you'll get his job."

"I'll tell you what you want to know if you'll let me live. Okay?"

Arsen unfolded his arms and once again pushed the drill's ON button. "Talk."

Spitting more blood from his mouth, Arturo uttered, "Carlos meets a married woman every Sunday and Wednesday at the Hotel del Rio on Avenida Juarez about two blocks from the Santa Fe Street Bridge."

"What time?"

"Always at two in the afternoon. I'm usually the only one with him."

Shaking his head in disgust, Arsen dropped the drill on the bed and walked into the bathroom.

Returning with a hand-towel in one hand and the Glock in the other, he placed the towel over Arturo's head. His body started to bounce on the bed, even though his head was held fast by the duct tape.

"Careful there, big boy. You could break your neck."

Arsen placed the tip of the barrel to Arturo's forehead. "The young lady in the next suite was the wrong person to invite to your party."

He pulled the trigger twice in succession as the silencer whispered its deadly promise.

Returning to suite 900, Arsen quietly knocked on the door and was met by Leela.

"Kasie's in the bathroom. She'll be ready to leave in a few minutes."

"How's she doing?"

"She wasn't assaulted, and she says that she's okay physically, but as you saw, she's pretty shaken. How's our dental patient?"

"He just had his last appointment."

"Where's Carlos Delgado? I'm surprised he wasn't here to meet me."

"Carlos was going to meet you tomorrow afternoon. He's in Mexico City, and Arturo was supposed to pick him up at the airport tomorrow at four . . . along with six or seven bodyguards. I believe Carlos was expecting to have some kind of party. Evidently, you and Kasie were going to be the guests of honor."

"Are you and I going to be waiting here and have a little surprise party for Carlos?"

"Nope." Shaking his head, Arsen repeated, "Six or seven bodyguards."

Comprehending the brief explanation, Leela said, "I think I understand your logic. You don't want to confront Carlos and his men here at the hotel. Right?"

"Yep. This isn't some James Bond movie. I don't like the odds of you and I going up against an experienced team of Sinaloa killers. I can wait another day and a half."

"Day and a half?"

"I'll explain later. We're going to attend a rendezvous Carlos is having with his girlfriend at another hotel on Sunday."

———————•———————

As the elevator descended to the lobby, Kasie was still shaken, her head against Arsen's shoulder.

Leela was still curious. "Did our dental patient divulge any other interesting facts?"

"Well, Carlos is not exactly a huge fan of Jack Pope. Arturo's exact words were: *Carlos thinks Jack Pope is a pompous dumbass.* I got his cell phone and I left a *Do Not Disturb* sign on the door. He's probably not going anywhere, but no need for the maids to bother him," he said, leaving out the gory details because Kasie was present.

"Interesting."

"By the way, we have one more problem to solve. Kasie doesn't have her purse with her, and therefore no driver license, and obviously no passport. We may have trouble getting her across the bridge."

Leela was quick to respond. "Give me a second."

The elevator reached the lobby level and the doors opened as Leela made a phone call. The lobby was still crowded, mostly with bikers, the noise from the bar still blaring.

Leela put her phone in her pocket and said, "Okay, here's the news. You and Kasie take your car and catch up with each other on the events of the day. I'll take my car and you can follow me to the Santa Fe Street Bridge. If for some reason we get separated, just remember to go through lane eight. They're numbered. Lane eight. Okay?"

Arsen nodded in understanding. *Nils is a magician.* "Got it. One more thing. Would you mind if Kasie spent the night with you? No need for her to be alone tonight."

"Sure. Let's meet on the street just past the bridge and Kasie can get in my car." Addressing Kasie, she said, "We can have our own little slumber party. I'll take you back to your apartment in the morning."

Kasie nodded.

The forty-minute drive to the Santa Fe Street Bridge consisted of questions and answers regarding the abduction, mixed with periods of awkward silence. Kasie was still traumatized and trying to remember exactly what had happened. She explained how the tall woman with the red hair hit her with a glove, and then all of a sudden, several men were holding her in her apartment. She didn't remember the trip to the hotel until five minutes or so before the trunk lid opened, and then there were memory flashes of being drug up a fire escape and placed on a bed.

Kasie leaned back, arms tightly wrapped, and whispered, "I need to sleep."

"I think it would be best if you stayed awake for now. Try to keep your eyes open." Arsen had witnessed individuals with shock and combat fatigue and he knew the signs. He wanted to stop the car and hold her in his arms, but his first priority was to get across the bridge.

East bound traffic was backed up in all ten lanes. It appeared that only two guards were at lane eight checking the cars and trucks attempting to cross. One guard questioned the drivers, while the other used a mirror attached to a pole in order to check underneath the vehicles. After a fifteen-minute wait, Arsen stopped under the portico by the guard shack and lowered his window.

The guard made a simple request. "Passports, please."

Arsen took note of the plural use of the word *passports*, but only handed the man his.

Thumbing through the document, the guard said, "Man, you've done some travelling the past couple of years!"

"I try to stay busy."

Leaning down and looking at Kasie, the guard nodded and said, "Stay safe and have a good evening."

Leela was parked one block past the bridge. Arsen stopped behind her car and got out of the Lexus. The late-night, warm breeze felt soothing compared to the constant air conditioning he had experienced during the drive from the hotel. Kasie opened her door before Arsen could walk around the car.

"I'm feeling better. Thanks for making me stay awake."

Arsen took Kasie's hand and walked with her to Leela's car. Leela was standing on the sidewalk, arms crossed.

"Have any issues at the bridge?"

"None."

"As I mentioned, I'll take Kasie to her apartment in the morning around eight."

Arsen put his arm around Kasie's shoulders and said, "I hope to have this situation wrapped up by tomorrow or the next day. I hate to ask you to withhold information from your parents, but if it's okay with you, I would suggest that you not tell them about your awful experience until this whole thing is over."

Placing her head on Arsen's chest, she began sobbing. "I won't tell them for now. It would only upset them more. I'll go to the hospital in the morning and check on Jamie. He'll probably be released tomorrow."

Leaning down and brushing his lips against her forehead, Arsen whispered, "It'll all be over soon."

"I'll be fine."

"What's our next move?" Leela was all business.

Arsen had already started to formulate another plan. "What do you think about meeting in your office at nine in the morning?"

Putting her hand on her chin, Leela hesitated, and said, "Great idea. I'll clear my social schedule and try to be on time."

31

El Paso, Texas
Saturday, July 8th

Jack's plate was on the verge of overflowing with the syrup he had poured on his pancakes. The early morning ambiance at Denny's wasn't helping his pounding headache.

"Uhh, Jack, I'm glad you had the foresight to order some pancakes with your syrup." Robin sounded grumpy. "I didn't want to get so up early and I didn't want to eat breakfast."

"I don't know what happened to me last night. It was probably food poisoning or some such thing. I was so weak that I had to sit down in the middle of the floor."

Robin took a sip of coffee and said with a sigh, "Jack, you fucking passed out. You didn't sit down in the floor, you crumbled like a cookie."

"Things have been stressful the past couple of days. Maybe I'm just over-worked . . . and under loved."

"As I recall, your love thing wasn't working last night. You do remember *that*, don't you?"

Ignoring the comment and the question, Jack said, "Where did you go after getting me on the couch?"

"Hospital," she lied.

"Oh crap! I totally forgot about Patterson. Is he okay?"

"Don't know. They wouldn't let me see him."

"It's all coming back. Gus and Melton went to the hospital with him. Call one of them."

"It's too early. Besides, they would've called if there were any news," Robin said as she gazed out the window, the sunlight fractured by the low clouds in the east. "Let me further refresh your memory. Surely you haven't forgotten about the kidnapping we pulled off yesterday, have you?"

Jack responded by frowning and pressing his lips together. For some reason, kidnappings didn't seem as glamorous in the early morning as they did late at night. "Are you going to tell her parents what happened. You know, a warning call?"

"I'll call them tomorrow. Isn't that when they're going to bring her back? You and Carlos came up with the idea."

"Carlos!" The name triggered a response from Jack's foggy memory bank. All the events of yesterday came back in a flood to Jack's already tired, muddled brain.

"Carlos called about his sister. She didn't make it back to Juarez. I'm supposed to find her. She's not my responsibility! She's his sister, not mine!"

Jack's voice started rising with every word he spoke. There were few customers at Denny's this early in the morning; two men sitting at the counter, and a young couple seated at another booth.

Unenthusiastically, Robin said, "Have you taken your morning dose of Ritalin yet? After all the syrup you've ingested, I may be pulling you off the ceiling before long."

"Whatever." Jack was not in the mood for suggestions related to his health. "What time are we meeting with the crew this morning?"

Slowly shaking her head, Robin responded without taking her eyes from the parking lot. "This is Saturday. Our meetings on Saturdays are scheduled for one in the afternoon. Correct?"

Despite a mouth full of pancakes, Jack managed to say, "Doesn't seem like Saturday." After swallowing, and running his tongue over his lips, he said, "Oh yeah, you can get us a report from our three distributors today. You know, match up their day-one sales to their inventories. See if they need us to deliver any more product. What do you think?"

Robin carefully placed her coffee mug on the table before answering. "Jack, it's only been one day since these distributors got their first product." Lying, she said, "Oh yeah, I forgot to mention that the owner of Muscle Madness called last night. He indicated that not a single person visited him yesterday looking for . . . *product*. So, don't let your expectations run wild."

Jack's headache was beginning to subside and he knew it was time to resume his leadership role. "Look, Carlos assured me that his people would contact all the appropriate individual buyers they have in their files. I've given him the addresses and phone numbers of all three distributors. Remember, he said it would be like a *rave*, a chain letter. All their friends, and all of their friends', friends. You know, anyone who wants to add a little spice to their boring life."

Robin leaned back in the booth and said firmly, "Let's give them a full weekend before we begin following up. It'll take a few days before the chain letter, or *rave*, or whatever you call it takes effect. Okay? Besides, what are you going to do about Delgado's sister?"

Jack pushed away his half-eaten plate of pancakes, placed his elbows on the table, and pressed his index fingers to his temples. Speaking louder than necessary, he said, "First, Burk disappears. Next, Patterson gets beaten up. And worst of all, Delgado's sister doesn't make it home. Tell me, what's going on? What's the solution to these problems? Huh?"

"The only solution I can think of is finding out if Patterson recognized the person who busted his head, and then maybe we'll have a starting point. If we can find out the *who*, maybe we can discover the *why*. I think it's the only way to unravel this mystery. As for Delgado's sister . . . screw her. She's not our problem."

"Let's go to the hospital and see if Patterson can talk. What do you think?"

"It's only six in the fucking morning!" Robin was definitely not an early morning person. "Visiting hours probably don't start until seven or so. Another thing. Gus shot a young man at the grocery store. Remember? It was the owners' son and he may still be in the hospital. Since they know both of us, it could turn messy if we happened to cross paths."

Jack's headache was making a comeback. "Damn. Why is everything so difficult? Okay, okay. You call Lester and get him to visit Patterson. With his new mustache and goatee, no one will recognize him. Tell him to pump Patterson for information about what happened. We need answers."

Jack left cash on the table and started for the door, Robin trailing behind. One of the men at the counter stood and blocked Jack from proceeding down the aisle.

"You're a loud mouth son-of-a-bitch. I think maybe you should pay for my steak and eggs."

The greasy overalls and the scowl on the man's face took Jack by surprise. Jack's first impulse was to reach for his wallet and pay for another breakfast.

Robin saved Jack ten dollars by stepping forward and throwing a vicious straight-right fist directly into the man's throat. He staggered backwards, eyes wide, both hands on his neck. Robin took two more steps forward and was about to hit him at the base of his nose with the heel of her hand when she saw the frothy blood starting to flow from his mouth.

"Come on, Jack, let's get out of here." Flexing her fingers, she said, "Jeez, that probably hurt my hand more than it hurt his larynx."

Jack, with a surprised look, said, "I don't think so."

They hurried to the parking lot and got into the van. Robin called Lester and gave him instructions to visit Patterson.

Jack was still in panic mode. "Let's get out of here. No telling what damage you did to that guy's throat."

"Fuck him."

Jack reacted with a start when his cell phone rang. "What now?"

His face turned pale when he saw Carlos's name on the screen. "Yes, Carlos, how can I help?" Trying to sound unaffected, Jack quickly added, "We just finished eating pancakes. Wish you were here."

"Where . . . is . . . my . . . sister?" Carlos slowly emphasized each word. "I've been calling her since yesterday morning and she doesn't answer. I told you to find her."

"Carlos, please. It was only last night that you called. I haven't had time to find out where she is. I'm sure she's okay. Just a young girl doing young girl things. Don't you think?"

Carlos hung up. The line was dead.

"I'm fucked! I'm fucked!"

———————

After Robin's call, Lester drove to El Paso General Hospital. The sign next to the entrance indicated that visiting hours were from 7:00 a.m. until 9:00 p.m. Robin had told him that in order to redeem himself for getting sick at the bar the previous evening, he needed to speak with Patterson.

"Good morning. Can you tell me which room Jimmy Patterson is in. He arrived last night."

The receptionist at the front desk was polite, but firm. "He's in room two hundred; however, visiting hours don't start for twenty minutes."

Lester sat in the chair nearest to the reception desk and waited . . . until the receptionist walked through a door behind her desk. Walking quietly past the desk, he entered a set of swinging doors and continued down the hallway to room 200. The door was closed, so Lester hesitated, trying to determine if any of the staff were in the room. Slowly opening the door, he peeked inside and saw a silent figure lying on the bed in the semi-darkness.

Lester partially opened one of the window blinds and pulled a chair next to the bed. Patterson's entire head appeared to be swollen. A heavy bandage had been placed across his nose. "Patterson, can you hear me?"

"Lester." The sound was garbled, a groan combined with a word. His mouth was full of metal braces and wires.

"Who did this to you?"

"Don't know."

"What did he want?"

"The girl." The words were slurred, but intelligible.

"You mean the girl we grabbed yesterday at the apartment?"

"Uh huh."

"What did you tell him?" Lester was as persistent as an FBI agent trying to get a death bed confession.

With great effort, Patterson managed two words. "Arturo. Juarez."

Lester could see that Patterson was in no shape to have a conversation. "Okay, buddy. I'll check on you later today."

As Lester stood to leave, a young man entered the room wearing a white smock, a clip board, and the ubiquitous stethoscope hanging around his neck.

"How's our patient this morning?" The doctor was pleasant and seemed unconcerned about official visiting hours.

"What were his specific injuries? I would like to be able to give a report to his boss and fellow workers."

Looking at the clip board, the doctor said, "Well, your friend has a broken jaw, three missing teeth, a cut on his nose that required twenty-seven stiches, a dislocated right shoulder, and a concussion." Smiling and showing his bedside manner, he added, "Other than that, he's in good shape."

Jack and Robin were sitting in the living room of their apartment when Robin's phone rang. Lester explained Patterson's injuries in excruciating detail, and then recounted his short conversation.

Robin was not pleased. "He told the guy that beat the shit out of him about Arturo and Juarez?"

"Everything he said was being strained through a bunch of wires, but I'm pretty sure that's what he said."

Regaining her composure, Robin calmly said, "Call Gus and Melton and remind them of our one o' clock meeting this afternoon. Okay?"

"We'll be there."

Robin turned and looked at Jack. "You're absolutely correct. We're fucked."

32

Mexico City
Saturday, July 8th

Carlos hung up on Jack and stared at his phone.

Pancakes my ass! I knew Jack was worthless. I should never have tried to help him. Now my sister is missing and he was the last person to have seen her. He may have done something to Antonia. He's finished.

Carlos had already tried to call Arturo twice this morning. He tried one more time with the same result, no answer.

Something's not right. He's supposed to meet me at the airport this afternoon. Where the hell is everybody?

His next call was to Santiago, his number two man after Arturo.

Santiago is as ruthless as Arturo, maybe a little psychotic. He probably deserves a promotion.

Santiago answered promptly. "Yes."

Without preamble, Carlos said, "Where are you?"

"At the compound."

"Have you heard from Arturo?"

"No. He's at a hotel near the airport waiting for you. He's supposed to leave the hotel and meet you later this afternoon."

"Have you seen my sister today?"

"No. I haven't seen her since Thursday night. I know she left early Friday morning with three boxes of material for your friend in El Paso. She took the flower van."

What's happened to Arturo? Where's my sister? They always return my calls.

"Pick me up at the airport at four this afternoon. Bring four of your best men. We've got to get to the bottom of this."

"Will do."

33

El Paso, Texas
Saturday, July 8ᵗʰ

Arsen awakened at 4:30 a.m. He had been asleep exactly three hours. The first thing on his mind was the carnage he and Leela had precipitated at the airport hotel: two dead bodies in the hotel room closet, and a dead body on the bed. He briefly wondered why the pain and death he'd inflicted didn't bother him in the least. He knew he'd become completely agnostic to the fact that he was a trained killer.

His next thought was about Kasie. She had been mostly quiet during their drive from the hotel to El Paso. She was shaken, if not in a state of mild shock, but nevertheless, she was so quiet. He tried to relive each moment following her discovery on the hotel bed. The hug he received after cutting away the tape from her hands and feet was the last bit of affection she had shown. Surely it was because of the trauma she had endured.

I've only been in El Paso for barely five days and look what's happened. Death, destruction, and love. How can all three of those items play such an important part of one man's life? Can they all exist at the same time on an ongoing basis? Do I need to make a choice?

Arsen rolled over and attempted to go back to sleep, but his mind was in overdrive. He couldn't explain the feeling in the pit of his stomach. Was it all because of his profession as a contract assassin, his feelings for Kasie . . . or was it something else? His conscious thoughts continued to vacillate between Carlos Delgado and Kasie. He finally got out of bed at 5:00 and dressed.

Maybe some eggs and hash browns will bring me around.

Arriving in the lobby, Arsen realized that the hotel coffee shop was not yet open. There was no one behind the registration desk and the lobby was vacant at this hour, so he walked outside into the warm, dry morning air.

A brisk walk will help clear my brain. Maybe I can find someplace open for breakfast.

Twelve minutes, and three blocks later, a flashing OPEN sign appeared in the window of Sunberg's City Diner. Arsen entered the door, stopped, and took a deep breath. The simple tinkling of the tiny bell on the door was a prelude to the breakfast aroma of bacon, eggs, biscuits, and coffee. Two early morning diners were sitting at one of the few tables in the small establishment, the eight stools at the counter were empty.

After taking seat at the counter, Arsen was studying the items on a one-page menu when a glass of water was placed in front of him.

"Coffee?" The proprietor, a middle-aged man with a pleasant smile, posed the question from behind the counter.

"Sure, black."

"Anything to eat?"

Arsen placed his order and then put both elbows on the counter, holding the coffee cup in his hand as if it was a priceless heirloom. The sound of the metal spatula on the hot grill, and the gurgling of the coffee pot faded into the background as he sipped the hot, black liquid and continued his self-examination.

Something's not right. What is it? I'm not concerned about Carlos Delgado. Hopefully, I'll meet him face to face tomorrow at the Juarez hotel near the Santa Fe Street bridge. If I kill him, will I feel guilty? Hell, no. Is it Kasie and her strange behavior last night? Probably not. She was traumatized. What's going on with me? Is it the job? What is it?

The solutions to his questions remained unanswered as the eggs, bacon, and hash brown potatoes arrived. Also arriving was another patron who seated himself at the counter. Arsen had not heard the faint, melodious sound of the bell when the door opened, and was somewhat surprised when the most recent customer at Sundberg's diner sat down.

"Good morning. I must say, this is a peaceful time of the day. Absolutely peaceful. Don't you agree?" The gentleman had a distinct British accent.

Must be from Scotland. His voice sounds exactly like Sean Connery.

Arsen nodded in recognition of the question as he took a bite of bacon. "Not a lot going on in El Paso at this time of the morning."

The newcomer had a striking appearance: deep voice, square jaw, short hair, that contrasted with his bushy mustache.

"Come here often?"

"Nope." Arsen was chewing a mouthful of hash browns.

The stranger placed his order as Arsen was finishing his breakfast.

"It's a peaceful time of day, but you don't seem to be at peace with yourself."

Arsen slowly turned and looked at the man who was only two seats away. "Excuse me?"

"We all have to decide who we are and where we're going before we can truly be at peace with ourselves. Your body language seems to reflect something different. Don't you agree?"

"Sure," Arsen said as he placed a twenty-dollar bill on the counter, not waiting for the change.

"Have a good day."

I didn't realize El Paso had so many kooks.

The sound of the bell bid Arsen goodbye as he walked through the door.

———————

After showering and shaving at his hotel, Arsen called the hospital to confirm visiting hours.

He'd decided to see Jamie and give him an abbreviated update on his activities over the past few days. He also was hoping to be there when Kasie arrived.

During the short drive to the hospital, he still had many things on his mind: *Who was the guy in the diner? Must have been a preacher. Peace, my ass! Meeting with Leela at nine this morning. I'll fill her in on my plan for Carlos Delgado when he meets his lover tomorrow at the hotel in Juarez. Hope Kasie has fully recovered.*

He knew his thoughts were random and disjointed. He knew he needed to slow down and get back to his customary logical, detail oriented, detached self. In the far recesses of his mind, he was starting to visualize the source of the problem.

Arsen walked into the hospital lobby at 8:00 a.m. He went straight to Jamie's room and was relieved to find that no other family members were present. Jamie was sitting up in bed with a pillow supporting his back. The overbed table contained the remnants of his breakfast.

Holding up a glass of orange juice in a toasting gesture, Jamie said, "Hey, stranger. I was beginning to worry about you. Everything under control?"

"Look at you. Fine dining and beautiful nurses. I'm sure you're being pampered."

"Not exactly. I'm being discharged this afternoon and it can't come soon enough. I can walk, but my side is extremely sore, so don't be asking me to help you move any heavy furniture."

Becoming serious, he said, "Making any progress?"

Arsen pressed his lips together and hesitated for a second. He couldn't tell Jamie all the gory details about what had transpired over the past two days, but he didn't want to leave him without hope regarding his family's well-being. "I think you know me well enough not to ask specific questions about all of my activities. However, I feel I can bring this problem to a conclusion within a day or two. Okay?"

"I trust you. Let me know if I can help."

Changing expressions, Arsen said, "Let's talk about something important. The NFL season starts in a couple of months, who's going to the Super Bowl this year?"

They talked about everything and nothing for the next forty-five minutes, but before they could solve all the world's problems, Kasie arrived.

"Well, hello, boys. Room for one more?" She walked into the room and gave Arsen a semi- hug on his shoulder.

Jamie perked-up when he saw his sister. "Good to see you, little sis."

Arsen smiled and said, "I didn't realize that beautiful women got up this early."

"The beautiful women are probably still asleep," Kasie said, without showing any emotion.

"How did you like the Hoppy Monk?" Jamie asked.

Kasie looked at Arsen and answered the question. "We had a good time. Too bad you couldn't make it. I continued with our tour of El Paso with a dinner at Mi Piaci Thursday night. Excellent food."

"Wow. I've been missing out. Where did you go last night?"

Hesitating for a second, Kasie said, "I was kind of tied up, so we didn't make it for dinner last night."

Arsen was impressed with Kasie's double entendre. *This girl's quick. No doubt about it, she's fully recovered.* Looking at his watch, he turned his attention to Kasie and said, "I have a few things to take care of, so maybe I'll see you later today. Jamie, let me know if you need any assistance getting out of here this afternoon."

"I'll be fine. My parents will pick me up, since I'm staying with them. Thanks, anyway. Keep me informed, okay?"

"Will do. See you guys later."

Arsen glanced at Kasie, but she stood steadfast by Jamie's bed. He was concerned, if not a little depressed, as he walked through the hospital lobby. Kasie had seemed fine . . . but, distant, detached. It was one of those hard to define feelings one has on occasion. It's not something a person says or does. It's just an intuition, a feeling beyond conscious reasoning.

———————◆◆———————

Although Arsen arrived early at the Dunleavy Funeral Home, Leela was waiting for him in the lobby.

"You're a few minutes early, but I think I can work you into my busy schedule."

Even in his current state of mind, Arsen couldn't hide his amazement. "How in the world do you maintain such a positive attitude all the time?"

"I love my work."

Trying to be nonchalant, Arsen said, "So, tell me. How was Kasie last night. Did you notice any physical or mental issues?"

"Like I told you at the hotel last night, she wasn't physically abused, but she was pretty well shaken after what she endured. You know, the sedative, the trip in the trunk of the car, and the horror of not knowing what was coming next put a big time scare in her. She seemed better this morning when I took her to her apartment."

That has to be it. She's still a little traumatized. That's all. "Let's go into your office and I'll tell you what I *extracted* from our dental patient last night."

Leela sat in the same desk chair that Spencer had been sitting in two days before. The room had been cleaned, but Arsen could still feel Spencer's presence.

Leaning back in his chair, Arsen said, "Our boy became quite talkative near the end of his procedure. He says that Carlos Delgado meets a woman each Sunday and Wednesday at a hotel in Juarez."

"Where exactly, and at what time?"

"The Hotel del Rio on Avenida Juarez. It's only a couple of blocks from the Santa Fe Street Bridge. They meet at two in the afternoon."

"You have to be kidding. Why would one of the most wanted men in Mexico risk going to a hotel that near the border?"

"As a kid, we had a saying. A stolen watermelon taste better than one you have to buy."

Rolling her eyes, Leela said, "Whatever. So, what's the plan . . . as if I didn't know."

"Couple of things going on. According to Arturo, Carlos thinks Jack Pope is a dumbass, even though he owes him some kind of debt. I want to take care of Carlos tomorrow and then I'll deal with Pope."

"We'll take care of Carlos and we'll deal with Pope." Leela put the emphasis on we'll.

"You've got me up to my neck in this little operation. Might as well see it all the way through."

"Appreciate it."

"I understand the sequence of events. No need to alert Carlos and unleash the long-term revenge thing. Carlos first and Pope second. Correct?"

"Correct."

Arsen spent the next ten minutes laying out the outline of his plan. It was relatively simple, with several critical details yet to be determined. He used Leela's desk computer, including the Google Earth feature, to examine the exact location of the Hotel del Rio and the surrounding business establishments.

He had one last topic he wanted to mention. "This will sound unusual coming from me, but I had a strange experience this morning at breakfast. I was at a diner near my hotel and a stranger sat down beside me and made a couple of personal observations. He implied I wasn't at peace with myself and that I didn't know where I was going in life. Is that crazy, or what?"

Smirking, Leela said, "Did he have a British accent?"

34

El Paso, Texas
Saturday, July 8th

Jack was moving slowly, both physically and mentally. The dark puffiness under both eyes contrasted with the paleness of his face. He and Robin, who was leaning on the desk, were looking at several sheets of paper containing a business forecast.

The three remaining members of the crew had seated themselves on the couch, and were quietly engaged in small talk, mostly about Patterson and the events of the past several days.

Even the kidnapping didn't seem as exciting as it had the previous evening.

Lester was providing an update on Patterson, including his own personal observations.

"His face is ruined, his teeth are ruined, and he'll never be back here. I feel sorry for him, but he's done . . . and I mean done."

Looking up from his desk, Jack said, "Lester, what were you saying about Patterson?"

"Patterson's a mess. No telling how long he'll be in the hospital. The guy that beat him up asked about the girl we kidnapped. Patterson gave him Arturo's name and mentioned something about Juarez. That's all I could get out of him."

Placing his hands on his forehead, Jack blurted out, "Why would he mentioned Arturo's name? Dog doo! Why would the idiot do that?"

Gus leaned forward and added his opinion. "It had to be someone associated with the grocery store, but how did they know the girl was gone. Patterson got cold-cocked within an hour after the abduction."

Melton had been unusually subdued during the conversation. Crossing his legs, leaning back, and placing his hands behind his head, he said, "Think about it. Burk carved the seven in the old lady's shoulder, and he disappears. Patterson was involved in the kidnapping, and he gets the shit beat out of him. Gus, you shot the owners' son, so you'd better watch yourself. Don't you think?"

Even though Jack had taken his medication, he was fidgeting in his chair, his eyebrows furrowed with anxiety. "Carlos Delgado's sister is missing. She's the one who delivered the drugs yesterday morning." He was no longer leading; instead, he was lowering himself into the morass of worry, fear, and self-doubt being expressed by other members of the crew. "In addition to everything else, none of our distributors have sold any product yet. Right, Robin?"

Standing up, Robin asserted herself into the desolate conversation. "Hold on, boys. Time to man-up. It's been barely twenty-four hours since our distributors received the drugs. For Christ sakes, give it another couple of days. Now, as for the other issue, I've given it some thought. Arturo has the Rodriguez girl somewhere in Juarez, so that problem is solved. Surely, whoever messed-up Patterson, knows nothing else can be done about it. It would be one person against the entire Sinaloa Cartel."

"Makes sense to me." Lester nodded in agreement.

Robin wasn't finished. "Delgado's missing sister is not our problem. She's probably shacked up with someone, either here or in Juarez, and will show up sooner or later. I'll call our distributors Monday morning and check on their sales. It may take longer than we think for this business venture to achieve lift off."

Listening to Robin's logic being expressed, Jack took a deep breath and his face began returning some of the missing color. "Robin is probably right. It will take a while for the word to get around regarding the service we're providing for a certain element of the local citizenry. And I'm certain that Carlos's sister has various self-identity issues, since she's associated with a drug cartel at such a young age. I wouldn't be surprised if she were at this very minute sharing her most intimate thoughts with some young man."

He would have continued pontificating, but his cell phone interrupted.

"Yes." Jack answered and listened to Carlos as he screamed threats and obscenities for the next several minutes.

"We'll keep looking," Jack said before carefully placing his phone on the desk, the coloring of his face once again returning to the washed-out look.

Robin knew it was not good news. "What was that all about?"

Jack spoke softly, the distant look returning to his eyes. "Carlos called from his private jet. His sister is still missing."

The word *missing* had barely left his lips before Jack passed out for the second time in two days, his forehead gently hitting the desk top.

35

El Paso, Texas
Saturday, July 8ᵗʰ

Arsen raised one eyebrow as he said, "British accent? You've got to be kidding! That was Nils?"

Displaying the innocence of a five-year-old, Leela said, "I didn't say it was Nils. I only ask if it was someone with a British accent. You know, it sounds like something a visiting Brit might say to a total stranger."

Arsen shook his head, frustration apparent. "We'll talk more about this later. I need to get to Juarez and implement the first phase of the *Carlos* plan. See you in the morning."

As Arsen walked down the sidewalk in front of the funeral home, his cell phone rang.

After glancing at the incoming number, he answered in a hopeful, upbeat manner as he sat down on the bench in the front lawn. "Hello."

"Arsen, this is Kasie. I hate to make this call, but we need to talk. I should tell you this in person, but I know I couldn't do it if we were face to face. It's about . . . about us. I think we've both been moving in the same direction. Actually, we've been moving rapidly in the same direction." There was a hitch in her voice and it was evident she was on the verge of crying. "I put a lot of thought into this last night and this morning." She hesitated before continuing. "You saved my life last night, but . . . but we can't continue this relationship in the way it's headed. I must sound small and ungrateful, but the world you live in frightens me and I need you to know how I feel before it's too late and someone really gets hurt. I'm sorry, I'm just rambling."

For some reason, Arsen had been expecting this conversation and was not totally surprised.

"What if I changed my occupation and settled down doing something different? It wouldn't be difficult. I could live in El Paso."

He hadn't seen her coming, and he didn't want to see her go.

"Arsen, although I've only known you for a few days, I think I know who you are. I know what happened at the hotel, and I suspect I know what's about to happen. You're a fiercely driven man and I respect your dedication, but we're so different. We're too far apart for anything to work-out longer term. And I think you realize it just as I do."

The intense feeling returned to the pit of Arsen's stomach, similar to the feeling he'd experienced the first time he met Kasie. This time it wasn't elation.

"You're sure about this?"

"Yes."

A thousand thoughts went through Arsen's mind in a flash: rationalizations, excuses, justifications. The final introspection was crystal clear. He'd killed six individuals in the short span of five days. Whether or not there were mitigating circumstances made no difference. Six was the number of lives he'd taken this week. Kasie was a naïve recent college graduate, he was a killer.

"I fully understand. Knowing you, even for such a short period of time, has been one of the highlights of my life. I'm sure we'll both be fine."

After saying goodbye, Arsen sat for a few minutes staring at his phone. A slight breeze rustled the leaves in the tree shading the bench. It was the perfect setting for a rejected lover . . . but not for Arsen. Something was still bothering him, something beyond Kasie.

I need to finish this job and get back to growing tomatoes. I also need to call Nils.

Looking at his phone as if it were the source of all his problems, Arsen dialed his mysterious boss.

Nils answered promptly. "Yes."

Arsen was all business. "We can talk about breakfast at a later date. Two things. First, I need two Glock seventeens and two switch blades, all with ankle holsters, delivered to me tomorrow at noon in Juarez. It will be too risky for me to carry them across the bridge. I'll be sitting at the bar in the Kentucky Club, which is two blocks from the Santa Fe Street bridge."

"I know where it is."

"The other item is Leela. She'll be with me. I'm going to eliminate Carlos Delgado."

In his finest Scottish brogue, Nils said, "Best of luck. You'll need it."

———•———

After checking-out of the Gardner Hotel, and stopping at an Applebee's for lunch, Arsen found a parking space on the street a block from the bridge. He removed his carry-bag from the trunk of the car and began the walk down the street. He was soon caught-up in the flow of visitors and locals funneling toward the Port of Entry. The considerable amount of Saturday afternoon pedestrian traffic caused a short delay at the toll booth. After paying the fifty-cent fee, he entered the chain-link covered walkway and began the walk over the Rio Grande. Ten automobile lanes separated him from the foot traffic on the other side of the bridge, all headed in the opposite direction toward the United States.

Looks like this human migration will result in a net equal exchange. Other than the tourists, where are these people going? Are they students, professionals, or just ordinary every-day-souls trying to fulfill a short-term dream . . . such as making enough money to exist.

Slanted concrete walls ran along both sides of the almost dry gulch of the wide river bed. Tall weeds, automobile tires, sacks, and other types of garbage littered the banks. A railroad bridge crossed the Rio Grande a few hundred yards to the right.

How do they inspect each and every one of the railroad cars for contraband before they cross? No wonder it's so easy for the cartels to stay in business.

Arsen tried to focus on the purpose of his visit as he weaved his way through the crowded, fenced tunnel, but he couldn't shake the thought of the phone call from Kasie. The empty feeling in his stomach was a constant reminder of the conversation.

Border security guards, dressed in black, were stationed at the tunnel exit, automatic weapons hanging at their sides. The stern looks on their faces served as the primary check on the arriving masses, although they would occasionally stop someone and conduct a random search of their belongings. Even though Arsen's bag contained only a black tee shirt, cargo pants, a change of underwear, and toiletries, he avoided eye contact with the guards as he looked ahead at the city of Juarez.

Avenida Juarez was bustling with activity. After walking for a block, Arsen stopped and made several observations. The street was lined on both sides with shops and businesses of various types, all of which were painted a clean white, some with flashing neon signs begging attention to their various products and services. Some tourists were trying out their best negotiating skills with street vendors, while others had come to conduct business with the many dental offices, eye doctors, and pharmacies.

A half-block later, Arsen looked to his right and saw a large painted window on a single-story building exclaiming the "World Famous Kentucky

Club and Grill, Since 1920." Across the street and thirty yards up the block, the Hotel del Rio was in full view.

The Kentucky Club provided tables and chairs on the small patio next to the street, all empty due to the afternoon heat. Arsen sat at one of the tables near the entrance to the bar and focused on the Hotel del Rio. The initial phase of the *Carlos* plan was coming together. The research he had conducted with Leela was on target. Nils would have the Glocks delivered tomorrow at noon.

Perfect location to view the hotel. I can drink on the job and not worry about a reprimand.

He tried to remove himself from the recent developments with Kasie, but the unsettling feeling in his mind and body persisted. He'd discovered how an inner conflict can be more painful than a physical wound.

After gazing across the street for ten minutes, Arsen decided to go inside the famous club. His initial impression was that he was entering a dive bar from the seventies. A long, battered bar stretched out the length of the green-hued interior. When Arsen's eyes finally adjusted to the dimness, he counted customers in seven of the swivel, low-backed chairs at the bar, couples seated at three separate tables, and all four chairs occupied at another table. He seated himself midway down the bar, placed his bag under his feet, and was greeted by a friendly bartender in a red shirt.

Before the bartender could ask, Arsen said, "Corona, please."

Turning slightly in his chair, Arsen again examined his surroundings. More table seating was available on the other side of a half-wall, several television screens were visible, and the red and green color scheme was on full display. He assumed an exit was near the restrooms in the back.

The bartender returned with the beer, along with a menu. The red and green letters on the cover of the menu caught Arsen's attention: *La Casa de las Margaritas.* The Kentucky Club claimed the honor of inventing the margarita, although two other establishments in Mexico boasted the same achievement.

Sometimes my research turns up the most trivial bits of information, but for history's sake, maybe I'll try one tomorrow.

Arsen's mind didn't want to leave the peaceful, coolness of the bar, but after paying for his beer, his body headed for the door. Phase Two of the Carlos plan needed to be implemented.

As Arsen crossed the street, the exterior of the Hotel del Rio did not meet even his expectations. He'd expected a boutique hotel, but not a small, two-story, run-down, white building with a definite skid-row appearance. The Yankee Bar, with a drawing of the Statue of Liberty on the window, was on the left side of the hotel, and a pharmacy on the other. The building was so narrow, only five windows were showing on the street side of the hotel's second level. There were no alleyways visible for the entire length of the block. Google Earth had shown that the hotel was adjacent to another two-story building in the back. Building codes were from lax to non-existent.

Arsen entered the front door, and surprisingly, was met by a neat, well-appointed interior. The registration desk was on the left, and two couches facing each other were situated in the center of the room. A bar, with only four chairs, occupied the right side of the lobby, along with a hallway leading to the first-floor rooms and a stairway to the second floor.

Approaching the middle-aged lady at the registration desk, Arsen said, "Good afternoon. Do you have any rooms available? I need one room for two nights. There will be two of us."

"Yes, we do. It'll be twenty-seven dollars a night." The desk clerk's appearance and demeanor would have easily qualified her for a position at the Ritz-Carlton in San Francisco.

Arsen and Leela had discussed the possibilities of Carlos's room location. They determined that he would choose a second-floor room for purposes of security. A sentry would be placed in the lobby and could easily keep an eye on the narrow stairway. They also figured Carlos would be in a corner room, probably at the far end of the hall.

"If possible, I would like a room on the second floor facing Avenida Juarez, not too close to the stairway."

Arsen assumed the hotel staff would be aware that the weekly meetings between Carlos and his woman were some kind of ongoing tryst. He also assumed that the staff may or may not know exactly who Carlos was, but that they probably received enough cash on the side to keep the meetings confidential.

After laying three twenties on the counter, Arsen noticed a board on the wall behind the desk clerk containing keys hanging on hooks. The keys were numbered from one to twenty-five.

The desk clerk didn't show any suspicion as to Arsen's intentions, and said, "Here's the key to room twenty-one, and your change. I hope you enjoy your stay. Let me know if there's anything I can do for you."

Interesting. She didn't ask me to fill out a registration form or show any kind of identification. Fine by me.

No one else was in the lobby as Arsen made his way to the stairway. He counted eight stair-steps to a small landing, and then after a left turn, eight more steps to the second floor. For some reason, he expected an old, musty smell, but was pleasantly surprised by the complete absence of any odors. The narrow hallway led past doors on each side numbered sixteen through twenty-five.

Midway down the hall on the left, Arsen stopped in front of his door.

I'm fairly certain Carlos will be at the end of the hall in twenty-five, or maybe across the hall in twenty-four. Probably twenty-five. For security purposes, he may have paid for both rooms. I'd bet on it.

Before entering his room, Arsen looked out the large window at the end of the hallway. It opened to the rooftop of the adjoining building housing the Yankee Bar.

Fine. I'll check it out later. It should work in case of an emergency.

Arsen stood at the door of his room and listened. Nothing. Not a sound. There was no street noise, no sounds from downstairs, nothing from the other rooms, only quiet.

This place must be well constructed and heavily insulated. Come to think of it, I haven't seen any other guests.

The room was small, but neat: double bed, side table, dresser with a wooden chair, closet, and bathroom. A portable air conditioner situated in the corner was doing its best to keep the room cool. The window was facing the avenue, with the Kentucky Club in full view.

Arsen placed his bag on the dresser before taking a closer look at the window. It had a single thumb lock, and he had no difficulty raising it to its full height. After lowering the window, he removed his cell phone from his pocket, took off his shoes, and dialed Leela.

"Yes." Her voice was smooth and professional.

"Phase Two complete. I'll see you at the Kentucky Club at eleven-thirty in the morning."

"I look forward to our Juarez sight-seeing trip. Goodbye."

Arsen placed the phone on the side table and stretched out on the bed. It had been a week of ups and downs, stresses and strains, hope . . . and even Arsen's version of love.

36

Juarez, Mexico
Saturday, July 8th

Carlos Delgado's private jet landed on time at the Ciudad Juarez International Airport. He squinted and shielded his eyes as he walked down the steps of the plane. Santiago and three other men were waiting next to an idling, black Mercedes.

"I knew it! Something's wrong. Arturo should be here." Carlos looked around the tarmac as if he expected to see Arturo walking toward the jet.

Santiago raised his eyebrows and frowned. "I've tried to call him several times today. He doesn't answer. I assumed he would be here. Do you think he forgot?"

"Arturo never forgets. Let's get in the car. I need to make a couple of calls."

Carlos sat in the back seat, between Santiago and another bodyguard. He punched Arturo's speed dial number for the sixth time in the past several hours. Same result. Voicemail. Next, he tried to call his sister, Antonia, but again, no answer. After several minutes, he found the number for the Hotel Azteca Aeropuerto.

"Hotel Azteca Aero----" The person answering the phone was cut-off in mid-sentence.

"Connect me to Arturo Hernandez's room." It was a demand, not a request.

"Sir, are you an associate of Mr. Hernandez?"

"What the fuck difference does it make who I am! Connect me to his room!" The other men in the car looked wide-eyed at Carlos as he screamed.

The desk clerk remained calm. "Sir, the bodies of Mr. Hernandez and two other men were found in one of the rooms this morning. It's now a police matter."

Carlos's mouth was open, but he didn't speak. He ended the call and whispered, "Arturo and two of his men are dead. What's going on? Let's get back to the compound. Now!"

Santiago was frowning as he said, "It's the Juarez Cartel. The bastards are stepping it up."

Carlos quickly regained his composure and mused aloud. "Juarez Cartel, Pope, or whoever . . . we'll kick the shit out of them. Santiago, I have a meeting at the Hotel del Rio tomorrow at two. I want you to pick two of your men to go with me. Okay?" Even the death of his second-in-command and two other men couldn't quench his sexual desire.

Fully understanding the word *meeting*, Santiago said, "I understand. I'll have two good men go with you." Arturo had previously told Santiago about the twice weekly arrangements that Carlos had with his girlfriend. "I'm also aware that a special desk clerk will be on duty during your visit."

"Yes. He's well paid." Carlos didn't care who knew about his extracurricular activities. He considered it a badge of honor to have a variety of women at his disposal.

"There will be no problems. I assure you."

"We need to have a meeting in my library tonight after dinner. Notify the team leaders to be there at seven. We have many items to discuss. Santiago, with Arturo's demise, you're now my second-in-command. Comprende?"

"Yes, boss. I'm always here to serve."

"I have another special task for you. We'll discuss it at the meeting."

———•———

The men sat quietly in the library as Carlos angrily paced about the room and related the details of his meeting in Mexico City. His bosses were concerned about the progress of the Juarez Cartel in the Juarez-El Paso corridor and the potential threat of other cartels making inroads into their business. Carlos continued to rant about Arturo's death, and his missing sister. He was agitated. He was tired, not only from the meetings he had attended, but also from the extracurricular activities at his hotel with the multiple blondes.

"The Juarez Cartel will pay for what they did to Arturo!" The veins on Carlos's neck stood out as he screamed.

All his men nodded vigorously in agreement.

"Jack Pope had something to do with the disappearance of my sister." Looking at Santiago, Carlos settled down and said calmly, "You know all about Jack Pope and his operation in El Paso. Right?"

"Right, boss."

"I want you to make plans to have him here at our compound tomorrow morning or early tomorrow afternoon. I want him to be here before I return from my two o' clock meeting. Understand?"

"No problema."

"Plan it carefully and use as many men as you think necessary. He can come peacefully, or you can hit him in the head. Just get him here. Duct tape and a straw. He should still be breathing when I get here. Got it?"

"Duct tape and a straw. Got it."

37

El Paso, Texas
Saturday, July 8th

Jack slowly raised his head. He was soaked in sweat, color still missing from his face. Robin was standing over him with a wet towel.

Jack conjured-up a lame excuse for his physical condition. He was alert enough to remember that effective managers never admitted mistakes or shortcomings. They made simple explanations and moved on.

"I think I had some bad pancakes this morning. I probably should sue the damn restaurant." He picked up a ballpoint pen and made a few notes on a pad of paper.

What's wrong with me? Grown men don't faint. I'll make an appointment for a physical. I'll get a blood test. I've got to regain control of my life.

Robin draped the towel around Jack's neck and took charge. She had the distinct feeling that the crew was on the verge of abandoning their fledgling drug distribution business.

"Listen up. Here's how we proceed. Burk is gone and Patterson isn't coming back. We'll find a couple of replacements next week. Won't be difficult. I'll make calls to our three distributors Monday morning and check with them regarding their weekend sales. No, I have a better idea. Let's meet here at eleven tomorrow morning and I'll call them with all of you present. All three of the businesses are open on Sunday. Plus, I have several more possibilities for distributors we can investigate. Any thoughts about what happened to Patterson?"

Jack sat impassively in his chair while the crew speculated about Patterson, Burk, and Carlos's missing sister. The three male members expressed their opinions, even though nothing of substance came from their comments.

Robin listened and nodded in agreement on occasion. When the discussion finally ran its course, she said, "I'll call the police department and inquire about Antonia. Of course, I won't use my name, but I'll ask about any young women being arrested in the past couple of days, murders, accidents, and so forth." Addressing the men on the couch, she added, "I want you guys to split-up the four major hospitals in the city and make similar inquires. We'll discuss our findings at our meeting in the morning. At least we can tell Carlos about our efforts to find his sister." Robin hesitated for a moment and glared at the remnants of the Seventh Avenue Crew. Raising her voice, she made her closing reprimand. "Are you a bunch of weak-sister bitches, or are you real men? If you're on the team, let's make some shit happen!"

Lester was first to speak. "Damn right! Let's make this thing work."

Melton and Gus nodded in agreement, while Jack leaned back in his chair with a blank look on his face. He was certain the crew had lost respect for him and that was unacceptable. This new approach to drug distribution was his idea. Not Robin's, not anyone else's. It was his idea. He paid the $2,000 a month salary to each member of the crew. He, and he alone, was providing the potential for each of these ingrates to make more money than they could make at any other job. Time to show them who's really the brains behind this operation.

Jack slowly rose from his chair and stood with his arms crossed. He knew this was a "power position" for a big-time executive. "I've been listening to all of your ideas, and they have merit. However, we need to be bold. Really bold. Here's what I recommend in order to get things rolling."

The crew sat quietly, all eyes on their boss.

"Our most immediate problem is related to Carlos Delgado's sister. We all know about the gang rivalry between Carlos's Sinaloa Cartel and the Juarez Cartel. Right? I have the cell phone number for Carlos, and a great idea to fix the problem. One of you can call Carlos, disguise your voice, and tell him you're with the Juarez Cartel. After you have his attention, you can say that you've kidnapped his sister and want a large ransom. You know, like five million dollars. Some outrageous number. Then hang-up and the problem will be solved. Since he'll never hear back from anyone, he'll think the Juarez boys killed his sister. What do you think?"

There was no response from the group. Robin broke the silence.

"That's the dumbest idea I've ever heard. You guys get on with the hospital calls. We'll see you at eleven in the morning."

Jack sat down, worried that he might pass out again.

After the meeting ended, Gus and Melton walked to their cars in the parking lot.

Gus was short and to the point. "Jack is an educated fool. I've had about all his pandering condescension I can take. He's going to get us all killed if we're not careful."

"I'm not sure what you just said, but I agree about the killing part. I'm beginning to think that prison or death could come before financial independence in this job."

"Yep. Tomorrow may be my last meeting with the Seventh Avenue Crew."

38

Juarez, Mexico
Saturday, July 8th

Arsen opened his eyes and blinked several times. It took him several seconds to realize he wasn't at home in Odessa, not at the Gardner Hotel, but instead, at a small hotel in Juarez. Looking at his watch, he was surprised at the time. He rarely took naps, and he rarely slept soundly for three straight hours, especially when a cheap air conditioning unit was humming and rattling nonstop. The events of the past week had taken their toll.

Must be getting old. I'll be thirty in a couple of years.

The late afternoon sun barely filtered through the white window curtains, but Arsen knew it would stay light for at least another two hours. He had several items on his to-do list: locate all of the entrances and exits to the building, take another look at the window at the end of the hall, determine exactly where Leela would be stationed, and buy some bottled water.

After showering and shaving, he put on his black cargo pants and black tee shirt. The conversation with Kasie earlier in the day had not affected him as much as he thought it would. He'd been surprised at how his feelings for her had surfaced almost overnight. And now it was over. He wondered if anyone else on the planet had ever had such a brief, mentally intense love affair . . . almost five days.

Why am I feeling so nonchalant about the whole thing? Part of me is actually excited about the possibility of killing Carlos Delgado tomorrow. I am who I am. I know it, and Kasie realized it in a very short time.

After locking his door, Arsen walked toward the window at the end of the hallway, stopping in front of Room 25.

The window in the room faces Juarez Avenue, the same as mine. What a ballsie bastard! The plan is to somehow get through his door, shoot him, and get the hell out of Dodge. Simple, except for figuring out the best way to get through the door. Kick it down? Knock, and say "room service?" Open the unsophisticated lock with a credit card? Probably the latter. Can't make a lot of noise because he'll have a bodyguard sitting in the lobby. Of course, we may have to kill the bodyguard as well.

The window at the end of the hallway had two thumb-screw latches on the bottom of the frame. After unlocking both latches and raising the window to the top, Arsen immediately felt a warm breeze in his face as he gazed at the flat, tar and gravel roof of the adjoining building. He decided it was too light outside to explore the roof as a means of escape, but instead to walk around the block and examine it from street level.

Removing a credit card from his wallet, Arsen walked back to his room and stood in front of the door. He inserted the card into the vertical crack between the door and the frame. He carefully tilted the flexible card toward the door handle and pushed it into the crack as far as possible. The last move was to bend the card away from the handle and push on the door at the same time. This forced the bolt back into the door and in a matter of seconds, it opened.

This hotel is a piece of shit. What about the first floor? Since there's no alley next to or behind the hotel, how could there be a first-floor exit at the end of the hallway?

As Arsen descended the last stair-step, he could see the desk clerk talking on the phone, her back to him. He turned and walked to the end of the first-floor hallway and confirmed his suspicion . . . solid wall, no exit.

This place is a firetrap. Absolutely no building codes.

Other than the desk clerk, who was still on the phone, the lobby was deserted when Arsen emerged from the hall. He stood by the registration desk for a few minutes hoping to get her attention.

Ending her call, she turned and looked at Arsen with a pleasant smile. "Did you find your room to be satisfactory?"

"Oh yes, it's fine. I was wondering if you could recommend a restaurant within walking distance?"

Arsen was not concerned about being identified by the desk clerk. The locals were known for their silence in police matters, especially when drug activities were involved.

"A very nice place for dinner is Garcia's." Pointing, she said, "It's only about five blocks down the street, on this side. You mentioned when you checked in that two of you would be staying in the room. Will the other person be joining you tonight?"

"No, she'll be here tomorrow. We'll be sightseeing. You know, tourists."

"I could arrange a companion for you tonight if you would be interested."

She made the statement in the same tone a desk clerk would use when enquiring about a wake-up call.

"Ahh, no, not tonight, but thanks for the offer."

Arsen exited the hotel and made his way down the crowded sidewalk. He passed a dental clinic, two pharmacies, and an optometrist. An Oxxo convenience store was across the street. Juarez Avenue had been razed following the height of the drug war between the two major cartels and many of the strip shows, nightclubs, and whorehouses were gone and replaced with the whitewashed buildings containing random businesses. People were out and about on this warm evening, optimistic about the future, oblivious to reality.

Weaving through the evening throng of shoppers and sightseers, Arsen counted exactly sixty paces from the hotel entrance to the end of the block. He turned left off Avenida Juarez onto a side street and continued to another narrow thoroughfare located behind the jammed-together building complex. Making another left turn, he counted sixty paces before stopping and surveying the surroundings. He was standing beside the two-story building with the tar and gravel roof.

I should be in line with the second-floor hallway of the hotel.

A one-story extension of the building appeared to have been recently attached. It was constructed with exposed metal beams and the same stucco finish as the buildings on the main avenue. A narrow portico extended from the corner of the building to an entrance about twenty paces away.

Three dumpsters were pushed against the wall, one of them next to the portico. A car was parked next to the entrance, but no other signs of life were to be seen.

If necessary, Leela and I could exit the hallway window on the second floor, cross the two roof lines, jump down to the portico and then to the dumpsters. Easy as pie. However, it would be so much easier to walk out the front door of the hotel. But at least, we have a backup plan.

Arsen made his way back to Juarez Avenue and found it still busy with Saturday evening pedestrian and automobile traffic. The air was warm, the neon lights were bright, but even the steady, excited hum of the crowd couldn't create a diversion from the day's activities oscillating through his brain. Part of him wanted to be carefree, satisfied, and untroubled as he perceived the people around him to be, but another part of him was disturbed and dejected.

Damn women. Another one of my excuses. I've brought this on myself, and I know it.

The unexpected sound of his phone caught Arsen by surprise. "Yes?"

"Arsen, this is Nils. Let's meet for dinner."

How does he know whether or not I've had dinner? "Where would you like to meet?"

"You name it."

"You must know that I'm in Juarez. How about Garcia's on Juarez Avenue?"

"Fine. See you out front in ten minutes."

This is unbelievable, but for some reason it doesn't bother me.

Garcia's red, white, and green neon sign was impossible to miss. So was the tall, well-built, fortyish man with the short hair and bushy mustache. He was wearing tan pants and a short-sleeved shirt with Hawaiian print that clashed with a canvas bag he was holding in his left hand.

Extending his hand, he said, "Arsen, nice to *formally* meet you in person. It's been three years since we first talked."

"And to what do I owe the pleasure?"

"Let's go inside and talk. Too crowded here." Looking at his watch, Nils said, "We have reservations right about now."

Arsen shook his head in amazement.

Garcia's was packed. A hostess seated the two associates in a dimly lit corner booth at the back of the restaurant.

Nils placed the canvas bag next to him and got straight to the point of the meeting. "This bag contains the merchandise you requested. In addition, it contains thirty-five feet of quarter-inch, double-braided nylon rope, a set of handcuffs, and a magic marker. I'll explain about these items later."

"You're delivering the merchandise now, rather than tomorrow at the Kentucky Club. Right?"

"Correct. Less complicated. Now, let me explain why I'm here."

"Please do."

"We're entering into a new era of fighting the drug wars, gun running, forced prostitution, kidnapping, etcetera. Take drugs for example. Our so-called justice system started out by arresting drug users, then street corner dealers, and with limited success, the higher-ups in the distribution chain. We have El Chapo behind bars in the United States, but not much has changed on the ground. The Sinaloa Cartel, the Juarez Cartel, and a number of others are still operating full steam ahead. We're going to take a slightly different tact going forward."

"Tell me more."

A waiter arrived and took their drink and food orders. From the noise being made by Garcia's Saturday night crowd, it seemed more drinking was taking place than eating.

"We will be sending a message to the cartels and to their potential recruits. Instead of attempting to lock up the people at the top of these organizations, we're going to eliminate them . . . in a very public way. In other words, we're going to adopt the very tactics they use."

"I see."

Arsen was enjoying the conversation as a thought flashed through his mind: *Kasie was right. We're different. Really different. This is me. This is what I like. This is what I want.*

"Our new approach will come with higher risks. Instead of one-person operations, two operatives will be involved in all further events. These assignments will be complex and dangerous. I think you and Leela would make a very effective team. Your thoughts?"

Arsen didn't have to think about the proposal. "Yes. In the short time I've known her, she's been outstanding. Count me in. If it's okay with her, it's fine with me."

The drinks arrived and the conversation was temporarily suspended. After a friendly toast, Nils changed topics. "Arsen, you're one of our best. I study people and I've always been curious about what motivates them and what makes them good at their job . . . this one or any other kind. What's your secret? Your military experience, or something earlier in your life?"

After taking a sip of his martini, Arsen said, "Earlier. It was my second year of junior college. I'd gotten into weight training and was working-out one afternoon at a VillaSport health club which was near the campus. It was much nicer than the weight facility the school had for the jocks, so a lot of them used it. Anyway, a hotshot football player and three of his buddies thought I was taking too much time on one of the squat racks and started giving me some shit. I'd seen this guy in the weight room from time-to-time. He was the type that was always shooting off his mouth and posing in front of the mirrors. You know, that kind of stuff."

"I like your story. The outcome is predictable."

"The football player outweighed me by thirty or forty pounds. He was one of those guys that probably started shaving when he was seven. After placing his shoe on my foot and twisting, he said he was going to kick my ass. I lowered the weights to the rack, stood up, and looked him in the eye. I guess he expected me to be scared shitless. You know how it is when someone is scared or feels threatened. Their facial features tighten, their entire body stiffens, their eyes widen, and their voices goes up at least half an octave. Well, none of that happened with me. For some reason, I was looking forward to the altercation. I don't know to this day why, but I was. I stared at him and my body became completely relaxed. For lack of a better term, it was a relaxed intensity. I mean really intense, and really relaxed. To make a long story short, I hit him twice and he bit the dust. His friends watched and just shook their heads. I actually think they enjoyed it as much as I did. So there. That could have been my motivating moment. Since that time, I've always tried to stand for the underdog. Corny, huh?"

"Not at all."

The food arrived and small talk ensued. Politics, the weather, and sports. Arsen refrained from asking Nils any penetrating questions about the agency or for whom he worked. He knew Nils would volunteer any information he wished to divulge.

The meal completed, Nils brought the conversation back to the present. "Now, the rope, the handcuffs, and the magic marker. Let's discuss how we're going to move forward."

Arsen leaned in closer. This was the part he wanted to hear.

39

El Paso, Texas
Sunday, July 9th

Jack Pope sat quietly at his desk watching Robin conduct the meeting. Lester, Gus, and Melton were seated on the couch. The one-way mirror provided Jack with a view of the two early-morning patrons at the bar.

Robin paced the room with her hands on her hips. "Look, I'm fully aware of the unease that exists among you guys. I've provided Jack with the names of two new candidates for the crew. Both come highly recommended, and they both will fit in well with you gentlemen. We'll contact them this coming week and hopefully things will work out."

As usual, Lester was enthusiastic. "Are they local? Tell us about their backgrounds."

"Wait until Jack and I personally screen them. It'll be soon. Now, let's discuss our findings with the local hospitals. Any news about Antonia, or any yet unidentified young women having been admitted in the past few days?"

Lester and Gus reported that they had called four area hospitals with no luck. Melton had contacted two emergency clinics with the same result.

Robin shrugged and said, "We've reached a dead-end regarding Antonia. I called the El Paso police department. No murders, no missing persons, no luck."

Jack's spirits were lifted as he noticed three more customers enter the bar . . . but not for long. He sat up straight in his chair when he saw one of the men lean against the bar and say something to Shelly. The other two were standing behind him looking around the room. The looks on their faces, their posture, everything about the three newcomers bothered Jack. He was especially concerned when the man at the bar looked directly at the one-way mirror, and then turned and motioned the other two to follow him to the office door.

They entered without knocking. Two of the men were now holding handguns at their sides.

In a matter-of-fact tone, the apparent leader of the three men said to no one in particular, "Good morning, folks. Sorry to interrupt, but I need Jack Pope to accompany us." Looking directly at Jack, he said, "Carlos Delgado would like to meet with you."

The entire crew had surprised looks on their faces. Jack blinked several times, his mouth hung wide open, but words were stuck in his throat. The two men with guns lifted Jack out of his chair and guided him out of the office. The three male members of the crew stood next to Robin and watched through the one-way mirror as Jack left the bar with his three escorts.

Gus was first to speak. "That was some serious shit!"

"Wha...what's going on?" Lester stood, slack-jawed. "Robin, what happened?"

Robin stood in silence for a few moments and then answered with several random thoughts. "Jack and Carlos have been friends for a long time. Carlos owes Jack a favor. This is Carlos's way of getting a point across. You know, the tough-guy cartel approach. He only wants to get Jack's attention."

"Well, he damned sure got mine." Gus's mind was made up. Looking at Melton, he said, "Let's go my friend. This drug bullshit is over."

40

Juarez, Mexico
Sunday, July 9th

Arsen had been standing outside the Kentucky Club for five minutes when he saw Leela approaching. She stood out in the uneven flow of bodies on the crowded sidewalk. She had a confident stride; not rushed, not lingering. Her exotic features and jet-black hair mocked the late morning sunlight. She was wearing a short-sleeved white blouse over dark blue, wide-leg pants. Her tennis shoes and hand bag perfectly matched the pants. She was striking. Arsen was surprised at how pleased he was to see her. A bulb was flickering in his head, but he refused to acknowledge it.

I'm about to engage in a very risky undertaking. I've got to focus, focus, focus.

Leela greeted Arsen with a hug and a kiss on the cheek. Whispering, she said, "I'm supposed to be meeting my hotel lover, aren't I?"

"Indeed. Any trouble getting over the bridge?"

"No, but there were lots of tourists on their way over here today."

"Yeah. Most of them are either getting their eyes checked or having a tooth pulled. Let's go inside."

The interior was still dim, with a green glow seeming to seep from the walls. The cool interior was a welcome change from the heat outside. There was no room at the bar, so they sat at one of several vacant tables.

"Is this place green, or what?" Leela turned and looked at the surroundings.

"This place is known for their margaritas. Want one?"

"Not now. It might interfere with my concentration. Know what I mean?"

"Yep. Same here. How about iced tea and chicken fajitas for a quick lunch? I'll place the order with that fellow over there."

"Sounds good."

After returning, Arsen said, "I suppose you know who I had dinner with last night."

"Yes. Did he make his proposal to you?" Leela always seemed to be a step ahead.

"He did . . . partner. And I hope it's okay with you. I think we'll make a good team."

"I agree; however, let's see how our little party goes this afternoon. If things go south, one or both of us may not be around to be part of a team."

Arsen was curious about the "real time" information flow between Nils and Leela. "Did Nils mention the new approach to cartel *shaming*?" He put the emphasis on shaming.

"Yes. I've been briefed on the . . . the *rope* method of getting someone's attention."

"Are you nervous?" Arsen was looking for a specific answer.

"A little."

"Good. I like that. You should be."

"What did you find out about the hotel and the surrounding area?"

Arsen explained the hotel layout, the window in the hall, the flat roof escape route, and his assumptions about the room Carlos would potentially be occupying. The fajitas were served while the final details of the plan were being outlined. For the next fifteen minutes, they discussed Leela's background: growing up in South Dakota, college, and her experience working for various government agencies.

Arsen shoved his plate aside, glanced at his watch, and said, "It's now twelve-thirty-five. Let's go to the hotel and wait until they arrive. We'll have a good view of the street and sidewalk from our room. We'll have to play some of this by ear, but basically, when they're both in their room, you'll go to the lobby and observe the guard's location. Who knows, he may bring ten of his men and place them next to the door of his room. When you return, we'll initiate the final phase of the operation."

"The Glocks, knives, and ankle holsters are in the room?"

"Yep. Not a problem."

Leela, with a hint of self-confidence, said, "Excellent. We can suit-up before the big game."

Arsen continued with his assumptions. "I'm certain they won't arrive in the same vehicle. Carlos will be the first to the hotel, and she'll be there soon after. He and his bodyguard will be easy to spot from our window. When he arrives at his room, we can listen and try to determine which door he uses. She'll come next and you can be standing in the hall fiddling with your purse and see where she goes."

"Makes sense to me." With a half-smile, Leela mentioned a topic that both of them had been pondering. "What if they don't rendezvous today?"

"Then we'll come back on Wednesday." Arsen was determined.

"What if they have a room on the first floor?"

"You worry too much. I don't really care which floor they're on or which room they're in. I only want them in this hotel. Today."

"One last worrisome question. How do we avoid collateral damage to other guests in the hotel?"

"Since I checked in yesterday, I haven't seen any other guests in the hotel. I have a feeling that most of the hotel's business comes from 'in-and-outs,' you know, 'touch-and-go' activity."

"Touch-and-go?"

"In other words, the hotel does most of its business in the evenings, or at night, with rooms rented by the hour."

Leela smiled. "Got it. I'm just not familiar with your Odessa lingo."

The lady at the front desk nodded as Arsen and Leela walked across the lobby to the stairs. Arriving at his room, Arsen stopped and said, "Look at this." Using his credit card, he unlocked the door in a matter of seconds. "That's how we're going to get into Carlos's room."

"Arsen, you're so special."

Good, she's back to her wiseass self.

Attempting to further reduce the tensions of the events to come, Arsen said, "How many paces from this door to the registration desk?"

"Exactly forty, including the sixteen steps up the stairs." Leela looked at him as if he had just asked her to add two plus two. "In the event the lights go out, you need to know that kind of information. If you have any problems, you can hold on to my skirt and follow me."

"Might be difficult since you're not wearing a skirt."

After closing the door, Arsen placed the wooden chair inside the closet and stood on it as he lifted one of the soft ceiling tiles. He removed the bag Nils had given him and handed it to Leela.

She opened the bag and said, "Well, would you look at this. Guns, silencers, knives, ankle holsters, rope, and . . . handcuffs? Partner, are we trying to start a war or film a pornographic movie?"

Ignoring Leela's last question, Arsen said, "As you said, let's suit-up."

Arsen decided not to use the ankle holster. He put the switch-blade knife in his pocket and the Glock in his waist band. Leela put the knife in her hand bag, and then strapped on the ankle holster. Due to the length of the silencer, the Glock extended several inches from the holster, but it was accommodated by her wide-leg pants. Arsen moved the chair to the window and motioned for Leela to have a seat. He stood as they viewed the Sunday afternoon sights on Avenida Juarez. It was nearing 1:30 p.m. and the sidewalks on both sides of the street were packed with shoppers and tourists. Arsen noticed two yellow cones designating an improvised "no parking" space on the street directly in front of the hotel.

"Those cones weren't there a few minutes ago when we arrived, were they?"

"Nope. Maybe there're expecting some important visitors."

Small talk ensued while the new partners surveilled the crowd passing by the hotel entrance.

Arsen clumsily asked, "You were dressed to the nines the other evening when we met in your office. I hope I didn't cause you to miss out on a dinner or some other important engagement."

Leela's answer was just as clumsy. "Not really. I was supposed to meet a friend of mine for dinner. He's a DEA agent stationed in El Paso. We attended college together. He's just a friend."

"I'll try to give you advance notice next time."

"Sorry I haven't asked, but how's your girlfriend doing? She experienced a traumatic experience the other night."

Hesitating, Arsen said bluntly, "Not sure girlfriend is the correct term. She called yesterday morning and broke-off whatever it was we had or would have had."

"Oh, sorry. I don't mean to pry, but how long had you known her?"

"Less than a week. Not much difference between the beginning and the end, huh? Guess that explains life in general."

Leela pointed to the street. "Look at the black Mercedes pulling into the reserved space."

Two men, one from the passenger seat and another from the back seat, got out of the car and began surveying their surroundings. After a few seconds, one of them opened the back door and Carlos Delgado made his appearance.

"There he is, in the flesh." Arsen was speaking more to himself than to Leela.

Carlos and both men entered the hotel. The driver of the Mercedes remained in the car.

Leela took a deep breath. "Humm, one more bodyguard than we

planned for, plus a driver. You listen at the door, and I'll keep an eye out for the arrival of the young lady."

It wasn't long before Arsen heard the sound of approaching footsteps. A few seconds later a door opened and closed somewhere near the window at the end of the hallway.

Arsen turned and whispered. "Not sure which door he entered."

"You're worthless. Still no sign of his woman out front."

And I was worried about her being nervous.

Arsen returned to the window and they both saw a long-haired beauty exit from a taxi parked next to the Mercedes.

"Carlos has good taste." Leela sounded serious.

"Okay, let's execute the plan we discussed at the Kentucky Club. Good luck."

Their eyes met briefly as they fist-bumped.

I would rather give her a big hug but got to focus.

Leela stood in the hall, shuffling items in her purse. Carlos's woman arrived at the top of the stairs and quickened her pace as she made her way down the hall. Leela never raised her head as the woman passed.

Leela turned her head slightly and watched the woman enter Room 25.

Arsen opened the door almost before Leela finished her gentle tap.

"Twenty-five." Leela whispered. "You won't have any problem locating her. Her perfume smells like she got a direct hit of Agent Orange."

Arsen nodded and watched his new partner walk down the hallway toward the stairs.

Leela entered the lobby and was met by the piercing gaze of the two guards who were sitting across from each other on the two couches. This was one more guard than initially anticipated; however, the man standing behind the registration desk was a total surprise.

Leela assumed a composed, unconcerned manner as she strolled leisurely across the lobby, her hand bag dangling at her side. The guard's laser beam stares were concentrated on every inch of her body. Instead of proceeding to the hotel entrance, she seated herself at the bar, hand bag in her lap.

Addressing no one in particular, she said, "What is this, self-service? Where's the bartender?"

One of the guards got up from the couch and ambled over to the bar. He hesitated momentarily and then seated himself next to Leela. With narrowed eyes and a discernable smirk, he turned his head toward the registration desk, and nodded. The man behind the desk walked to the hotel entrance, locked the doors, and returned to his station behind the desk.

Still smirking, the guard said, "You here alone?"

"No, my husband is showering. He'll be down shortly."

"Tourists, huh?"

"Yes."

"Want to see my big banana?" The guard skipped the preliminaries and got straight to the point.

Leela could hear the other guard on the couch snickering as the man beside her put his hand on her forearm. His hands were strong, his grip was tight. He was so fixated on Leela's face that he didn't notice her other hand in her purse.

"Your husband won't mind if you take a look, will he?"

This was the last question the guard would ever ask anyone. Leela lifted the switch blade knife from her purse and simultaneously pressed the release button. She was fully aware of the two external carotid arteries running on both sides of the guard's neck. A lightning fast movement sliced through the left artery, and almost before the blood began spurting from the wound, she backhanded the blade through the right artery.

The man jerked backward, blood gushing from the deep cuts. Both of his hands were on his throat causing blood to spew through his fingers, while a guttural sound came deep from within his chest. The guard on the couch stood and watched in horror as his friend stumbled in a semi-circle before falling to the floor.

Leela bent over, lifted her pant leg, and in a flash, removed the Glock from the holster. She kneeled, left hand steadying her right arm, and fired two shots at the man near the couch. The first bullet hit him in the throat, the second in the forehead.

The third man behind the desk raised his hands over his head. It was a white flag of surrender, but it came too late. He shouldn't have been holding a revolver in his hand, and he shouldn't have locked the front door. Leela's silencer spoke twice, and both bullets hit him squarely in the chest. His body bounced off the wall and disappeared behind the counter.

Leela walked around the puddle of blood forming near the bar, jogged up the staircase, and then slowed to a fast walk on her way to Room 21. After a light tap, Arsen opened the door.

"Where have you been? I was about to go down to the lobby and check on you."

"The drug industry is now short three people."

Looking at several blood spots on her white blouse, Arsen said, "I hope that's not your blood."

"No. It belongs to Banana Man, but he doesn't need it anymore. I'll tell you about it later. Let's get on with the plan."

Holding the bag Nils had given him, Arsen said, "Bring your purse. Based on what you just said about the lobby, I'm thinking a fast exit across the flat roof will be in order after we finish our business. Follow me."

No sounds could be heard from Room 25 as they stood on each side of the door. Arsen laid the bag at his feet, slid the credit card between the door lock and the frame and pushed. Nothing happened. It didn't feel right, only a quiet click. He went through the procedure again, turned the handle, pushed, and the door opened a few inches. Arsen removed his Glock from his waist band, while Leela picked up the bag with her free hand.

They quietly entered the door, the short entrance-way blocking a full view of the bed, but the entwined, lower half of two bodies was clearly visible. The window shades were open and the room was flooded with early afternoon sunlight. The air conditioner in the corner of the room drowned out most of the noise the lovers were making.

Arsen stood over the nude bodies for an instant, fully expecting a shout of alarm from at least one of them. The face of the woman was facing toward the intruders, but her eyes were pressed shut while she emitted a constant, low moan.

Arsen slammed the butt of his gun against the back of Carlos's head. He rolled over stunned, but not unconscious. The startled woman shrieked, prompting Leela to place her index finger on her lips.

Emptying the contents of the bag on the edge of the bed, Leela said, "Honey, sorry to interrupt, but we're just getting started."

Carlos began struggling and yelling obscenities as Arsen jerked his arms behind his back and cuffed him.

Arsen rolled the nude body off the bed and said, "Shut-the-fuck-up." Grabbing the rope from the bed, he said. "Carlos, my friend, I have some good news and some not so good news for you. The good news is that as a young lad, I was a Boy Scout. The bad news is that I learned how to tie a slip knot."

Arsen took the coiled rope from the bed and quickly created a noose, which he placed over Carlos's head. He leaned over and tied the other end of the rope to the bed frame. Carlos knew what was about to happen and started to kick and flop about on the floor. Arsen once again hit him with the butt of his gun.

Using the magic marker, Arsen printed five large letters vertically down Carlos's back . . . DRUGS. Turning the limp body over, he duplicated the same five letters on his chest.

"Leela, open the window."

Leela released the thumb lock, and with some effort finally raised it. The clamor of street noise and exhaust fumes filtered into the room. Arsen lifted Carlos from the floor as easily as one would lift a small child, and sat him on the window sill, his bare feet dangling.

The woman on the bed sat up, regaining some of her composure. The rest seemed to happen in slow motion as she grabbed a gun from under a pillow, pointed it at Arsen, pulled the trigger, and was dumbfounded when nothing happened.

Leela shook her head as she watched the woman on the bed fingering the safety latch. Raising her Glock, Leela walked toward the bed and shot the nude woman in the head.

Carlos had a serene look on his face. He didn't appear to have any regrets, no apologies, no remorse. He had lived the life of a criminal, a murderer, and a philanderer. He uttered one phrase as Arsen pushed him into the bright sunlight. "Madre, mi Madre."

Bring it on home.

Arsen watched the rope uncoil, and then tighten in a sudden jerk, causing the bed frame to move a few inches. Moving closer to the window's edge, he could see Carlos Delgado's body swaying back and forth, his neck at an odd angle. Screams and shouts from people on both sides of the avenue became louder and louder.

I don't care if he has a family or not. He got what he deserved. If and when it's my time, I'll go with no complaints, too.

Glock in his right hand, Arsen slowly opened the door and looked down the hallway, and then toward the exit window. As he stepped out the door and was about to motion Leela to follow him, he heard rapid footsteps on the stairway at the end of the hall. A man appeared from around the corner and immediately started firing at Arsen. The sound of the gun was deafening as it echoed down the hallway. The first round hit the exit window frame with a loud thud, and the second one was on target. Arsen kneeled, and was sure his forehead was shattered, warm blood about to pour down the side of his face. The stinging sensation would only be a prelude to his brain exploding inside his head.

So, this is what it's like to die. This is how I'm going to go. Fucking hotel in Juarez.

Extensive training and strong determination overcame the pain. Arsen raised his Glock and fired twice in succession at the figure running toward him. The man's forward motion was counteracted by the impact of the two bullets in his chest. He appeared to be going in two directions at the same time as his feet left him and he dropped to the floor in an uncoordinated heap. Silence returned to the hallway, with only the slight smell of gunpowder a reminder of what had happened.

Arsen carefully laid his Glock beside him and thought about putting his hand on the mess that used to be his forehead.

"That must have been the limo driver." Leela emerged from the room and peered down the hall.

"How bad is it?" Arsen was still in a kneeling position pointing at his forehead.

"How bad is what?"

"The fucking wound in my head!" Arsen was surprised that he was still conscious.

Leaning down and looking at Arsen, Leela said, "Looks like you have a small one-inch scratch on your head. Nothing else."

"I'm sure that I was hit."

"You're a big baby. It doesn't appear that the bullet even touched you. Looks more like a curling iron injury."

Arsen slowly stood, placing his hand on his forehead. With an embarrassed shrug and a sigh of relief, he said, "Let's exit across the roof. After we wipe down the weapons and dump them in a trash bin, we can get across the bridge before anyone knows what's going on. You can follow me in your car to our final stop of the afternoon." His day was not yet over.

"What makes me think we're headed for the Seventh Avenue Lounge?" Leela knew Arsen like she knew the back of her hand.

41

Juarez, Mexico
Sunday, July 9th

Jack Pope was on the verge of hyperventilating. He was in the basement of one of the houses in Carlos Delgado's compound. They had pushed him down the last few steps. His elbow was bleeding, his shoulder hurt, and he was horrified. The three men had laid him on the damp floor and were in the process of removing his clothes.

One of the men was standing over him waving a stun gun. "Don't move, motherfucker, or I'll light you up with this."

"Please, let me go. I didn't do anything wrong. Carlos's sister brought me a drug shipment and left a few minutes later. I swear. Carlos is my friend. I helped him."

Jack's explanation was of no interest to his captors. The men appeared to be having a good time watching him squirm. This wasn't their first party in this basement.

Jack's shirt was the last clothing item they removed.

The man with the stun gun leaned close to the nude body and said, "Now lie still. Let me show you what will happen if you interfere with what we're about to do." He placed the two prongs of the stun gun to Jack's bare hip and pulled the trigger.

Jack's body stiffened, his back arched, and he screamed. For the next thirty seconds, Jack lost all muscle control and was mentally disoriented. He was vaguely aware of his arms being duct taped to his sides. The tape had been wrapped around his body several times in order to hold his arms in place. His ankles were taped together, and someone had lifted his feet and was wrapping the tape around his legs. Panic morphed into pure terror.

"No, no, noooo!" When this involuntary response didn't bring relief, Jack started screaming, "Help me! Help me!"

Santiago, who was directing the tape job, said, "He sounds like the guy in the movie. You know, '*The Fly*.' Remember him saying 'help me, help me' when he got out of the time machine after he had been turned into a half-man, half-fly?"

Even though Santiago didn't correctly remember the details of the movie, he was amused at Jack's pleadings.

For the next twenty minutes, the duct tape was applied to every square inch of Jack's body, with the exception of his eyes, ears, nose and mouth. Duct tape was wrapped around his chin, his forehead, and his hair. Only sight, sound, smell and taste remained . . . for now.

Santiago had done his job well. "This straightjacket is of your own making. You don't fuck with Carlos's sister and get away with it." Handing pieces of paper to the other two men, he said, "Okay, let's write down our guesses on the paper. Remember, you have to include fifteen second increments. You can use hours and minutes or whatever time frame you want. Put a hundred dollars in the pot."

The words had no meaning to Jack. His brain had been disabled. Not only was he in a physical straightjacket, he was also in mental limbo. His entire mind had been duct taped into a cocoon of bewilderment.

No sooner had Santiago placed his hundred-dollar bill on the floor next to Jack, his cell phone rang. He listened intently for several seconds, the expression on his face becoming grim. Shaking his head in disbelief, he shrieked, "No fucking way, no! It can't be! That was our contact in the police department. Carlos is dead."

The other two men had startled looks and asked at the same time. "What happened?"

"He was thrown out of a hotel window with a rope around his neck. It had to be the Juarez Cartel. We need to notify everyone here at the compound, but first, get me the straw."

Santiago was wild-eyed. He continued the mummification process by slapping strips of tape over Jack's ears, eyes and nose. Jack's mouth was his only bodily part not covered in the gray tape. His breathing rate had become rapid and shallow. One of the men handed Santiago a short strip of tape with a small hole punched in the center. He pressed it across Jack's mouth and inserted the straw through the hole.

The three cartel soldiers started talking about past "duct tape and straw" wagers. The longest anyone survived breathing through the straw was for three hours. The shortest was five-minutes.

The men compared the time estimates they had written on the slips of paper.

Santiago won with a guess of fifty-five seconds.

42

El Paso, Texas
Sunday, July 9th

Robin was still trying to make sense of what had happened a few hours earlier. She was sitting at Jack's desk, Lester was seated alone on the couch. The late afternoon patrons on the other side of the one-way mirror appeared to be drinking and having a good time on this last day of the weekend.

Robin's facial features were expressionless, but the tone of her voice sounded worried, uncertain. "Sometimes these cartel guys can be unpredictable, but Jack and Carlos are friends. He'll be okay."

Lester had witnessed the three men take Jack by the arms and lead him out of the bar. "I don't know, Robin, those guys weren't very friendly. What if Jack doesn't come back? What if they come back for us?"

"They couldn't care less about us. Jack is their connection and he'll be fine." Seeing a familiar face walk into the bar, she said, "By the way, I invited Bill Hayes, the owner of Muscle Madness, to meet with us this afternoon. He just came in."

The timid knock on the office door didn't do justice to the hulk that entered.

Robin smiled, a sparkle in her eyes. "Have a seat, Bill. You remember, Lester."

Extending a large hand, he said, "How you doing, Lester?"

With a puzzled look, Lester shook Bill's hand, and said, "What brings you here?"

"Nothing much going on at the gym on a Sunday afternoon, so I accepted Robin's invitation to meet with you folks."

Robin filled in the blanks. "Bill, what would you think about being a member of the Seventh Avenue Crew? Jack will pay you a two-thousand dollar a month salary, plus a potential monthly bonus as business picks-up."

Bill answered enthusiastically, "Yeah, you bet. The gym business isn't exactly working out. No pun intended. When do I start?"

Robin and Lester exchanged glances. "Jack is temporarily out of town, but I expect him back in a day or so. We'll wrap it up when he returns."

Looking around the office, Bill said, "Where are the other guys that were with you at the gym?"

"They weren't tough enough for this team. We're in a rebuilding process. Okay?"

"Okay with me."

The couple speaking to Shelly at the bar caught Robin's attention. The man was wearing a black tee-shirt, and the attractive lady had stains on her white blouse. There was no knock on the office door. Instead, it opened, and the couple entered.

Without hesitation, Arsen spoke to Robin, since she was sitting at the desk. "The lady behind the bar informed us that Jack Pope was manhandled out of here this morning by three unsavory looking characters. Right or wrong?"

Robin was angry. "Who are you? What the fuck do you want?"

Leela stepped near the desk and said, "Watch your language . . . bitch."

Bill Hayes, muscles bulging through his sleeveless sweat shirt, stood and tried to solidify his position as the newest member of the Seventh Avenue Crew. His deep, baritone voice reverberated through the office. "Hey, this is private property. You can't barge in here like this!"

Arsen didn't even acknowledge the big man who was at least four inches taller and forty pounds heavier than he. Instead, he repeated his question to Robin, carefully enunciating each word. "I'll ask you one more time. Where is Pope? Was it Delgado's men that took him?"

Bill Hayes took a step forward, and at the same time threw a looping right hand at Arsen's head. Arsen spun to his left, grabbing Hayes' wrist with his left hand and a wad of sweat shirt with his right hand. Lifting, turning, and violently pushing the big body, Arsen literally threw Hayes over the couch and into the one-way mirror. Lester, still seated on the couch, looked in amazement as the much larger, but much less coordinated body builder, exploded through the window, glass shards flying into the bar area.

Five men sitting at the bar reacted with surprise and shock. In an involuntary, synchronized move, all five stood, raised their forearms in front of their eyes, and turned to run. It was reminiscent of a Fifties rock and roll group supporting the lead singer. Shelly Jones, standing at the end of the bar, kneeled in prayer.

Lester who had raised his hands in complete and unconditional surrender, started talking in unrelated, partial sentences. "Delgado's guys took him. They thought he did something to Delgado's sister. Gus is gone. Shot the grocery store son." Looking across the room at the closet, he continued to babble. "Robin can open the safe with the drugs. The gun went off."

Robin, with a letter opener gripped in her hand, stood and screamed. It wasn't a scream of terror; it was a scream of total frustration. "Shut up, you wimp!"

Leela calmly walked around the desk toward Robin. "Well, well. The 'Iron Lady' speaks. Aren't you just the Margaret Thatcher of the underworld."

Robin charged. Leela ducked. In one quick movement, Leela threw her right elbow into the red-haired beauty's face, the point hitting the side of her nose and her eye socket simultaneously. A sharp sounding crack ensued as Robin fell against her chair, and then the floor.

Arsen opened the closet door and examined the safe. Noticing the finger print sensor, he dragged Robin to the closet and placed her finger on the glass sensor. She half-heartedly resisted, blood flowing into her mouth. The shelves in the safe contained replenishment drugs for Jack's distributors. Drugs they wouldn't get . . . or need.

"Leela, call your DEA friend. I'm sure the lady at the bar has already called the police.

Arsen jerked an extension cord from the base of a lamp next to the couch and cut it into four pieces. Lester offered no resistance while his hands and feet were being tied.

As Leela completed her phone call, Arsen handed her the other two segments of cord and said, "Mr. Motor Mouth is hog tied. Do the same to your friend, and then let's get out of here."

The Sunday evening customers were still in a state of turmoil after having witnessed the eruption of a body through the glass window. The big man was still behind the bar on his hands and knees. Numerous cuts were visible, his sweat shirt was shredded. Even though the one-way mirror was gone, no one seemed to notice, or care, as Arsen and Leela walked through the bar area to the parking lot.

Arriving at Leela's car, they stood for a moment without speaking. They appeared to be reading each other's mind. Police sirens could be heard in the distance.

Leela was fist to break the awkward silence. "Want to come over to my place and have a drink? It's been a long, stressful day."

"What's your address?"

"Just follow me. Surely you can keep up."

Arsen made one phone call during the short trip.

"Hello."

"Jamie, this is Arsen. How are you feeling?"

"Sore. I can't wait to compare scars."

"I'm sure mine is much more macho than yours."

"Arsen, any new developments?"

"Yes, and they're all positive. The Jack Pope gang no longer exists. He had a disagreement with his buddy in Juarez, and the gang has been disbanded. Tell your parents the problem has been solved."

"Can you tell me the details?"

"No, but there is something I want to tell you. In the short time I've known your family, they've made a big impact on me. They remind me of why I do what I do . . . and sometimes I need to be reminded."

"How can I ever repay you?"

"Next time I need stiches, I'll come see you, Doc. Tell your parents and your sister I said good-by. Let's keep in touch."

Leela's apartment was small, but neat . . . except for the clothes strewn on the floor from the front door all the way to the bedroom. As in a typical movie scene, Arsen and Leela were leaning against their pillows in the afterglow of making love. Content, talking quietly.

"Well, I guess this proves that there's one surprise after another in this business." Leela sounded profound, not flippant.

"On some level, you've been wandering around in my subconscious ever since the day I met you at the crematorium."

"How romantic. Sounds like a card a husband would give his wife on their fiftieth wedding anniversary." She smiled.

"A lot of complicated thoughts have been badgering me for the past several days. It's all your fault. I'm blaming you for my confusion."

"Poor, baby." Returning to her serious side, she said, "Hey, what do you think happened to Jack Pope?"

"Apparently, Delgado and his boys think Jack was involved in his sister's disappearance. Logic tells me that Jack Pope is no longer with us in this life."

"Too bad."

Curious about the mental makeup of his new partner, Arsen said, "Were you scared during your hotel lobby escapade?"

"I was pretty uptight, but those guys were awfully irritating."

"Uh huh." Arsen sat up against the headboard. "Where exactly did you get your training? CIA?"

"Yes. We had intense hand-to-hand and firearms training at Langley. Actually, I rather enjoyed it."

"What branch of the CIA are we in? Does Nils head up the entire organization?"

"Arsen, Arsen, Arsen. Didn't you ask Nils those questions? I thought you were the thorough one."

"Our dinner meeting in Juarez didn't seem like the time or place to be discussing sensitive information."

"All this time you thought you were working for the CIA?" Leela slowly shook her head and raised her eyebrows. "Nils is not in the CIA. He, like me, used to work for the Agency, but no longer. And you, Mr. Arsen, have never worked for the CIA. Sorry to disappoint."

Arsen was silent for several seconds. "Okay, I give up. Who do we work for?"

"I have no idea. Nils won't tell me, and I doubt he'll tell you. He says it's better not to know."

"You mean to tell me that you got transferred out of the CIA into a job you know nothing about?"

"I only report the news. I don't make it up."

Arsen turned toward Leela and said, "There are so many things I don't know about you. I have at least a thousand questions."

"Save them for when I'm not so mellow."

Arsen had put some thought in what he was about to propose. "You and I are going to be splitting the half-million-dollar bonus for Delgado. As you know, I've had several big pay days for my work during the past few years. Have you ever thought about retiring at a young age? We could retire together and raise tomatoes."

"I must have a ringing in my ears. I thought I heard you say something about raising tomatoes!"

"I have a house and a nice little tomato patch in Odessa."

"Odessa fucking Texas? Are you sure we wouldn't die from boredom?" With a sly grin, she continued. "Tell me more about it. Nothing wrong with considering early retirement."

Arsen rolled over toward Leela, wrapping his arms around her. She pressed her forehead to his chest while his hands slowly moved down her bare back. The buzz of his cell phone interrupted the intimate moment.

"Yes."

"Arsen, this is Nils. Have you ever been to El Salvador?"

ACKNOWLEDGMENTS

Once again, thanks to my wife, Jan, for her support and understanding during the writing of this novel. Even though she rolled her eyes at some of the language and content, her comments (and corrections) during the initial "home edit" of the book were extremely helpful. And thanks to Erin Brown at Erin Edits for her very helpful Manuscript Evaluation.

My sincere gratitude goes out to Phil Rushing who read and provided insights to the narrative during the writing of the first draft of the story. I am also grateful to other friends who read early chapters and provided feedback: Bob Campbell, Frank Sunberg, Van Hubbard, and Tom Monahan.

The research I conducted in both El Paso and Juarez was invaluable. The border guards on both sides of the Rio Grande were not only open and communicative, they also contributed to several of the storylines in the book. A number of El Paso and Juarez residents had interesting insights into "the bridge," drug smuggling, and the "border wall."

And finally, thanks to a number of individuals in law enforcement who assisted in my research, and who wish to remain anonymous.

ABOUT THE AUTHOR

Jim Tindle is a former U.S. Army lieutenant who served in Vietnam. He is the author of the novel **DOUBLEWIDE**. Jim lives in Southern California with his wife, Jan, and their calico cat, Rosie, where he is working on the second book in his ARSEN series.